"I can keep yo **anywhere near you. I just need you to trust me."**

"Please, Carlos. We're fine here for now." Faye thought of her missing sister and shuddered. "I don't want you to get involved. If he causes trouble, I'll let you know, but until then, I'd rather just be. He doesn't know where I am. Not yet."

"But, Faye..."

"No buts. If you really do care..." The words didn't come out. Couldn't. "If you care, you'll listen to me."

She allowed herself to imagine—to feel—what could be. She hated leading Carlos on. Lying to him about her "ex" instead of telling him about the abusive brother-in-law she was hiding from.

She wanted more. Carlos felt like...home. *Safe*.

But she had to keep him out of it. His duty was to the law. She'd broken it.

And yet she knew with every cell and every breath that by not telling him, she could lose the only man she'd ever felt a connection with. And a chance at love.

Dear Reader,

What lengths would you go to help a loved one? Would you abandon your career, your home... your identity? Would you commit a crime if it meant saving a life? Love isn't always easy and it can force us to face moral dilemmas or to make difficult choices.

In *Caught by the Sheriff*, dog trainer Faye Donovan abandons her home and business, assumes her twin sister's identity and kidnaps her baby niece—all in the name of love. Given the past (no spoilers), she can't trust the police. And to make matters worse, she finds herself falling for the one man she can't trust.

As the sheriff of Turtleback Beach, Carlos Ryker—whom many of you met in *Almost a Bride*—is sworn to protect the town and uphold the law. But what happens when he falls in love with Faye, who he thinks is a single mother hiding from an abusive ex, only to find she's been lying to him all along? Will he risk breaking the law to protect her...or will he arrest her?

My door is open at rulasinara.com, where you'll find my newsletter signup, social media links, information on my books and more.

Wishing you love, peace and courage in life,

Rula Sinara

HEARTWARMING

Caught by the Sheriff

——

Rula Sinara

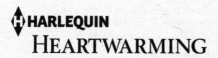

HARLEQUIN

HEARTWARMING

**HARLEQUIN®
HEARTWARMING™**

Recycling programs
for this product may
not exist in your area.

ISBN-13: 978-1-335-88964-5

Caught by the Sheriff

Copyright © 2020 by Rula Sinara

This edition published by arrangement with Harlequin Books S.A.

For questions and comments about the quality of this book,
please contact us at CustomerService@Harlequin.com.

Harlequin Enterprises ULC
22 Adelaide St. West, 40th Floor
Toronto, Ontario M5H 4E3, Canada
www.Harlequin.com

Printed in U.S.A.

Award-winning and *USA TODAY* bestselling author **Rula Sinara** lives in rural Virginia with her family and wild but endearing pets. She loves organic gardening, attracting wildlife to her yard, planting trees, raising backyard chickens and drinking more coffee than she'll ever admit to. Rula's writing has earned her a National Readers' Choice Award and a HOLT Medallion, among other honors. Her door is always open at rulasinara.com, where you can sign up for her newsletter, learn about her latest books and find links to her social media hangouts.

Books by Rula Sinara

Harlequin Heartwarming

From Kenya, with Love

The Promise of Rain
After the Silence
Through the Storm
Every Serengeti Sunrise
The Twin Test
The Marine's Return

Turtleback Beach

Almost a Bride

A Heartwarming Thanksgiving
"The Sweetheart Tree"

Visit the Author Profile page
at Harlequin.com for more titles.

To Mom. I love you forever.

CHAPTER ONE

HAD FAYE DONOVAN known she'd be a child kidnapper and fugitive by afternoon, she would have skipped her second double shot of espresso that morning. The extra caffeine had helped her survive grooming a 130-pound Newfoundland, who'd assumed his owner had created the muddy, busted water pipe disaster in his backyard just for him to swim in, but the residual buzz was doing nothing for her pulse at the moment. If it raced any faster, she'd have a heart attack before her crime was committed, and that simply wasn't an option.

She pulled her aging, powder blue Beetle up in front of a two-story colonial flanked by a barren weeping willow on its left and an oak, clinging stubbornly to its shriveled brown leaves, on the right. A poinsettia wreath still graced the door, despite it being well into the second week of February. The knot in her stomach cinched even tighter as she double-checked the address she'd jotted down on the back of one of her Dog Galaxy business cards.

This was it.

She glanced back at the rear-facing car seat she'd managed to buy and install only an hour ago—a process that had nearly driven her to tears given the almost impossible fit. She'd handle grooming a massive canine any day over what parents with babies had to handle. The amount of equipment and accessories babies required was downright mind-boggling, not to mention expensive. But what she was about to do was more than worth it. She knew that. She didn't doubt it for a second. What she doubted was her ability to pull this off. What if she failed? It wouldn't be the first time she'd fallen short or let someone down. Family, especially. Only this time a child was involved. She took a deep breath and held it a few seconds to push back a wave of nausea.

You've got this. Just get in there and back to the car as fast as you can without looking suspicious. You're running out of time. The baby seat is secure enough.

The store clerk had suggested visiting a police or fire station to check the install. Yeah, right. That wasn't going to happen. Not today, anyway. She couldn't risk being identified once news broke that the child of one of the DC metroplex's most famous and successful prosecuting lawyers was missing. Besides, she wouldn't get far in this car—the car she'd pined for throughout college and had managed to buy used, shortly after starting her dog grooming and training business. She knew she'd have to trade it for something a little more generic before the kid's father put out an Amber Alert. Not that a new one couldn't be traced, but it would buy her time. All that mattered right now was getting out of town and not getting caught.

She started to open her door just as a siren blared past the intersection up ahead. She pulled the door shut, sank into the driver's seat and muttered a curse. She pressed both hands to her chest, but corralling a swarm of spooked bees back into their hives would have been easier than getting her heart rate back to normal.

"They're not looking for you. Nothing has happened yet. You've got this."

She closed her eyes briefly, gathered whatever courage she had, opened the door and tried not to run up the path to the house.

Play it cool. You've pulled off the twin switch plenty of times.

Somehow switching places with her sister, Clara, in high school to make it through exams didn't equate with posing as her twin in order to kidnap her baby. Her eyes stung and she briskly wiped the corners and blinked them dry. God, she hoped Clara was okay. Worry, frustration and anger all jumbled in the pit of her stomach, but she had to stay focused. She could fall apart later, but she couldn't fail now. Not this time. She wasn't going to back down no matter what the consequences. She wasn't going to let Clara cave in.

But what if it's too late? What if Jim took it too far this time? What if Clara's gone?

She picked up her pace, sucking in the icy air, hoping to freeze her train of thought and keep it from spiraling downward. She tried to channel the anger it brewed into the task at hand. He was not going to win. Not this time.

She checked the time on her phone, then stuffed it back in the pocket of her down jacket. It was one-thirty already. The car seat had taken up more time than she'd planned on. Heaven knows that Newfie had taken longer to clean up than she'd planned on too. She'd never washed a dog so fast in her life. She would have canceled the appointment, but she had not heard the desperate message from her sister until the dog had already been dropped off this morning. And the guilt of that plagued her. How many times had her sister accused her of putting her business first? How many times had she run more than an hour late for dinner at Clara's or had to skip it altogether? Missing out on spending time with her niece and sister. Avoiding it, according to Clara, who was convinced Faye liked dogs more than kids...or family. Clara had never forgiven Faye for all the times she had to cancel helping her shop for baby items before the birth a year and a half ago. She didn't seem to understand that Faye's business was demanding and that she was doing well because clients could count on her being there for them. *But your own sister couldn't count on you?* Clara had accused Faye of being better at coming through for strangers than she was at being there for family. Was that why Clara had stayed loyally by Jim's side? Was that Faye's fault too?

She shuddered at the memory of Clara's

bruised cheek and eye a month ago. The bruises Faye had seen on her sister's shoulder and back months prior to that, in a changing room mirror during a rare trip clothes shopping when Clara had shrunk a size, had triggered a heated argument between them. Clara hadn't expected Faye to open the changing room curtain to check on her. Faye was supposed to have been preoccupied with holding Mia.

Clara had insisted the bruises were caused by books falling off a closet shelf while she was cleaning. Then there was the broken ankle she'd explained away earlier. All Faye could do the entire time she was dog washing this morning was remember similar incidents in the past. The bruise on Clara's left arm after she'd supposedly bumped into the corner of her dresser. The one on her calf from slipping on the steps. The tears that were never triggered by anything more than "pregnancy hormones," even when Faye sensed tension between Clara and Jim. And the forced smile whenever her sister insisted that putting aside any professional career of her own was her idea as much as Jim's. Why had Clara been making excuses for it all? Shame? Was she afraid that problems with Jim would equate to her having failed at marriage? That it would mean disappointing her parents once again? She would have failed at the one thing she'd accomplished that Faye hadn't already done? The one thing her parents praised her for? But the black eye her sister had tried covering up with makeup four weeks ago? That was when Clara had finally admitted that she and Jim had gotten in an argument.

The way Faye saw it, he'd gone from being careful to make sure any injuries he inflicted weren't easily seen, to losing control and hitting her in the face. At that point, Faye had urged her sister to report the incident and leave him. She'd even driven her to the police station, but before Clara had spoken with anyone officially, someone notified Jim that his wife was at the station. He had shown up completely prepared. The doting, concerned husband. The lawyer who knew how to plant reasonable doubt in minds. The mention of a mugging and Clara's antidepressants. He had whispered something in Clara's ear that Faye couldn't make out. All she knew was that her sister's eyes had darkened and Clara had backed off. No charges were made. Clara simply claimed that she couldn't identify the man who had hit her.

Jim's friends at the station had looked the other way much too easily, especially when he slipped in a compliment about the new computer system. An upgrade one of his contributions must have funded. Faye had noticed the way the sheriff exchanged glances with him. Something silent passed between them. Not necessarily disregard for Clara's state, but perhaps a warning. Faye's gut told her it reeked of an "I've got your back, but I can only cover you for so long" warning. A brotherhood of sorts.

What would it take to break that kind of loyalty? Permanent injury? Death?

Clara had begged her, that evening, to let it go. She claimed that Jim had apologized profusely and agreed to counseling "at some point in the near future." As soon as he could work it into his schedule. That wasn't good enough. Didn't Clara understand that? Didn't she get that she was worth more than that? Faye didn't buy Jim's empty promises, but Clara had insisted that pressuring him would only make things worse. That she thought she could save her marriage and that she needed to. The idea of being a single mom, alone with a toddler and no job, scared her. Even worse was the potential fallout of pushing Jim too far. But from the looks of it, he was the one who'd gone too far this time. Clara may not have had the confidence to defend herself, but she would protect Mia at all costs. Jim had awakened something primal in Clara. It jarred each word in the message she'd left that morning. Faye could hear it in the way her voice cracked with her last words. It was the first time she'd heard from her sister in three days.

Take Mia and go. Hide her from him. And don't trust anyone. Especially not the police. He'll find out. He always does. I tried again and it only made things worse. Just get her far from here. There was a rustling sound and gasp. *He's coming. I have to go. She goes to a playdate at 222 Gretchen Street today until 2:00 p.m. Get there before him. Please, Faye. You're the only person I can trust. I love you.*

That was it. The first thing she did was try to check Clara's location on her phone's text app, but her sister…or Jim…must have turned the tracking off. The day before yesterday, when Clara hadn't returned her calls or texts, Faye had called the house. Jim, sounding more irritated than concerned, told her that Clara had left him and Mia. Not because of anything he'd done—he'd sworn profusely that he hadn't laid a hand on her—but because Clara had been suffering from depression and anxiety and clearly couldn't handle the pressures of motherhood. He said that the mild postpartum depression she'd suffered after Mia was born had returned with a vengeance. That her moods had been erratic. He claimed that she'd lost control of her emotions and had been taking it out on him. That it was actually Clara who had lashed out at him physically and anything he'd ever done was in self-defense. He said Clara had left a note telling him she needed a break. For Jim that was proof she had something to hide, even from her sister. That she hadn't told the whole truth when she'd gone to the cops with Faye. He said that maybe it was for the best that she'd left Mia with him. That Mia wasn't safe with her mother.

That didn't sit right with Faye. It just didn't. She hadn't picked up on any signs of depression in her sister since the first few months after Mia was born. Even then it had been relatively mild. Besides, Clara lashing out physically at Jim? No way. She didn't even swear or insult people. She didn't have it in her.

Faye had called her sister's phone relentlessly after that without success. She found it hard believing Jim, but the guy had a way of blurring lines and making a person second-guess themselves. Then yesterday morning, when she called Jim to see if he'd heard anything or needed help with Mia, he said that Clara had returned home late the night before, and she'd agreed to check into a mental health rehab center. He'd taken her there and said the center had a policy of no phone calls or visitors for the first week.

Wouldn't her sister have returned her missed calls before checking into rehab? As different as they were, the two of them had always been close. They had that twin connection. Surely, Clara would have confided in her. Wouldn't she? Or had falling in love and getting married weakened that connection more than she'd realized? Faye missed having her sister all to herself. Or maybe she was jealous. *No.* She was happy that Clara had married and started a family. Faye didn't want to be tied down at this point in her life. She had her business and the love of all the dogs she worked with.

But truth be told, she realized she'd been spending more time immersed in her work since her sister got married. Could she have dropped the ball again? Been so preoccupied with her own life that she'd missed picking up on whatever internal turmoil her twin sister was going through?

Faye had always been the go-getter, the first to start her own business. Their parents used to point out Faye's strengths all the time, not realizing that encouraging Clara to be…well…just like her twin…used to bother Clara more than she ever let them know. And when Jim had said that Clara had left him a few days ago, Faye knew her sister hadn't gone to visit their parents in Philly because, when she'd called up there to check, they'd immediately asked how she, Clara and Mia were doing. She didn't tell them what was going on. Worrying her parents wouldn't have helped matters. And Clara wouldn't want her to share private details with their parents. They had a tendency to side with Jim on everything. After all, he had status, power and money. And he was their first—and perfect— son-in-law. According to them, Clara needed to be there for him and count her blessings.

Sometimes Faye wondered if they'd wished they'd had twin sons instead of daughters. That, or maybe they'd missed the memo on women's lib. Or maybe they'd never understand how one comment like that could mince a person's self-respect and confidence into such tiny pieces it would take a lifetime to rebuild it. Or a lot of therapy.

The fact was, their parents might have approved of Faye applying herself, but nothing she did had ever been good enough. Any compliment they'd issued had come paired with a criticism and advice on how to do even better—from school projects when she was younger, to steps she'd taken when opening her business. Clara had nothing to be jealous of. She didn't need to hide what she was going through from Faye of all people. If you couldn't trust your own twin when your life was falling apart, who could you trust?

Except that you haven't always been there for her. Have you? No. She hadn't.

Clara's message this morning played through her mind again. The tremor in her voice confirmed what Faye had known deep down. Clara had reached a breaking point, alright. But it had nothing to do with depression and everything to do with Jim. Had he threatened her? Hurt her again? God, Faye wished she hadn't ignored her instincts when Clara didn't return her calls. Maybe she hadn't always been there for her sister, but she was here now. This time, even if Clara reappeared and said that Jim was the kindest man on the face of the earth, she wouldn't believe her. She wouldn't bend or break this time. If Clara needed strength to stand up for herself, Faye would be that strength. She just hoped she wasn't too late.

She hurried up the stone steps to the front door and rang the bell. If her brother-in-law had done anything to hurt her sister or confine her to some facility against her wishes, there would be hell to pay.

She looked down the street for any sign of Jim's BMW. She needed to hurry. She hit the buzzer a second time, remembering belatedly that Clara always had to remind her to knock softly in case Mia was napping. Did kids even nap at this hour? The door swung open.

"Oh, hey, Clara. Come on in. Did you have a nice lunch date with Jim?" A short-haired brunette in leggings and a red tunic sweater stepped aside and motioned her in.

Faye smiled on the outside and tried to channel her inner Clara. Leave it to Jim not to want neighbors and friends to know where his wife really was—assuming he *had* checked her into a mental health facility. He'd worry about gossip and his professional reputation.

"It was great, thanks." From what she knew of him, she doubted any date with Jim could be good. The man was full of himself. Judgy without realizing it. Or maybe he did, but felt entitled to be that way. He was liberal with his demands, yet conservative with his compliments when it came to her sister. So much like their parents it was disconcerting. Only their parents didn't believe in corporal punishment.

Clara always defended Jim and their relationship, but Faye noticed the little things. Clara seemed less confident in herself after marrying him, and she'd changed her mind about getting her master's in education. Witnessing their marriage only further convinced Faye that if she ever lived with another being it would be a dog. She rubbed her gloved palms together, thankful she'd had the foresight to cover the fact that she wasn't wearing Clara's wedding ring. "Something came up and he needed to head back to the office and I have an errand to run closer to home, so I thought I'd pick Mia up first."

She tucked her long brown hair behind her ears the way her sister always did. Faye usually wore hers twisted up in an alligator clip to keep it out of the way during work. She had deliberately removed the clip before driving over.

"He still working late all the time?" The woman peered out the door before closing it. "New car?"

"No, no. It's a loaner while mine gets an oil change. I hope Mia wasn't any trouble. Thanks so much for having her."

Jim did tend to work late, but she deliberately skirted the question. According to Clara, he was planning to pick Mia up today, which meant he was clearly adjusting his work schedule around Clara being out of the picture. No doubt he was lining up a nanny or planning to sign his kid up for daycare. He'd have to, given his work schedule. Faye seriously hoped he'd be running late right now.

"No problem at all. She and Zak had fun playing. She was pretty quiet, as usual. Maybe more so today. I hope she's not coming down with something. Her thumb was in her mouth almost the whole time too. You'd better watch out or she'll end up needing braces. I made sure to break Zak's thumb sucking as soon as I could." She interrupted herself and pointed toward the kitchen. "Are you sure you don't have time for a cup of coffee or tea? They're just now waking up from a nap."

Was that code for you woke them up with the doorbell?

"So sorry, but I really can't." Did she owe the woman money? Faye wasn't sure if her sister traded playdates with friends in lieu of paid babysitting. She had referred to a play-date in her message. Faye wasn't even sure why her sister was friends with such a competitive parent. Talk about relationship patterns. "If Mia's out of sorts, I should get her home in case she's catching a cold or something." Maybe that excuse would be enough to delay further invitations or babysitting fees, if she owed any. Not that Mia's being quiet was an unusual thing. Now in retrospect, Faye wondered if it had anything to do with the situation at home. She tended to be either extremely quiet or inconsolable.

She followed as the woman—Faye really

wished Clara had mentioned a name—motioned her down a short hall that led from the cozy foyer to a kitchen and adjoining family room at the back of the house. An extra-large, build-in-place playpen filled with a wonderland of toddler toys and a couple of small, padded mats for napping took up a good part of the room. Mia sat in the playpen, her blond hair sticking up on the right side of her rosy face, still looking groggy and sucking her thumb. The other child was trying to escape the penned space. If he was any older than Mia's sixteen months, it didn't look like it was by much, based on his size, but he was definitely more daring than her niece. Then again, the Donovan girls had been taught to follow rules for so long it had probably worked its way into their genes.

"Hey, sweetie," Faye said, as she scooped up Mia, nuzzled her cheek and gave her a kiss. "Time to go."

Mia pouted but didn't say anything. She just examined her aunt with the scrutinizing eyes of a toddler. Clara had mentioned once that she worried Mia wasn't saying as many words as some of her playmates, but right now, Faye was glad the kid didn't know how to say her aunt's name yet.

"Fa," Mia said, as if on cue. Faye closed her eyes briefly. Had her scent given her away? Whom was she kidding? Babies knew who their mothers were, even if they were identical twins. Her chest cramped and her heart beat even faster. Mia had just tried saying her name for the first time—at the worst time. Panic and pride swirled inside her. Her mouth felt dry and she swallowed hard. *Baby, I hope your mommy is safe. I'll keep you safe until I can find her.* She gave Mia another peck on the cheek.

"No, we're not going *far*. Just to the store and home. Come on, honey." She hoped the word cover-up would go over smoothly.

"That's really good! You didn't tell me she'd picked up a new word. Zak is up to five words already."

Was she keeping count? Did competition between kids begin before the age of two now? Why not get a head start on college choices?

"Oh, her jacket?" Faye asked, looking around the room. Clara usually brought the floral print bag full of baby stuff whenever she visited or they went shopping together. It had been one of the gifts Faye had given Clara at her baby shower. She didn't see it.

"Right here." Zak's mom reached into a coat closet and brought out the bag.

She took the proffered coat and set Mia down just long enough to get her bundled. The woman ducked her head in a small closet between the kitchen and living room.

"I have her diaper bag here too. They literally just woke up so I didn't have a chance to check her diaper. If you want to—"

"I'll have to change it at home. We'll be there soon enough." She knew she was probably sounding like a terrible mother, but if they didn't get out of there fast, Mia might start crying for her mama or, worse yet, her father would show up. She lifted her back into her arms and took the bag. The wall clock over the kitchen fridge read one forty-five. *Please be late, Jim. Please.* "Thanks so much. I'll give you a call to set up the next play time."

"I thought we'd agreed on next Saturday as our trade. I made reservations for Mat and I for our anniversary," she said, ruffling the hair of her escape artist, as he clung to her leg.

Shoot. Well, someone was going to be missing their reservation.

"Right. We did. I'm sorry. I do have that on the calendar," Faye lied.

"Great. You had me worried for a sec." The mom lifted Zak up and led Faye back toward the front door. They were almost there. She'd be on the road any minute. She was going to have to buckle Mia into that darned car seat in record time. A few more steps and they'd be outside.

The doorbell rang.

Faye stopped. Her face went cold. She couldn't breathe. She couldn't move. It took a second, after the door was opened, to register that a deliveryman had rung the bell. Not Jim. She gripped Mia a little tighter and rushed forward.

"Thanks again," she blurted, as she squeezed past the guy with Mia on one hip and her bag slung over the opposite shoulder. She didn't look back or wave to Zak's mom. Jim could drive up any moment. And even if she drove off before he did, it wouldn't give her much time to get out of town or ditch her car. She threw the bag in the car and frantically worked the car seat straps around Mia. She'd have to get rid of the bag, once she emptied the contents into her duffel. The baby bag was unique. Too recognizable, not to mention she'd had it inscribed with Clara's name. She was also leaving behind her Beetle, her business…her home. And possibly her freedom. But as much as it all meant to her, she'd throw it away a hundred times over if it meant ensuring that Mia would be safe. She'd give her life for her sister and this little girl. She glanced down the street again, before she closed the back door and got in the driver's seat. *Please be late.* Of all days, she prayed that today Jim would be slammed with an overload of prosecution cases.

She just hoped she wouldn't end up being one of them.

A BRISK GUST of wind flapped the collar of Sheriff Carlos Ryker's uniform as he stood at the end of the pier, watching the horizon turn a fiery crimson over the Atlantic. White-tipped waves raced toward the shoreline and tumbled against the sand. The Turtleback Lighthouse stood like a sentinel down the beach to his left, and several cottages, each nestled in its own private stretch of dunes and reeds, trailed along the beach to the north and south of town.

He closed his eyes briefly, taking in the crashing surf and hoarse cries of gulls in search of their morning meal. He'd never tire of this dawn ritual. It fueled him. It reminded him of when his mother would walk out here with him when he was a kid and tell him stories about his father, focusing only on good memories. It reminded him of the time he'd brought her out here in a wheelchair because cancer had made her too weak to walk and the treatments they'd sought at hospitals hadn't been effective. She had insisted that if she was going to leave this life, she wanted to be home. She wanted her spirit to ride the waves and wind. Coming out here every morning was a way of honoring her. Of remembering how her laughter would carry through the air. Her laugh was warm, heartfelt, and she never held it back.

Another gust ruffled his hair and the cold numbed his ears. He didn't bother zipping up his jacket. He loved everything about the town of Turtleback Beach, especially winter, with days in the midfifties, crisper nights and brisk, early mornings like this one. The small town still attracted off-season tourists, as did neighboring towns like Rodanthe and Cape Hatteras along North Carolina's Outer Banks, but the pristine beaches along the southern tip were even less crowded in winter than they were in summer. Life seemed a little calmer this time of year—especially with New Year's behind them—even if his job as sheriff still demanded his attention.

He took a bite of the cinnamon pecan muffin he'd picked up at The Saltwater Sweetery, the town's only bakery, but one whose growing reputation drew tourists down from the busier northern towns of the Outer Banks. Heck. It drew people from North Carolina's mainland too. Darla, the owner, was gifted. Downright magical when it came to baking. She also never failed to have his usual order ready by sunrise every morning. Coffee, no cream, and his favorite muffin. The routine was just as comforting as going home to his place on the sound side of town at the end of a long shift. The alone time was grounding. Reassuring. As complicated as work could get sometimes, he made sure he kept his personal life simple. The only greeting he needed when he got home came from his rescue mutt, Pepper.

He took a swig of the coffee and let its warmth steel him. The ocean shimmered with the first rays of sun as it broke past the horizon. He ate the rest of his muffin in two bites and headed down the weather-worn pier that led to a short boardwalk. Turtleback's main restaurant hadn't opened yet, but apart from the aroma wafting through town from the bakery, he could see a light on in Castaway Books, a quaint used bookstore with a rickety wood sign carved with a palm tree on an island and a washed-up boat full of books. Eve was an early bird and was probably shelving new arrivals. A person could see most of the town's shops from here. They lined Turtleback's main street in bright, albeit weather-faded, colors. All of them were raised slightly on stilts due to the region's hurricanes and tropical storms.

He held on to his coffee and tucked one hand into his jacket pocket for warmth as he made his way back to the bakery, where he'd left his sheriff's SUV. He was officially on shift in fifteen minutes. His deputy Jordan Daniels, who'd been on duty last night, would be waiting at the station on the edge of town for relief. He picked up his pace, scanning the town partly out of habit and partly, he had to admit, because he loved the sight of it. Turtle-back looked like a picturesque town plucked from an oil painting.

The sky was getting lighter by the minute. He caught sight of an old, blue Accord he'd never seen before parked along the side of the bookshop. He was certain it hadn't been there earlier when he'd gone into the bakery. He'd have noticed it, even in the dark. Eve hadn't mentioned anything yesterday about having guests coming to town. In fact, he'd specifi-cally asked if she had plans to visit relatives, since bad weather had caused her to cancel a trip up north at Christmas. She'd said no and made no mention of anyone coming down in-stead. And tourists were definitely not out and about at this hour of the morning, not to men-tion the shop didn't open until 10:00 a.m. It seemed rather early for anyone from a neigh-boring town to be dropping off donated books.

Eve's head popped up as she tried to pull a large bag out of the back seat of the car. It seemed to be caught on something. Guess it wasn't too early for someone donating books.

He put his coffee in his vehicle, then took double strides across the street.

"Bright and early, I see. Here, let me help," he said, grabbing the oversize duffel bag, unhitching the bottom where it had caught on a long rectangular box with a playpen label. A child's car seat occupied the rest of the space.

"You know what they say. The early bird catches the bookworm," Eve said, tugging a cable-knit cardigan across her chest when a gust blew past.

Carlos raised a brow at her and shook his head as she shut the car door behind him.

"I don't think that's what they say."

"Oh, come on," Eve explained. "The early bird catches the worm, but I'm a bookworm and sell books, so…never mind."

"I'm laughing on the inside." Carlos adjusted his grip on the bag.

"Okay, I'll admit, that wasn't even close to funny. But I haven't had my coffee yet."

"Excuses, excuses," he teased.

"Thanks for the help, by the way. I could have handled it, but I do appreciate it." She hurried ahead of him and the shell-and-bell chime tinkled as she held the shop door open.

"I know you could have carried it yourself,

but it's no problem. Anything else to unload before I head to the station?"

"Nope. That's it, Sheriff in Shining Armor."

He chuckled and set the bag down in front of the live edge wood counter where her cash register sat.

"Now *that* is funny. No shining armor here. Just a helping hand."

His mother had raised him to open doors and to always help out, even before the Air Force had reinforced the chivalry and respect she believed in. More than once, his behavior had inadvertently offended the opposite sex. He was all for women's rights, equality and empowerment. It simply wasn't in him to stand by and not offer help if heavy lifting was involved or a tire needed changing or whatever. He did have to explain that once to Eve, back when she was trying to recover from hurricane damage. She was almost as bad at accepting help as he was at taking compliments. Even those laced with her quirky, book-based sense of humor.

A whimper and whine had him glancing over at the children's book area, which was decorated whimsically and used for story

time. A woman in black jeans, a green, form-
fitting sweater and piercing blue eyes lined in
dark makeup stood stiff as a mannequin. She
sported a rather daring shade of burgundy
hair cut in a short bob. A little redhead, who
looked no more than a year and a half, clung
to her leg with a tear-streaked face. No doubt
the woman was the car owner. He gave her a
quick nod, but it was hard not to take his eyes
off hers. Mainly because of the cold stare he
was getting in return.

"Oh, Faye, this is Carlos Ryker, the town
sheriff. And Sheriff, this little pumpkin is
Nim. Faye and I went to college together,"
Eve said. She stole a quick sip of coffee from
the pottery mug that sat on the checkout counter, then went and scooped Nim up into her
arms and bounced her gently on her hip. The
redheaded woman kept a hand on her daughter's shoulder.

College friends, then. The stilted smile
Faye gave him didn't soften her gaze. Clearly,
this woman didn't like seeing a man in uniform. At least not a cop. He never had that
problem back in the Air Force. He gave her a
reassuring smile. Many folks equated a cop
with getting a speeding or parking ticket. He

was used to the cold shoulder from tourists who assumed he was out to get them, rather than to keep them safe. The excuses and lies he'd heard over the years from people trying to get out of a ticket were pretty creative at times. Everything from having eaten bad seafood and needing to get to the nearest bathroom pronto—only to find them at the local restaurant eating joyfully twenty minutes later—to flat out begging him not to ruin their birthday. But there was something about this woman's body language that said a whole lot more than an old friend visiting.

Eve had once confessed, after a few beers during a beach bonfire, that she'd lied to cops before. Back during her college days. All in the name of protecting helpless women and children on the run from abusive relationships. He couldn't really fault her for it. He'd heard about secret groups that did that sort of thing. Heck, he'd kept plenty of secrets himself. But he was in law enforcement. She wasn't.

Just last summer he'd helped hide the town vet as a federal witness, before Gray's cover was blown, putting several lives in danger. Maybe that recent—almost deadly—incident with Gray was why his senses were still on high alert. He needed to stop looking at every situation through police eyes. He couldn't help it, though. Protecting Turtleback Beach was on his shoulders. Noticing things that were out of the ordinary was what made him good at his job.

Carlos held out his hand and Faye paused before placing hers in his. There weren't any rings on either of her hands. Single mother?

"Nice to meet you, Miss…?"

He was still in uniform and, regardless of Eve introducing her friend by her first name, he preferred keeping things formal with town visitors. Establishing his position as sheriff helped to maintain the peace, especially when tourist season hit. He had to admit, though, with Eve's friend, there was something else that made him feel the need to keep that line drawn. Something he couldn't quite put his finger on. Something that stirred in his chest, despite the fact that she wasn't his type. Too much makeup and too little warmth. And he wasn't interested in complicating his life. She glanced over his shoulder, then met his gaze.

"Potter… Faye Potter. Nice to meet you," she said.

Her grip matched the firm line of her lips. There was nothing helpless about this woman. Her skin felt warm against his palm.

Eve blinked at her friend and her brow pinched ever so slightly. Faye quickly reclaimed her hand and folded her arms.

"Welcome to Turtleback," Carlos said. "Glad you made it across the inlet safely. Most people wait until the sun's up to cross that bridge. Safe as it is, it can be a little disconcerting in the dark if you're not used to it, especially with waters this rough," he added. That might explain why she looked like she needed to de-stress after her drive.

Crossing over to Hatteras Island in the dark with rough waters was a haunting drive for anyone not used to it. The bridge connecting the southern stretch of barrier island with the more populated northern end rose less than one hundred feet above the water and ran just under three miles across the Oregon Inlet. It was certainly safer and higher than the old bridge, but still a daunting experience to cross. An upset child in the back seat would have been an added distraction.

"Well, you know how it is when kids cry

at night. Driving them around lulls them to sleep, so I took advantage," Faye said.

No, he didn't know how it was. He'd been an only child and had never had kids. And the one woman he'd planned on having a family with had left him when he was honorably discharged from the Air Force in order to care for his ailing mother. Not only had his life gotten too complicated for her, his mother's needs meant it was time for him to return home for good...a fact that made her realize she wasn't ready to put down roots, let alone in Turtleback...a town she had no ties to.

The toddler started whining and doing something akin to knee bends. Faye looked flustered and tried taking the child from Eve. She set her down to readjust her grip, but the squirming kid dropped her weight to the floor and let out a scream that had him wincing.

"Nim, do you want a book?" Eve suggested.

"Mi, mi," the tot said, in a tearful, yet stubborn tone. Faye's face flushed. She managed to hoist Nim into her arms and patted her back awkwardly. "Mi!" Nim insisted as she swatted away the book Eve held out. Faye pressed the little one against her shoulder and shushed her again.

"Everything is mine, mine, mine or me, me, me at this age," Faye said, brushing off the outburst with a flick of her hand. Carlos couldn't help but wonder why, if everything had to be "mine," Nim didn't claim the offered book. Faye gave him a tired smile, then sucked in the corner of her lip as she glanced at Eve.

"Um, someone's tired. I think I should get my guests settled in," she said. Carlos took the hint, pausing just long enough to look back at Faye, then at Eve..

Eve had not been involved in harboring runaways since her college years, as far as he knew. And he made it his business to know everything that went on in Turtleback. With only one road that led in and out of town, it was easy to keep watch. Turtleback was a nice place for a beach vacation…a place to hide out, so to speak, especially during the summer. But it wasn't an ideal choice for someone on the run. They'd be easily cornered down here. Unless…they knew they'd be protected.

He was doing it again. Overthinking things and reading more into situations than existed.

Was he that desperate for excitement? Had the adrenaline rush from the whole witness protection ambush been that addictive? Had it given him a taste of the more adventurous life he'd had back in his Air Force days? For crying out loud, maybe he needed to channel his imagination into writing one of those thrillers Eve kept stocked on the second level of Castaway Books.

He scrubbed a hand along his jawline. He needed less coffee and more sleep. Faye Potter was nothing more than Eve's guest. Years in the Air Force and working in law enforcement taught him to trust his instincts, but instincts weren't foolproof. If they were, he'd have never had his heart broken. He tipped his hat at them.

"Sure thing. I'll leave you all to your day. Enjoy your stay in Turtleback. And Eve. Let me know if you need anything. Same for you, of course," he added, cocking his head at her friend.

The bells jingled as he closed the door behind him and he squinted at the bright morning light. Out of habit, he burned the plate on Faye's car to memory, noting the expiration sticker, then crossed the street.

Visitors came to Turtleback to relax, but those two looked anything but relaxed. Was Eve getting back into the business of helping abused women and children disappear, the way she did during college? Or was she just helping one friend in need? Faye Potter had a fire about her. There was nothing frail about her handshake or the way she looked at him. But he couldn't seem to ignore his gut. The protective hand on Nim. The tension in the room. He slipped into the SUV that had Sheriff emblazoned on the side and took a swig of lukewarm coffee before starting the ignition. He trusted Eve and if she said all was well, then he had to go with it. He wouldn't interfere. But that didn't mean he wouldn't keep an eye—or two—on her friend. He wasn't the bad guy. Protecting people from those on the wrong side of the law was what he lived for. That and keeping criminals out of Turtleback.

JIM PACED BACK and forth, then smacked the box of cereal that he had left out that morning on the otherwise pristine granite countertop. He'd gotten used to Clara cleaning up after him so that he could get out the door in a hurry for work. He cursed at the mess

he'd made—of the kitchen and his life—
and reached under the sink for a dustpan. It
wasn't there. He slammed the cabinet shut
and stormed over to the pantry. She kept the
stupid thing somewhere around here.

He flicked the light switch on the inner
wall of the pantry and looked around. The
paper towels were stacked just as he'd in-
structed her to do. Labeled side of the pack-
age facing forward. That way, they wouldn't
obstruct the door and things would look neat
if one of his guests happened to open the pantry and look inside. Appearances mattered
if he was to keep climbing up in the world.
First impressions were everything. He needed
people to know he could maintain control of
any situation. That he paid attention to detail
and could get the job done, whether it was
taking on a high-profile case or moving beyond that into the world of politics. He'd rise
up the ranks in the court system. He'd attain
more power. People would listen to him. Respect him.

No dustpan, but the handheld vacuum
charging on a wall unit would have to do.
He hated the whirring noise it made and the
fact that she'd gone and bought it without him

approving the expense. It didn't work as well as a dustpan, as far as he was concerned. She'd gone and broken their regular vacuum by clogging it with one of Mia's toys. Carelessness. Given no other option, he grabbed the hand vac, paused to straighten the jars of olives so that the labels all faced forward and proceeded to clean up the floor.

He'd get Faye for this. His sister-in-law, the bane of his existence, would regret what she'd just done. He had had everything under control until yesterday afternoon, when he went to pick Mia up. If he wasn't the sharp-minded man he was, he might not have caught on so fast when Karen told him his wife had picked up their daughter earlier. He was furious. Faye had egged Clara on, dragging her to the station last month. She'd come so close to getting Clara to file charges against him. Who was she to interfere in his marriage? In his personal life? She didn't understand what he dealt with on a daily basis. She had meddled where she had no business. And then there was Clara.

He pinched a piece of cereal the vac refused to suck up and threw it in the trash. His Clara. He'd given her plenty of warn-

ings. What had she been thinking? Going to
the cops…or even to Faye…hadn't been her
smartest move. Attempting to do it again earlier this week? Unforgivable. Utterly foolish.
Didn't she appreciate the life he was building for their family? How could she risk it
all? The family name and reputation? All
he'd worked for? He muttered another curse.
They could have lost everything. That femi-
nist sister of hers put a few ideas in her head
and that's all it took to risk everything? No
wonder Faye was still single and, from what
he understood from Clara, didn't even have a
boyfriend. What guy would put up with her?

He returned the hand vac to its holder, then
loosened his tie. Family. As if he didn't have
enough to take care of at work. He and Clara
had an understanding. She was supposed to
help manage their home and social life. Keep
things running smoothly. People liked the
image of a family man. The attractive wife.
The cute child. The dependable provider.
They were supposed to be a team. But Clara
didn't get it. She had done fine until Mia was
born and then motherhood had jumbled up
her priorities. It had taken him forever to convince her to use babysitters so that she could

make it to his work-related social events. He needed her there, by his side. But no. She had wanted to stay home. She hated the public eye. She seemed to think it wouldn't be good for their child.

That's not what they had agreed on when he'd first talked about marriage and their future. Plenty of kids grew up in politics and the public eye. They ended up in renowned schools because of it too. He knew what he was doing. She needed to listen to him.

Faye just had to interfere in their lives again. Clara had denied contacting her the past few days, but he couldn't imagine Faye acting on her own—leaving that dirty dog business of hers behind and running off with his daughter. He knew Clara had confided in her sister. He made sure she understood he knew. She'd never overstep again.

At least right now he had Clara where he could keep her quiet until she remembered how things were supposed to be. The problem was that his boss and his wife were supposed to come to dinner tonight. He looked at his watch and thrummed his fingers on the counter. He'd have to cancel. No, wait. He'd tell them that Clara had gone to visit her parents with Mia for a few weeks and suggest dinner out. They knew Clara was the one who could cook.

An easy excuse. It would buy him time.

If he reported Faye taking Mia, there would be questions. Too many questions. Authorities would want to talk to Clara too. He couldn't have that. Not unless he had a plan.

All he could think of right now was that he'd need to go after Faye himself. He had contacts. He could lie about why he wanted the information. And he'd track her down. He'd find her and destroy her reputation, credibility and her life if it was the last thing he did.

CHAPTER TWO

FAYE COLLAPSED IN the bookshop's wingback reading chair as soon as the sheriff left. That was close. Too close. When Mia started insisting on her correct name, Faye thought it would be over. Of all the times to start trying to say her own name, she had to pick now. Faye rubbed her thumb against the pressure building along her brow. How long would it be before little Mia really started giving their true identities away?

What if their pictures were already plastered in every police station along the East Coast? This Carlos Ryker was asking questions and he kept looking at her. Not exactly in a mean, scrutinizing way, but he'd taken her in alright. Had he been one of her business customers back home, she might have assumed he was interested in her—personally—but that obviously wasn't it. As ruggedly handsome as he was, she wasn't interested either. Not given her present situation, at least. And certainly not with a cop of all people. This was the internet era. If Jim had reported the kidnapping, the sheriff would have her and Mia's photos on his computer by now. She could only hope that the extra makeup, boxed hair dye she'd used on herself and the more child-friendly natural henna dye she'd used on Mia last night in a hotel room would work to keep suspicions at bay. There was also a chance that, since Jim had something to hide, he'd try negotiating with Faye one-on-one. In all honesty, she wasn't sure what his game was or what would happen next and the not knowing—including not knowing where Clara was or if she was okay—was killing her.

"Potter? What happened to Donovan?" Eve asked, bringing another mug of coffee over and handing it to her. Faye licked her dry lips and stretched her neck from side to side. The tension in her muscles wouldn't give.

Here we go. One lie always leads to another.

Last night, she'd decided, while staring in the mirror at her new look and having no real plan, that of all her old friends and acquaintances, Eve would be the only one she could trust. Plus, she lived far enough away to make Faye comfortable…buy her time…for a few days, assuming she was correct in betting her brother-in-law might try to avoid a media fiasco. But even if he didn't spare a second in coming after her, she figured a small beach town in the middle of winter would be the last place Jim and his buddies in the system might look for her.

It had been almost three years since she'd last seen Eve in person. They had kept in touch over social media during the first year out of college, but the number of interactions and depth of them had dissipated thereafter. Life had a way of doing that. Making a person so busy that they figured when it came to saying hi or checking in on someone, there would always be tomorrow. Well, there was nothing like danger to wake a person up. Tomorrows weren't always guaranteed. It shouldn't have taken a crisis to get her to visit an old friend. Plus, Eve had always loved kids. Eve had also volunteered with a group back in college that helped abused women and their children disappear. She'd mentioned it to Faye once, in confidence. But that was years ago. Faye had no idea if Eve still did that sort of thing. To be safe, she wasn't planning on telling Eve the entire truth. She couldn't come clean with her, at least not yet. Clara had warned her not to trust anyone. She'd given her sister her word. But Eve still felt like the safest person to hide out with.

She shifted her weight in the chair and adjusted "Nim's" position on her lap. She needed to start using their new names even in her thoughts. She seriously hated lying. She had decided against changing her own first name because Eve knew her as Faye, but last names were a different game. Keeping her real one would make her too easy to track.

Here it goes. Please forgive me.

"Potter is my married name. I recently got a divorce—a really ugly one—and needed to get away for a while."

When the sheriff had dropped in unexpectedly, she spotted the entire series of Harry Potter books on a shelf nearby and a new surname was born. It seemed appropriate enough, considering her disguise attempt was as close as she could get to pulling off a magical transfiguration spell.

"Oh, goodness, Faye. I didn't know. I'm so

sorry. When you called last night to say you were coming to visit, I didn't realize there was more to it."

You have no idea.

Faye had left her cell phone behind, before picking Mia up. She'd seen enough suspense movies to know credit cards and calls could be traced. Everything had happened so quickly. Even the name Nim had been chosen on the spur of the moment, only seconds after she'd arrived at Castaway Books. One glance at the titles of the children's books on the shelf behind Eve and she'd introduced her niece with a name inspired by *Nim's Island*. It seemed appropriate. She knew the name had to be different. Something short and easy to remember that was close enough to get past Mia. But with the baby's whining and calling out "Mi," she was beginning to wonder if she'd made the right choice. In any case, it was too late to change it now. They'd have to get used to Nim. And lying.

"It's not exactly the sort of thing you call out of the blue to tell someone," Faye said, cradling Nim. Thank goodness the crying had stopped. Eve crouched down near the chair and held out a small board book for Nim to look at. This time, she actually reached for it.

"Did he try to fight you for custody?"

"No. No, he wasn't interested at all. Not the father type. He…uh…had an affair. Several, in fact."

She could weave a story if she wanted to. She was surrounded by inspiration. She wouldn't be surprised if there was a book somewhere in the shop about a woman on the run with a child who wasn't hers. Hopefully not in the children's section, though.

"Oh, man. You didn't deserve having that happen to you. No one does."

"Thank you for saying that."

"If there's anything I can do to help you get through this, just say the word. I'm here for you."

"You're the best. I knew I could count on you to lift my spirits." She felt like dirt. Muddy, worm-infested dirt. Scum. *Keep your head about you. Clara is counting on you. You're lying for her and a helpless child. Stay focused or you'll screw this up. You can't let her down.*

Eve cupped her hand over hers and gave it a squeeze.

"Well, I'll start with the truth. I love your short hairdo and the red really brings out your eyes."

Faye smiled, unsure of how to respond. Start with the truth? Rub it in. And here all her friend intended to do was to make her feel better. She fingered her new burgundy-red hair and a zing of panic shot through her. What if Eve mentioned to someone that Faye's hair used to be long and brown? Within earshot of the sheriff?

"Oh. Thanks. I wanted to try something different. My ex liked long hair. You can imagine why I didn't hesitate to chop it off. But do me a favor and don't tell anyone my hair was brown before. I'm trying to feel better about myself."

A part of her wished that this nightmare was all part of a wild dream. That she'd wake up and be right back at Dog Galaxy caring for pooches and Clara and Mia would be happy and healthy and Jim a super nice moral guy. Maybe that was the case in some parallel universe. Unfortunately, not this one.

"Faye, I hate to tell you. That's not a natural shade of red. However, you needing a change because of the past is not anyone's business, so mum's the word. And, just so you know, you look beautiful. I'm not used to seeing you in eyeliner, but you look wonderful. It makes your eyes pop. Feel *good about yourself.* Don't let any guy ruin your self-worth and confidence. Got that?"

What confidence? Funny that she'd tried giving Clara the same advice three years ago at her wedding rehearsal. She wished her sister had listened to her. The only thing Faye was confident about was working with dogs. She had either gotten fired or quit every job she'd tried to hold through college and the year after. The issue was politics. People stepping on each other, backstabbing, prying, complaining, beating around the bush... She hated it. People always seemed to want to pin someone down and get them to fit a mold. Jim did it to Clara. Faye's parents had done it to both her and her sister. Employers did it all the time. Sure, she ran a business that tied her to one place, but it was her passion and her choice.

Outside of work, she had always been free to do what she wanted. She had learned pretty fast that being self-employed was the only way she'd survive. She was surrounded by

dogs at work. It was perfect. And they provided a sort of buffer between her and their
owners. Doubly perfect. She might have more
confidence than her sister, but that wasn't saying much. She knew how to fake it sometimes
or use anger, like when she had taken Clara to
the police station, but the fact was that con-
frontations like that made her excruciatingly
nervous. They depleted her. Left her limp and
drained. It was a wonder her adrenal glands
were still working after the kidnapping. She
wasn't sure she'd ever be able to let down her
guard again. Or feel free.

"You have always been straightforward,
Eve. Sweet as pie, but straightforward. That's
what I love about you," Faye said.

"Ditto, my friend."

Eve stood up and held out a hand to Nim.
The kid, surprisingly, didn't hesitate to take it.
She slid off Faye's lap and toddled after Eve,
who led her to the corner of the room where
a miniature, lime-green wingback chair sat in
a corner dedicated to board books. A mobile
of fairies and stars dangled overhead. The entire room had a fantasy and fairy-tale theme,
from a dragon and prince mural to fairies and
woodland critters. Faye felt like she'd been

whisked away to another land. Another world. She needed that feeling more than anything right now, if only for a moment.

"This place is amazing. Do you live here?" Faye asked.

"No, but I spend most of my time here. It was once a house, but got converted to a shop, as many of the stores along this row were, and I took it over. Each room has a theme. Upstairs houses reference books, military history, suspense and mysteries and downstairs I have this area for children's books and two other rooms in the back for romance and general fiction. I tend to host reading time for the kids here. It gives parents a break, especially those trying to enjoy a bit of vacation in the summer. As for me, I have a place down the beach from here. It's just a small, two-bedroom cottage, but there's plenty of room for you to stay with me."

"I couldn't put you out like that. I was planning to pay for a room at one of the B and Bs or rentals."

"Nonsense. Besides, I don't think I could part ways with this little munchkin. She's too adorable."

Nim eyed Eve from under her lashes. She

had her thumb in her mouth and fingers curled over her button nose. Faye would make a terrible mother. She'd end up with all her kids in braces. She didn't dare force Nim to stop sucking her thumb. It was a comfort thing and heaven knew both of them needed that right now. Surely, thumb sucking wasn't keeping her from talking as much as other kids her age. Was it? Most kids didn't hesitate to try to ask for something if they wanted it. Unless they'd witnessed or heard things— yelling or hitting—that scared them into staying quiet. Mia *had* always been quiet and shy for her age. Faye thought of her own work with pets instead of people. Silence could be a buffer too.

"Well, let me pay you rent, then. I'm not sure how long I'll be here. Maybe a few days. A week tops." She hoped she had enough cash to cover the stay. She had used a huge chunk of it after she ditched her car in in the suburbs of DC, took a bus to North Carolina, then paid for the partly rusted Accord she had seen in a front yard with a for-sale sign taped inside the windshield. There was nothing like cash to satisfy a young, inexperienced seller and keep him from asking for too much personal information. Registering the car was something she couldn't think about right now. She'd probably leave it behind if it came to that, but since no buses traveled to Turtle-back, she had needed the four wheels. She'd also used cash to pay for a night at a motel just inside the border of North Carolina. She needed to be frugal.

Eve went over to where her coat hung behind the checkout counter and pulled out a set of keys.

"Take these. If you go left at the only intersection in town, then drive a quarter of a mile, you'll see my place on your left. You can't miss it. It's bright blue with a yellow front door. And I have a policy, the first week with me is always as a guest. After that, we can talk. Though I warn you, I'll try my hardest to get you to forget about rent. Seeing you again is a treat in itself."

"You totally just made up that policy."

"Guilty. But don't argue. And seriously consider staying longer. It's February and…" Eve sucked in her bottom lip and crinkled her nose. It took only a moment for Faye to realize what she was getting at. Valentine's Day. And she was supposedly freshly divorced.

"Don't worry about me. I've got this. No silly holiday is going to bring me down," Faye said.

She couldn't help but worry about what it would do to her sister. She had tried calling Clara's cell phone again, using a prepaid card and a public phone at a rest stop in southern Virginia, but there was no answer and she didn't dare call again from North Carolina. If Jim was tracking missed calls, she'd be laying out a trail of bread crumbs. What she needed was computer access so that she could try to track down whatever rehab center Jim claimed to have checked her into. Assuming he had been telling the truth. Clara had sounded so desperate. Was Jim trying to establish her as an unfit parent? Was he intending to take Mia from her? He was smart at his job and successful, but the man had an emotional IQ of zero.

On second thought, maybe he was such a good manipulator because he understood emotion *too* well and used it to his advantage. He knew how to bruise a person's self-esteem and break their spirit without ever looking like a villain. People like him sought out people who were weaker…less confident. Like

Clara. Faye had tried to point it out to Clara once, but her sister had gotten defensive. She had insisted her marriage was just fine. She had even told Faye to get her own relationship to worry about. Those words had cut deep.

"I don't believe you," Eve said. "Valentine's Day annoys and depresses most singles and it's gotta sting even more when it comes after a breakup. You can't be alone. I won't allow it. Besides, you being here means I won't have to spend it alone either."

"You don't have a boyfriend?"

That was hard to believe. Eve was adorable with her pixie cut, big green eyes, welcoming smile and big heart. However, it wouldn't have surprised Faye if Eve's past work with abused women had made her skeptical of relationships. She and Eve still had a lot in common in that respect.

"Nope. My hands are full enough with this shop. And most of the other singles in Turtleback are really more like friends. We've all known each other for so long. I had a summer crush two years ago, but he headed back to New Mexico after a week. Trust me, it was for the best. Anyhow, you, me and this cutie are going to spend February 14 together."

"Trust me, I won't be depressed." Well, maybe she would be, but not because of her fake divorce. For all she knew, she could end up spending Valentine's Day in jail. Plus, she was worried sick about Clara. She rubbed her palms against her jeans. "Getting rid of toxic people in our lives is cause to celebrate. But I honestly don't know if I can stay that long. We'll see."

Sooner or later she'd need to make some money, and that posed a whole new set of problems. Job applications required giving information and showing ID. Her temples were beginning to pound even harder. Maybe catching up on some sleep at Eve's was a good idea. Figuring things out would be easier if she wasn't sleep deprived and suffering an adrenaline crash.

"You came here to get away. Stick around and relax," Eve insisted. "There's a bonfire down at the beach every year on Valentine's Day, weather permitting. If it's too windy or rainy, everyone ends up crowding into the restaurant, but there's nothing like standing in front of a glowing fire on a nippy night. And it's not just couples. A bunch of us started it a few years back because we had nothing better to do on Valentine's Day."

"Why do anything at all?" Faye said. "It's such a commercialized holiday, isn't it? It puts pressure on couples who half ignore each other all year only to cram all that romance into one day."

Even *she* had taken advantage of the day from a commercial point of view, tying red and pink bows on any dog she groomed or trained in the week leading up to February 14 and offering a discount for services. "Show your pup some love" was what she had printed on her coupons last year. Love at a discount. The concept was pitiful, in retrospect.

"You're being such a cynic. Since when were you so negative? Think of it as a reminder. A once-a-year spark to keep the flame from going out. Or a day to celebrate love for all. It doesn't have to be romantic. It's only a few days away. You're coming with me."

"I don't know. We'll see." Faye shrugged as she went to put the rubble of twenty or so books Nim had pulled off the shelf back in place. Hanging out at a bonfire and socializing was too much to wrap her head around after all that had gone down in less than twenty-four hours. Man, her head was throbbing like nobody's business.

"Don't bother with picking up. I have time before opening shop. These shelves are here to be explored. Let her explore. She seems like the quiet book type. She's in her element."

Maybe that's all it was. Her niece was a quiet book type. Faye rubbed the back of her neck.

"Yeah, not always quiet—you heard her scream earlier—but for the most part she seems content to play on her own. Not a big talker, which worries me sometimes," Faye said, hoping that maybe Eve would have some insight. Eve folded her arms and watched Nim pushing books around until one with kittens on it grabbed her attention.

"Ca!" Nim squealed. She looked up and smiled a rare, beaming smile at Faye and Eve before turning the pages with her slobber-soaked hand.

"You know, I'm not a psychologist, but with my experience back in college, I saw a lot of kids who'd put up walls, emotionally speaking. Some dealt with the emotional burden of having been in an unstable home by rebelling and becoming difficult. Others became more withdrawn. They didn't want to make waves or cause trouble. I have no idea how things were between you and your husband, but even babies can be sensitive to tones of voice, yelling, arguments… You get the idea. If that's the case, I'm sure she'll come around, now that you're out of that situation. Don't worry too much. Give her a little time. Or get her a pet kitten," Eve teased. "Pets do have a magical way with connecting with kids." She reached over and squeezed Faye's shoulder. "It takes a lot of courage to leave a bad relationship. I'm proud of you. You should be proud of you too. You're a strong woman, Faye Potter, and a great mom."

Faye nodded and swallowed back a lump in her throat. All she could think of was Clara. Clara was the strong woman. Not Faye. Maybe Clara wasn't the most self-assured person out there, but she was the one who'd endured Jim's treatment for the past couple of years. She was the one who'd taken a risk by contacting Faye because that's what real moms did. They risked everything for the sake of their children. Faye was nothing but an imposter.

"Thank you, Eve. For saying that."

"You look tired. Beautiful, but tired. Why don't you two go to my place and rest from your long drive? Help yourself to whatever's in the fridge. If you need anything, call me." She handed her a business card with the shop number and cell phone on it. "There's a grocer in town if you'd like something in particular for Nim."

Nim had abandoned the book, rolled on her side, then started whining as she stood. She got her balance in check, then toddled over to Faye and cried softly against her jeans. Faye scooped her up.

How could she forget? The food jars and snacks in the baby bag were almost done. Maybe that's why Nim was fussy right now. That and, no doubt, she wanted her "real" mommy. And a diaper change.

"Gosh, I forgot. I need to change her. No wonder she's upset. Do you have a bathroom I can use?"

If that sheriff hadn't walked in and thrown her for a loop, she would have remembered. Poor kid. It didn't help that she'd consolidated their things into her duffel so that she'd have less to carry and because that diaper bag had been so identifiable. It had gotten thrown in a dumpster.

"Absolutely. It's right through that door behind the steps. But after you're done, please take the keys and go settle in at my place."

"Okay. You win. I really appreciate it." She put the keys in her pocket, adjusted Nim on her hip and disappeared into the bathroom. She put a dry diaper on her niece. "Now, let's go settle you in and get you some food."

"Nanana."

"No idea what you're saying, but it rhymes with banana." Nim clasped her hands together. "Okay. Banana it is. Let's go." She made her way back up front. "Um, Eve. If anyone comes or calls around looking for me, could you keep them off my back? Act clueless, maybe? My ex didn't take his loss so well and nor did his parents. I don't want to subject Nim to any more stress."

That part wasn't totally a lie.

There was a short pause, then Eve cocked her head and frowned. Faye really hoped she wasn't raising her friend's suspicion.

"Yeah, sure. Of course. I've got your back," Eve said.

The rims of Faye's eyes burned. She felt like she had been holding her breath since her sister's message, and hearing that someone had her back made her want to cry away all that pent-up stress. But letting her guard down wasn't an option. She was just tired. She hadn't slept a wink. It was all catching up to her.

"Thanks again." She gave Eve a big hug, carried Nim, then exited the shop. A gust of wind caught her off guard and made her eyes flutter shut for just a moment. She opened them and glanced around to get her bearings and her back stiffened.

Sheriff Ryker was sitting in his vehicle, parked just down the street...staring right at her.

Carlos didn't smile. He looked away when Faye noticed him. He didn't want to freak her out. He certainly didn't want her thinking he was suspicious. But he couldn't shake the feeling that something was wrong. He hadn't missed the way Eve had eyed her friend when Faye Potter had introduced herself and shaken his hand. And Faye had flinched ever so slightly when he'd brought up driving at night. And just now, when their eyes met through the window, he saw fear behind hers.

She quickly strapped Nim into her car seat, then got in the driver's seat and backed out. He didn't need to follow her to know where she was headed. The left she took would lead her straight to Eve's place. Good sign. At least he hadn't rattled her enough to leave town then and there.

He pulled out and in less than five minutes he was parked in his reserved spot at the police station. The entire lot held no more than five cars and the building needed updating that they couldn't afford. It served its purpose, though. He didn't need bells and whistles to get his job done.

"Thought you were about to call in sick or something," Jordan said, as Carlos walked in and threw his hat on his desk.

"Sorry about that. I was welcoming a visitor to town."

"Since when?" Jordan lifted a brow at him and clasped his fingers together as he rocked in his desk chair. He grinned.

"Oh, no you don't." Carlos waved a finger at him. "It wasn't like that. She had a kid in tow. Wasn't even my type."

Jordan chuckled and got up to get his jacket.

"I was beginning to think you didn't have a type."

"Says the guy who is as single as I am. You're letting your tall, dark and handsome go to waste," Carlos said.

"I'm just trying to keep hearts from breaking."

Carlos laughed as he turned on his computer. The photograph of his mother on his desk sobered him, as he waited for the screen to load.

He used to have a type. Natalie. Back when he was in the Air Force. Natalie had been smart and tough as nails. Best pilot he'd ever known. She'd made him push harder to be a better pilot himself. They had had plans in life, or so he'd thought. As it turned out, hers hadn't involved settling down in one place.

His mother used to say that everything in life happened for a reason. She was a firm believer that life's challenges built character. That they were both revealing and empowering. They forced an individual's strengths and weaknesses to the surface. Life's hurdles tested relationships too. Only the ones that were meant to be survived. That's what his mother kept telling him after Natalie had moved on. Natalie didn't just love flying planes, she loved flying through life. The freedom of it. She had definitely not been ready to put down roots. She was a pack-light-and-leave-complications-behind type of person. And his life had gotten complicated, at least in the time before cancer had won the battle.

As much as he loved flying too, life-and-death situations had a way of making a person reevaluate their priorities. His mother had been his anchor. His mentor and guide after his father died. She used to help Carlos with his studies when he was younger, send him packages of the absolute best homemade chicken tamales when he couldn't make it home for the holidays, and she had tried to coax him into going after Natalie if that's what he wanted. His mom had been so unselfish. Always wanting him to be happy. But staying by her side and trying to help her survive the cancer battle had been all that mattered to him. She taught him the importance of family. He believed it down to his core. Her getting sick had simply reminded him that caring for and protecting people was what drove him and sometimes that was best

done by putting down those roots and standing strong.

"You need anything else from me before I
go?" Jordan asked.

"Get outta here. Say hi to Chanda for me
and thank her again for the casserole she
dropped off yesterday."

Chanda was Jordan's much older sister who
worked as an office manager at the vet clinic.
She treated Carlos like one of the family and
insisted on sending food over at least once a
week. She also never failed to point out that
he needed to find someone to grow old with.
Carlos knew she meant well, but he hated it
when folks took pity on anyone who was single. He saw absolutely nothing wrong with
being single forever.

"Will do. Later." Jordan started to leave,
but turned on his heel and motioned to the
latest photo he'd printed and tacked on their
board. "We had a few alerts come through
overnight. One was an escaped convict, found
two hours ago. That's the other." He pointed
to a second photo underneath the first.

Carlos got up and took a closer look at the
printout.

Those eyes.

CHAPTER THREE

THE WIND HAD died down and the sun was out in full glory. It was in the upper forties and rising already—a lot warmer than the DC suburbs in February.

Eve was right. Her place was hard to miss. Just as whimsical and vibrant as she was. The exterior was quaint with a gable over the door and clusters of ornamental grasses to each side. Colorful flowerpots were clustered here and there, though empty because of the season. The place wasn't much bigger than a large apartment. Raised on stilts because of its proximity to the beach, it reminded Faye of a simpler version of the house illustrated for "the crooked man" nursery rhyme in one of Nim's books handed down from Clara and Faye's childhood collection. There were only two other houses she could spot nearby: a slightly larger white one with a fenced yard, about fifty yards down and across the road,

and a green one with brown trim just beyond
it. That one had a front porch facing the Atlantic.

Faye carried the bag of groceries in one
hand and clung to Nim's hand as she made
her way, shuffling at toddler pace, to the blue
house with the bright yellow front door. She
had Nim sit down at the base of the steps for
a moment, then carried the duffel bag, followed by the playpen box, to the door. She
set them down and hurried back to carry Nim
up the stairs.

The inside of Eve's cottage was just as cute
as the exterior. Her style was boho-chic with
comfy chairs and lots of pillows. A macramé
planter hung near a patio sliding door and her
curtains looked like she'd fashioned them out
of oversize, sheer mandala wall hangings. The
console by the door was a plank of wood on
top of legs made from stacks of books. Faye
thought of the pile of books Nim had pulled
down from the shelf at Castaway Books and
wondered if the console legs and top were actually glued together. She was going to need
to watch Nim like a hawk.

"Come on, sweetie. Let's get you some
breakfast."

She pulled out a box of Alpha-O's cereal and a banana, then realizing they'd have to make do without a high chair, she rummaged for a bowl and set Nim in her lap at the table. The poor kid went at it. Faye used one hand to cut up the banana into small pieces and reached for a yogurt in the bag. She ripped the top off with her teeth and tried to offer Nim a spoonful. Nim grabbed the end of the spoon instead, getting yogurt all over her hand. She licked most of it off, then turned, smiled at her auntie and patted her goopy fingers on Faye's cheek.

"So, this is how it's going to be, huh?"

Nim went to reach for the cereal bowl and accidentally tipped it over. Little "O's" scattered across the floor.

Faye had based grocery shopping on the foods she'd seen her sister feed Nim.

Apparently, some were messier than others…

Nim stuffed her little fist in the yogurt container and sucked her knuckles, before "sharing" with Faye.

And apparently, high chairs served a purpose.

"I'm not so sure Eve's going to want us

staying here after she witnesses your lovely eating habits."

"Ma…ma."

Faye bit the corner of her lip and shook her head.

"I'm Mama, okay? You're Nim."

"Mama!" Nim's eyes glistened and her chubby face quivered and crinkled up like a tight coil on the verge of springing loose. Heaven help her. No more crying. The sound tore her up inside. She couldn't take seeing her niece upset, especially knowing that she was the one to blame. Well, at least in part. She was the kidnapper, even if Jim was the trigger.

Oh, Clara. I wish I knew what exactly was going on. I wish you would have trusted me sooner.

Faye drew her banana-and-yogurt-slathered niece against her chest and kissed the top of her red head. Her hair still smelled of earthy henna. Her squishy cheeks…of everything young, pure and innocent. Faye loved that baby scent as much as she loved the warm, cozy smell of puppies. She hated that little ones—of all species—were at the mercy of adult drama and bad behavior. She'd trained and groomed dogs that ended up in the middle of divorces. She'd met a lot of the kids, during pet drop-offs and pickups, who ended up right there with them...often getting separated from their pets in the process. She didn't wish that kind of mess on anyone, but sometimes the upheaval was better than the unhealthy—or even dangerous—status quo. She'd sensed for a long time that there was something not right about her sister's relationship with Jim. Faye could only hope the situation would be resolved with Clara and Mia reunited and safe. She gave that pudgy cheek another reassuring kiss.

"I know, I know. I'll find her. I'll figure out what's going on. I promise."

There had to be a computer around here somewhere. She scanned the living room that was no more than an extension of the breakfast area. Nothing techie. Not even a television set. Eve had to have a computer somewhere. Unless she kept everything work related at the shop and reserved her cottage for candles, throw pillows and mandala art work. Maybe the bedroom. That's where a person was supposed to really unplug, but hey, Eve was never one to do what was expected.

She wiped Nim's hands with a damp paper towel, set her and what was left of the cereal on the floor and quickly assembled the playpen near the couch. She moved Nim into the pen, where she couldn't get into trouble, then went to peek in the bedroom.

"Bingo."

Never had the sight of a laptop given her such a sense of relief and control. Her life had been spinning ever since Clara's plea. It still was, but being here in Eve's cottage with a laptop in sight gave her a chance to catch her breath, regroup and possibly find a lead or clue as to what was going on with her sister.

She shuffled over to the bed, her sock snagging on a chip in the old wood plank floor, and opened the laptop that lay at the foot of the bed next to a pile of red envelopes and Valentine's cards. It was hard to ignore the long list of names handwritten on a sheet of paper next to the envelopes. Faye shook her head and gave both temples a quick rub. She sighed.

"That is so like you, Eve. You haven't changed a bit."

Eve was probably the only person who would give Valentine's Day cards to everyone she knew, whether they were single, married, friends, the librarian or crossing guard. She even handed one to the grocery store checkout person back in college. Bless her heart. If Eve had a calling in life, it was to lift hearts and give people hope.

Faye had never gone as far as to hand out Valentines to total strangers, but she did send cards with hearts and puppies on them to all of her canine clientele. That counted for a little good karma, didn't it?

She took the laptop, silently apologizing to Eve for borrowing it without asking first, and hurried back to find Nim still busy playing with cereal pieces in her pen. Faye set the computer on a clean spot at the coffee table.

"I'll find her, Nim." She needed to practice saying the name as much as possible. Maybe that would keep her from slipping up, and it might get her niece used to it too.

"Mi."

Or not.

"*Nim.* It's cute like you," Faye said. The kid started crying and bouncing at the side of the playpen. Faye lifted her out and the crying stopped. "Okay. Play here instead."

She set her down next the table with a slobber-proof baby book and began searching for mental health facilities on the laptop. She narrowed the search down to places Jim would have been able to drive Clara to and still have had time to turn around and pick up Nim from whatever babysitting arrangements he'd made. Then she ignored the facilities limited to drug and alcohol addiction and focused on those which, based on their websites, looked like they admitted people for depression and anxiety. Her search results included a few related articles about admission procedures. In general, a person couldn't be admitted for more than seventy-two hours against their will without a petition and court order to keep them longer, assuming they were a threat to themselves. Clara had been out of touch with her for days prior to her message. If Faye was interpreting the rule correctly, Clara wouldn't be in a facility right now unless Jim had managed to use his connections to keep her there. She doubted her sister had checked herself in, not the way her voice had sounded. Clara would have called Faye back again if she was able to. If she was okay. The center websites all seemed to say that phone calls were allowed in most cases. Then why wouldn't she have called? *She's not in rehab. He was lying.*

Faye pressed her hands to her eyes and tried to think. Yes, Jim had connections, but according to the internet, he hadn't put out a warrant for her. At least she didn't find any alerts. Not for her, or Mia. What if she went ahead and used a blocking code before dialing from Eve's phone? Just a couple of calls to see if Clara was at any of the facilities or had been recently. What were the chances that anyone would be checking to see if Faye had called around looking for her sister? Jim valued reputation and privacy. He wouldn't have told anyone if he'd admitted his wife. If he did put out a wanted alert on her, she'd end up having to leave Turtleback immediately. But she needed to find something—anything—on Clara's whereabouts. She glanced at Nim. The girl stood up and started waddling over to the shelf where Eve had various objects on display, from shells to pottery and a few books.

"Oh, no you don't." Faye jumped up and grabbed her before any damage was done. Nim started crying. "Come on, sweetie. We need to find you some safer toys. Take my keys."

She plopped her back in the playpen with the keys, a wooden spoon from the kitchen and some plastic bowls. She had only bought a couple of actual toddler toys—a slobber-proof book with gadgets hanging from it and a stuffed, musical giraffe. Obviously not enough to keep Nim's interest for long. She needed to get more toys, but the kitchen items and keys would have to do for now.

"I just need a sec. We can play in a minute. Okay? Patty-cake? How about that?" she asked, trying to distract her. If Nim started crying, she'd have to hang up immediately.

Nim lasted through two calls. According to the staff she spoke with, Clara wasn't a patient at their facilities. She was lucky they'd shared that info. The fact that Faye had disclosed she was family had helped, though she figured if Clara was actually a patient of theirs, they might have been reluctant to share that information. She had to rock Nim to sleep before she could make any more calls. Same results. She cleared her search history, closed the laptop and slumped back on the couch. She knew deep down that Jim had to be lying. And lying meant he was hiding something.

Clara was in trouble. Not the *cause* of trouble, as he'd implied. But if Eve was supposed to keep her niece safe and hidden and not trust anyone, her hands were tied. She had to lie low. Her stomach churned and she curled her head down against her knees, digging her fingers into her shins. There wasn't anything she could do to help find her sister without Jim finding her. This was so frustrating. She had to make her little niece's days feel normal, no matter how stressed out she was herself. Eve was right. Kids could sense tension. That poor little girl had probably been exposed to more stress than Clara realized. That was one thing she could try to mitigate. Get Nim to relax. Not let the situation leave a permanent mark on her. She reached into the playpen and caressed Nim's baby-soft cheek. She looked so angelic sleeping there. So carefree.

"You'll be okay, sweetie. I'll make sure of it."

CARLOS USUALLY WAITED until afternoon before swinging by his place to check on Pepper. The girl had a doggy door and a fenced-in area, but he made a point of taking her for a walk and refilling her water bowl when nothing pressing was going on during his shift. He'd had a slow morning at work. Nothing but recognizing the photo Jordan had pointed out to him. The one of the man with one brown eye and one blue who had tried stealing sea turtle eggs from a protected nest on the beach last summer. The Outer Banks beaches, including Turtleback, were famous for their endangered sea turtle nesting grounds. The barrier reef was situated right along the turtle migration path, and the people around here took protecting the nests seriously. Apparently, the perpetrator had robbed a gas station up north in Duck recently. Some guys just didn't learn. They broke the law with no conscience. They had no respect for honesty. No consideration for others.

Witnessing how easily criminals lied or turned on their cohorts when given a plea bargain was disillusioning. It made time with his dog all the more precious. Dogs understood loyalty. They wore their truth on their sleeve…or paw. They loved unconditionally.

Natalie's face flashed in his mind and he shook the image away. Where had that come from? Bitterness pooled in his stomach. He gave Pepper a solid scratch behind the ears and latched her leash onto her collar. It had to be because Valentine's Day was creeping up on him. It brought back memories. Memories he didn't care to entertain. Last year, he had spent the occasion watching thriller movies all evening. This year, unfortunately, he was on the schedule to work. That meant keeping an eye on things in town with the bonfire and all. It was a family-friendly event, but he knew he'd have to witness lovebirds flirting and snuggling and whispering promises they might never keep.

He peered out one of the two windows that framed his front door. His gaze immediately shot down the street. Faye Potter. It was hard to miss the sun bouncing off that dark red hair. She was sitting on the top step to Eve's house with her forehead resting in the palm of her hand. For someone just visiting a friend, she sure seemed bothered. Or maybe she was one of those people who didn't know how to relax.

She's a mother. Out here on her own. Just like yours.

He scratched at the twinge of guilt in his

chest. He was judging the newcomer too quickly. If she was indeed a single mother dealing with a handful of a toddler, who was he to call her out on not relaxing? His own mother had barely taken time for herself. Everything she did was in the name of helping others or raising her son. And she never complained. She always claimed to be okay. Even when she found out she had cancer, she had been so upset with him when he told her he'd left the Air Force and was going to stay at home with her. She'd gotten downright angry, in fact accusing him of throwing away his life for nothing. But she wasn't nothing. She was his mother. She got over it soon enough and he knew she appreciated his presence and help. He couldn't have lived with himself had he not come home to help her.

He gave Pepper's leash a gentle tug.

"Come on, girl. We're going for a walk."

Pepper wagged her black, gray and white "peppered" tail and followed him out the door. One bark and Faye's head jolted up. Eve's place was a good five hundred feet away, yet when she looked over at them, he could see her lips part. She started to get up. *Didn't know the sheriff would be your neighbor, did you?* He picked up his pace just slightly, making sure not to go any faster than Pepper's old joints could handle.

"Hello again," he called out, not wanting Faye to disappear inside.

She stopped mid-retreat and turned toward him. Her smile didn't reach her blue eyes.

"Sheriff."

"Enjoying Turtleback Beach so far?"

"Absolutely." Her eyes softened when she spotted his dog. She seemed uncertain about whether to approach them, then rubbed her palms on her jeans and made her way down the steps. "May I pet her?"

"She'd love it." He tried to keep his attention on Pepper. It wasn't working. The officer in him couldn't tamp down the need to look deeper...past the terse smile and into the thoughts that seemed to be churning behind her eyes. *You, the sheriff, are interested. Not you, the man. You're just doing your job. Staying on top of happenings around town, including who comes and goes. Besides, like you told Jordan, she's not your type.*

Faye got on her knees and held her hand out for Pepper to sniff, but his dog wasted no time in licking her face and trying to climb into her lap. As large as she was, that was a lot of dog to handle. Faye laughed and gave Pepper a good rub and hug. The lighthearted warmth of her laugh stirred something in his chest and made his voice catch in his throat.

"She likes you."

"What's her name?" Faye asked. Her smile, real this time.

"Pepper. You can see why. No clue what breed she is. I haven't had her that long, actually. Just a few months. My last two didn't survive long."

Her eyes widened in horror.

"Why?"

"That didn't sound right." Carlos adjusted his sheriff's hat. "What I mean is that any dog I've owned has been an elderly rescue. I'm hoping she does better than my last two. Older dogs—especially if they have expensive health issues—don't get adopted so easily. I only adopt the older ones. It works out both ways since I'm not home enough for a puppy. She's past the point of needing much exercise or chewing up a place. Some days it's not easy getting off shift to walk her or to stop by the house, just so she knows she hasn't been abandoned again, but I think she's catching on. You ever have a dog?" he hedged. *She's putting her guard down. You'll find out more that way.*

"No." Her brow furrowed.

Not a dog person, then. She could have fooled him, what with the way she was gushing over his.

She gave Pepper a kiss and stood looking wistfully at her.

"I mean, I love them. I've worked with them before—just volunteering-type stuff," she quickly added. "I walked them for cash in college too. I just haven't had my own. Pepper here looks like she might have some Great Dane and Aussie in her."

There were a lot of pauses there. Clearly, she was carefully considering everything she said.

"Perhaps. Any reason you never got a dog?" he asked, bringing the conversation back to her.

"I don't know, really. I just never got one." She stroked her right hand down Pepper's back while she knelt in front of the dog, and because of the dog's height, the action caused the sleeve of her sweater to hike up an inch on her wrist. Carlos stilled. There was a nickel-sized bruise just above her wrist and multiple small wounds that looked like they'd scabbed over. All in a row, as if someone had dug their nails into her while grabbing forcefully. His jacket was suddenly feeling much too hot despite the brisk day. He gritted his teeth to keep from saying more than he should. She was obviously not the most trusting person. Could he blame her? The last thing he needed to do was scare her off, especially if she really was here seeking Eve's help.

Instinct was telling him that Faye needed help. Maybe she'd reached out to Eve because of her past work helping abused women. He'd read and heard plenty of reports about women whose complaints regarding domestic abuse were either dismissed after a brief questioning or ignored altogether. There had to be a reason Faye had gone cold when she first saw him at Castaway Books. He rolled his shoulders once and sucked in a breath of cold air. Was this why Nim had been so out of sorts? God help him if that kid had been hurt too. He rubbed his jaw and cleared his throat. He'd be keeping a closer eye on her and her kid. As far as he was concerned, by coming to his town, she'd stepped into his sphere of protection. And if her abuser was out looking for her, well, that meant he'd need to be vigilant about keeping everyone in town safe, along with Faye and her baby.

"Well, dogs need attention and you have your hands full with your kid and all," he said, hoping she might volunteer more information about her situation without realizing it.

"What? Oh, yes. Nim. She's napping."

"Cute kid."

"Thanks."

One-word answers were going to get him nowhere really fast.

"Eve probably told you there's a dog who helps out with her reading hour sometimes. Kids love Laddie and vice versa. He has a way of calming kids down and making them more interested in reading. He's a rough collie, like Lassie in the movies and books, and belongs to the town veterinarian. I think Gray said he was dropping Laddie off at the bookstore this afternoon. Nim might enjoy the reading hour."

"Right. I'll ask Eve about it. Thanks for letting me know."

"Oh, and don't forget about your registration." He nodded toward her car.

"Excuse me?"

"Your registration expired a week ago." He figured the last thing she needed was getting pulled over. He had noticed it when she was parked outside Castaway Books, but figured he had plenty of time to point it out. She was lucky she hadn't been stopped by a cop on the way down here. She paled.

"Are you here to ticket me? I promise, I'll take care of it. I've been so preoccupied with Nim and—"

"I'm not issuing you a ticket," he said, holding up his palm. "I just happened to notice it. You have eight days left on a grace period. If you need an emissions inspection, Roger can help you. He runs the only gas station in town. You can't miss it. If you're not sure, I can check and see if you need the emissions test."

"No. No need. I'm on it. Thanks for the warning. Um. I better head on up. I don't want Nim waking up and wondering where her mommy is. It was nice meeting Pepper." She hurried up the steps and gave a quick wave as she disappeared behind the yellow door.

Mentioning the registration hadn't been so much of a *warning* as a friendly reminder. Had he come off that harshly? Tone of voice? How often had she been yelled at before? He muttered a curse. He loved his life here in Turtleback but sometimes he hated the fact that he was no longer out there in the world fighting the bad guys. The rational side of him knew he was making a difference here, but there was a part of him that always wondered if it was enough.

"Let's get you home, Pep. I need to get back to the station."

The station, then Castaway Books. One advantage to being in law enforcement was access to information. Perhaps Faye didn't know she could trust him…and just about everyone in Turtleback for that matter… But she'd figure that out soon enough. If she needed protection, he would provide it. It was his job to do so. It wasn't unusual for abused women to think they were at fault…that they'd done something wrong to deserve punishment. It was all part of an abuser's brainwashing technique. He had learned about the psychology behind it during his training, but the topic hit a lot deeper. Natalie had been abused as a kid.

He'd never forget the night she told him about it. The thought that anyone could hurt another like that had infuriated him. He knew in that moment that he'd never let it happen to her again. It wouldn't happen to anyone if he had the power to intervene. And he'd wanted—believed—that he would be protecting Natalie for the rest of her life, but things didn't turn out that way. She wanted to protect herself. She had joined the military to empower herself. She made it clear that she loved and appreciated that Carlos had her back, but she had warned him not to stifle her with his protection. He hadn't intended to. He just cared about her. He hated what had happened to her. He hated what he suspected had been happening to Faye, as well. Faye needed to understand that she and her daughter were the victims, but that she also had power. She wasn't the lawbreaking criminal. Whoever cut and bruised her was the one committing a crime… And Carlos hoped when he ran Faye Potter's name, he'd find out exactly whom she needed protection from.

CHAPTER FOUR

FAYE NEEDED TO THINK.

Was the sheriff onto her? No. Wait. If he knew she was a kidnapper, he would have arrested her. There would be cops raining down on Eve's place right now. But all he had done was ask a few questions. Small talk and a dog walk. That's all it was.

She slumped down on Eve's couch and held her face in her hands.

For crying out loud, the man adopted elderly dogs. He had a heart.

The tightness in her chest gave way to an almost scary, fluttery sensation. She pushed her hair back, got up and marched straight to the kitchen for a glass of cold water, which she guzzled ungracefully. Her tendency to judge people on how connected they were to their dogs…how caring and attentive they were…was getting the better of her right now. Her mother used to say that a lot could be gleaned about a man by observing how he treated his mother. If he treated his mother with respect, admiration and kindness, then he very likely would respect his wife—the mother of his own children. And all women, for that matter.

Maybe this was true, or at least true most of the time, but Faye believed in watching how a person treated everyone else, including their pets. Animals didn't lie. Dogs and cats, in particular, had sharp instincts when it came to people. In fact, her brother-in-law never talked about his mother and he was adamant about no pets in his pristine house. Two strikes against him. She had even told Clara several times that she didn't like that about Jim.

But she didn't miss the love and gratitude between Carlos Ryker and his dog, Pepper, earlier. Sheriff Ryker was clearly kind and compassionate, yet dangerous to her. A man who could out her so easily. A man who, for some reason, she couldn't break eye contact with when he looked at her as if he *knew*.

The sheriff was only being neighborly. Of all people to have as a neighbor. And he had to go and be good-looking too, with his dark hair, full lips and kind eyes. Looks could be deceiving. Her brother-in-law was good in the looks department and bad in character. But Sheriff Ryker really did have kind eyes, and their deep brown seemed to swirl with concern when he talked about his dog. Maybe the guy had a heart. Maybe if she told him the truth, he'd help her find her sister and he'd convince Jim not to press kidnapping charges.

The shadow of a gull swooping low, just outside the cottage, brushed across the worn, gray wood of the deck off the back of the house, and its hoarse cry had Faye nearly jumping off the couch. For heaven's sake, now birds were startling her? What next? She padded over to the glass patio door and caught the gull diving dangerously close to the white-crested waves. It had to be a red-flag day with a surf like that, yet that bird was taking risks for survival. Diving into deep waters headfirst. Flying alone. Had that been the universe's way of warning her? Fly alone. Don't trust anyone. Had that been what Clara had been doing all this time? Trying to survive her marriage alone? Without trusting her own sister to step in until it was too late? *Was* it too late?

Frustration welled inside her and the pressure built in her chest. She covered her mouth to stifle a sob and glanced back toward the room where the small, portable playpen she'd set up earlier was doubling as a temporary crib. Nim looked so peaceful asleep. The sheriff was right about her being cute.

Don't trust anyone.

But what about Eve? Clara never knew her. She couldn't judge someone she'd never met. Sheriff Ryker's face flashed in her mind again. The tenderness in his eyes when he looked at his dog had to mean something. Didn't it? Maybe he could help. He wasn't in the same town or state as the cops Jim knew. Maybe…

No, no, no.

The gull reappeared and squawked fiercely before taking another dive. The saltwater mist in the air had to be rusting her brain. What was she thinking? Was she *that* desperate for a way out? For help? Clara had warned her not to trust any cops. Jim was too well connected. People owed him favors. People in elected positions knew how to play politics. They'd look the other way in a flash. They'd make excuses for their buddies. Sheriffs were elected positions.

And she had broken the law.

Carlos Ryker didn't owe her any favors and she was officially a criminal. If she got caught, Jim would take it out on Clara, if he hadn't already. She had no doubt he knew by now who'd taken Mia. She was the only person anyone could describe as looking just like Clara, plus Faye's shop was closed and she and her blue Beetle were gone. It didn't take a rocket scientist to figure out what she'd done. But if she was caught and had to testify under oath, he'd have proof that his wife was in on their daughter's disappearance and that Faye hadn't been acting alone.

Clara, I wish you could tell me that you're alright. That you're alive, at least. My gut tells me you are. That twin connection we've always had is telling me you are. I promise I'll do whatever it takes to make sure you'll be okay.

Her eyes stung with that last thought, but she refused to let a tear escape. She needed to be strong, for her niece and her sister. They'd get through this. They had to. She closed her eyes and listened to the rough surf. The weather would change. It always did. The waters would eventually calm down. But tides changed too, with the pull of the moon, and low tides uncovered things. So did full moons. Their brilliant light revealed things that would otherwise remain hidden in the dark. Just how long would she be able to stay in the shadows?

Seeing Eve again and staying here at her place had given her a moment of relief... a chance to catch her breath... But maybe coming to a small town wasn't such a good idea after all. A person could disappear into crowds. There weren't any here, at least not right now. Maybe there were during the summer months. To top it off, her friend happened to live within view of the sheriff's home. And Faye had gone and made calls. They'd been blocked, but paranoia was setting in. Maybe she shouldn't have, but she had needed something to go on. Something to prove her instincts were right and that Jim had lied to her. She needed to know that Clara was alive for sure.

Faye raked her fingers through her hair, then braced her hands on her hips. There was the issue of car registration too. Everything was getting complicated really fast. She looked back at Nim in the playpen. *Protect her.* She would. She couldn't let Clara down. If Jim was going to track Faye and take her down, he was going under right with her. She'd run long enough for other people in Clara's life to notice something was off. Long enough for him to stumble. She wasn't the only person who could make mistakes. Everyone did eventually. She just needed time. She needed to hold out as long as possible. And that meant one thing. She couldn't stay in Turtleback. She had to keep moving. Moving targets were harder to catch, weren't they? First thing in the morning, they'd be gone.

CARLOS GAVE THE door to Castaway Books an extra tug to get the latch to close.

"Back so soon?"

Eve tucked a stack of books on a shelf marked "50 Percent Off" and made her way over to him.

"Yep. Your door's swing mechanism isn't working."

"It's been acting up this week. I'll look at it later today. I keep forgetting my toolbox at home. I'm sure all it needs is a little adjustment."

"Need me to—"

"Thanks for offering, but I can handle it. You're busy with work and it's probably nothing more than a loose screw. Unless our salty air's done a number on the hinge again. But I'll figure it out. Bored at work and need a book?" she teased. He knew Eve was kidding. She appreciated the demands of being the town sheriff.

"Actually, I need your help with something that's possibly work related. Have any customers right now?" He wasn't about to discuss Faye within earshot of shoppers. Business was generally slower during the winter months for most of the shops around town, especially after the holidays, but it wasn't zero. Eve tipped her chin down and narrowed her eyes at him.

"My first for the day just left. What's up? Should I be worried? Are Gray and Mandi okay?" Eve, who had been friends with Gray ever since he started bringing his dog, Laddie, to reading time a few years ago, had recently reconnected with Mandi, a childhood acquaintance.

Mandi had grown up in Turtleback and had left Gray at the altar a few years back. It wasn't until she returned to town this past summer for the funeral of her grandmother, the town's beloved matriarch, that the two found their way back to each other. Granted, both had nearly lost their lives when criminals discovered Gray's new identity and tracked him to Turtleback Beach. The whole incident had townsfolk on edge for months. Danger around here usually consisted of sharks, riptides and hurricanes…not federal witness ambushes.

"They're fine. It's your friend—Faye—I have questions about."

"Faye? Man, Carlos. I know February can be slow around here, but you really are bored." She quirked a brow. "Or interested."

"Far from it. I mean I'm not bored or interested. But I am concerned. I ran into her earlier, while walking Pepper. Told her about your reading hour, so she might be by. Be honest with me, Eve. Did she come to you for help? Are you hiding her?"

Eve sucked in a deep breath and braced her hands on her hips. She glanced around the shop, as if mulling over what she should and shouldn't say.

"What makes you think that? A drunken confession once at a bonfire? I haven't helped abused women and children disappear since college. I told you that. Besides, Faye's a strong woman. She'd never let anyone mess with her."

"You sure about that? I ran her tags."

"You what?" The color rose in her face, and not in a good way.

"Her registration is expired. Turns out, the car was recently sold, but registration and title paperwork hasn't been updated yet. I made a call and the seller said the buyer's name was Donovan. Not Potter. She paid in cash, Eve. No one carries around that much cash on a trip. Either your friend is lying to both of us, or just to me."

Something shifted in Eve's face.

"Eve. I'm trying to help here. I'm not the bad guy."

If it hadn't been for seeing those marks on Faye's wrist before he headed to the station, he would have gone straight back to Faye for questioning. But the fact that she was Eve's friend and he suspected that she was lying about her name out of fear, rather than maliciousness, had him changing tactics. Carlos had no tolerance for lawbreaking, but his mother had a saying she used to repeat to him all the time: *Look beneath the waves because deep waters hide many things and skew perception. Danger can be alluring. Predators can be beautiful. But beauty can also hide the vulnerable...the prey.*

When he was younger, Carlos used to think she was talking about the coral reefs, sharks and smaller fish, but eventually he understood she'd meant so much more. She had whispered those wise words to him again, on the day he was sworn in as sheriff. He saw those marks on Faye's wrist. His eyes didn't lie. But something didn't jibe with the car and her last name. Victims didn't always fit the profile, nor did criminals. He knew that firsthand. Profiling and stereotypes didn't always work and were potentially dangerous tactics. He preferred facts. Something was going on with Eve's friend. He just needed to figure out for sure whether Faye was predator...or prey.

"She just went through a bad divorce," Eve confessed. "Please keep this to yourself. She didn't want me talking about it. I knew her as Faye Donovan. She told me Potter was her married name. My understanding is that the divorce got ugly and she doesn't want her in-laws knowing where she is because they weren't happy about her getting custody of her daughter. Divorce can be draining. She came here to clear her head. To give herself and Nim a little peace and quiet."

"She didn't mention anything else?"

"Like what?"

He rubbed the back of his neck, then leaned against the wooden checkout counter.

"Like why the divorce got ugly," he said, lowering his voice despite the fact that she'd said they were alone. "She had marks on her arm, Eve. She was petting Pepper and I caught a bruise and some wounds along her wrist. She doesn't know I saw them. I thought that maybe she came to you because of your work back in the day."

Eve's lips parted and he could tell the shock in her eyes was genuine. She covered her mouth and took several paces back before staring him down.

"She hasn't said anything to me. Yet. I mean, she just got here and I sent her to my place. We haven't had a chance to really talk.

She only mentioned the part about not telling anyone who might come looking for her that she was here."

"I get the feeling she's more than lying low. It looks to me like she's hiding from her ex. Afraid of him. I can be trusted to help, Eve. You know that, but she doesn't. My guess is that she's tried turning to the police for help before and it backfired."

"Oh, Faye." Eve closed her eyes. She knew what *backfired* meant. Controlling spouses didn't appreciate getting turned in to the police. It was a punishable act as far as they were concerned. "But she's here now. If the divorce went through, that means someone listened to her. That must be why she was more concerned about her in-laws than her ex. Maybe he got time or a restraining order."

"Maybe. You might want to talk to her after work. Let me know if there's anything I can do."

"I will. Thank you…for noticing and letting me know."

He hesitated, almost asking Eve to set up an intervention, then thought better of it and simply nodded and left the shop. Outside, a dark cloud was making its way toward town.

Another few minutes and it would obscure the bit of sun they'd been graced with that morning. *Deep waters and dark skies.* He scanned the street to his left and right. It was the only main street in town. On the far end he could see Joel Burkitt, the local lawyer, entering the yellow, two-story row house where his law office occupied the top floor. A yoga studio occupied the bottom level. Mandi slipped in behind Joel with a yoga mat rolled under her arm. Now Gray's wife, she'd had to come to the realization that her love for him outweighed the fact that he'd kept his true identity a secret from her for years. Secrets. How was it that such a peaceful, small town managed to harbor so many secrets? Perhaps it was a testament to the fact that something in the atmosphere of Turtleback made people feel safe here. Pride for his town fired up in his chest. Turtleback was home and he'd protect it, and everyone seeking refuge here, with every ounce of his soul.

Familiar faces shuffled in and out of The Saltwater Sweetery for an early afternoon pick-me-up. The rest of the shops that lined the street, sporting different colors from pastels to primary hues, gave the town its quaint, seaside flair. They'd all seen their share of damage when stronger hurricanes came through, but if the people here were anything, they were resilient. A few locals popped into Treasures, the only jewelry store in town, probably for Valentine's Day gifts. Nothing unusual going on. No new faces. But he'd be keeping an eye out for sure. If there was one thing Faye would find out soon enough, it was that she and her little girl would be safe here. If her ex, or anyone doing his bidding, set one foot in Turtleback, they'd have to face him first.

He glanced at his watch. No wonder his stomach was rumbling. His mind had been so preoccupied with work that he hadn't noticed the hunger pangs until now. *Work, huh?* Okay, so it wasn't as if Faye Potter was a case that had come across his desk. Nonetheless, his conscience couldn't ignore the fact that she wasn't in the best of situations... And he knew he could help, if she'd let him. The image of Faye holding Nim flashed in his mind. He rubbed the back of his neck and headed for his vehicle. Doug, one of the other officers on staff, had the next shift and Carlos had promised Chanda that he'd join her and Jordan for a late lunch/early dinner.

He clocked out at the station, then headed for Chanda's place a mile down the road from the veterinary clinic. The duplex wasn't large, but it never seemed to run out of room, regardless of how many people she invited over. And if folks simply dropped by, the door was always open, so to speak. That was Chanda. The woman had a heart of gold.

He knew from Gray Zale that Chanda was instrumental in keeping his veterinary practice running smoothly. He'd said more than once that there wasn't another office manager/receptionist who could ever replace her. She was efficient, organized and had both a best friend and mothering quality about her. She'd also raised her brother, Jordan, who was ten years younger than her, after they'd lost their parents—one to a heart attack and the other to a drowning accident. And she'd taken Carlos under her wing when his mother—her closest friend, despite the generation gap—had passed on. It didn't matter that he was an adult at the time. Chanda was a couple of years older, which, according to her, granted her the privilege of acting like his big sister. Chanda was simply an old soul.

The tiny, fenced side garden and front yard that cradled flowers of every color throughout the warmer months was cleaned up and barren, yet the evergreen wreath left over from the holidays and repurposed with bright red hearts stuck all over it maintained the home's welcoming charm.

Carlos parked next to Jordan's and Chanda's cars, made his way up the front steps and rapped the door twice before cracking it open and announcing his arrival. Chanda looked over her shoulder as she pulled a casserole dish out of the oven.

"Right on time. How's work today?" she asked, as she scurried over to the kitchen table and set the hot dish on a quilted trivet. Jordan greeted him with a quick "hey" and head jerk as he took three glasses out of a top cabinet.

"All good," he lied. He never discussed the details of work with her. He knew her brother didn't either. They had a policy at the station. Not that he didn't trust Chanda, but she could, at times, be a little meddlesome in a totally well-intentioned way. "Something smells fantastic. I hope you didn't go out of your way. I told you, you didn't have to have me over."

"Nonsense. What else would I do with the afternoon off from work? Cooking for you two is more fun than catching up on laundry."

"Hey, I totally agree with you, sis," Jordan added. "I think cooking for us is a much better idea." He grinned and planted a kiss on his sister's cheek.

"I bet you do." She chuckled and slapped his arm. "Grab the bottle of seltzer water from the pantry, would you?"

"What can I do?" Carlos asked, leaning over the table to get a closer whiff of the casserole. Bacon, broccoli and cheese with a side of rice. His stomach grumbled a little louder.

"You can pull out a chair and dig in, honey. Then you can slather me with compliments," she teased.

"You know I love your food." He turned toward Jordan as he grabbed a chair across from him. The kid had been working a lot of shifts lately. He had even tried signing up for one on the fourteenth, but Carlos had deliberately taken it instead. He knew it was all avoidance tactics. If Jordan had to work, he'd have a valid reason for watching the bonfire from a safe distance. The gathering wasn't about dating, but Eve would be there and Carlos had noticed that Jordan had been avoiding running into her more and more, the closer V-Day came. Carlos hovered his fork over his plate. "If you want to make use of that toolkit I got you for Christmas, the door at Castaway Books needs fixing."

Jordan paused, a heaping serving spoon in his hand, before quickly recovering and clearing his throat. He added a second spoonful to his plate and shook his head at Carlos. It was hard to miss the way the corner of Chanda's mouth lifted, but she started piling salad in her plate without saying a word.

"Since when am I the town handyman?" Jordan asked.

What a joke. The guy loved fixing things. He'd repaired plenty of house items for his sister alone, not to mention a dripping sink over at the bakery once, when the local plumber was out with the flu. And then there was the table leg that broke at the boardwalk restaurant when a rambunctious gull flew in and scared a waiter so badly he tumbled, along with a few others, into the table to avoid the winged customer. Heck, Carlos couldn't count the number of people Jordan helped in the aftermath of a hurricane. Not only maintaining peace, order and safety—an officer's duty—but putting homes and, thus, lives back together in the damaged aftermath. Everyone around Turtleback came to the aid of their neighbors with open hearts, but Jordan never seemed to tire. It was as if the more repairs he had to tackle…the more folks who needed help…the more energized he became. He was a good guy. A great officer to have on Carlos's team.

The fact that he was getting defensive at the suggestion that he help out Eve—specifically—only confirmed Carlos's suspicions.

"Since it's practically your nickname and Eve appeared to be too busy this morning to tackle it," Carlos said, stealing a glimpse at both Chanda and Jordan between bites of warm, melted cheese.

Jordan looked horrified and a bit flushed. Chanda looked all-out amused. Clearly, she'd picked up on the chemistry between Eve and her brother over the past year or two. No flirting or anything like that. The two were much too preoccupied with their jobs. But the way Jordan would lose his words in the one shop that was technically loaded with them…and the way Eve would eye him through shelves, or surreptitiously over the top of a storybook she'd be reading to kids, didn't escape anyone. The only ones unwilling to admit these two liked each other were Jordan and Eve. Especially after the time Jordan mustered up the courage to offer to help her move a heavy chair and she took offense and insisted she was capable of moving it herself. Typical of Eve. And just like Jordan to get bruised by having a pretty girl decline his help.

"Why didn't you fix it?" Jordan retorted.

"I didn't have time. I was on duty. You're not, this afternoon. I figured with the wind picking up, I'd hate for that hinge to give Eve or her customers trouble. Wouldn't want anyone getting injured." Carlos took a mouthful of casserole and closed his eyes. So good. He nodded at Chanda while pointing at his dish—his mouth too full to talk—to let her know he was in culinary heaven. She knew how to make rib-sticking comfort food like no other.

Jordan stuffed his mouth and didn't answer.

"Actually," Chanda jumped in, "I have a small stack of paperbacks I've been meaning to take to her. I really need them out of my way. I'm getting an early spring-cleaning itch."

"It's barely mid-February," Jordan said, furrowing his brow at her.

"Nothing wrong with doing it in stages. Decluttering first. I've been reading some books on feng shui, and decluttering helps with energy flow through a home. Please take this stack over to Castaway Books with you. Tell Eve we can settle how much they're worth later. It would be such a huge help if you took care of that for me." Chanda shot Carlos a wink when her brother focused on his plate.

"Don't think I don't know what you're doing, sis. And, for the record, it goes beyond psychological manipulation into the realm of guilt-tripping. You should be ashamed." Jordan failed at hiding the twinge of a smile that threatened to blow his fake stern voice. "I'm telling you both, I'm positive Eve knows how to fix a door and would probably rather do it herself."

"You're totally right, come to think of it," Carlos mused. "I'm sure she'll find time in between shelving books, doing inventory, hosting her children's hour today and such. She told me she could manage when I carried in a bag for her this morning—naturally, I told her I knew she could do it before I dared touch the thing. Probably the only reason that I survived the encounter and am here right now enjoying this fine meal. That woman can be downright scary."

"That horrible, sweet girl," Chanda quipped. Her sarcasm nearly had Carlos choking on his swig of water.

"If—and I mean *if*—I have time, I'll drop your books off. But that's it." Jordan picked up his empty plate, gave it a quick rinse at the sink and popped it in the dishwasher. "In fact, I'm about to swing by the vet clinic to look at a litter of puppies. Newfoundlands from that pregnant mama Damon rescued around Christmas. If you want me to drop off the books, hand them over."

Damon was in charge of their lifeguard and water rescue team. Carlos had known him since they were kids, but Damon had become a Navy SEAL back when Carlos had gone the Air Force route. No other dog could come as close to loving water as much as that man did than a Newfie.

Chanda disappeared and returned with three books. Quite a stack. He'd bet his life she'd made up the whole thing and grabbed the first books she found on her nightstand. One still had a bookmark sticking out of it. Someone was going to be losing sleep over how that story finished. All in the name of orchestrating a real-life happy ending. It wouldn't be the first time she'd meddled. Not that Carlos was all innocent here, but he wasn't matchmaking. That match already existed to anyone paying enough attention. Jordan just needed courage and a little nudge.

"How long's it going to take before you hunt your book down at Castaway and finish reading it?" Carlos asked, as soon as Jordan closed the front door behind him. Carlos went to the sink to take care of his plate.

"You noticed, huh? A sister's gotta do what a sister's gotta do. That boy has too much pride."

"Is there such a thing?"

"You wouldn't know. When are you going to give in and find someone to come home to?"

Carlos dried his hands on a towel printed

in pink and red hearts, then hung it on the oven handle to dry.

"Look who's talking."

"Me? Boy, I have my hands full with my furry friends at the vet clinic, and everyone working there is family to me. Then there's you and Jordan. My heart runneth over. But you? All work. Same with my brother."

"I have Pepper at home. Plenty of friends. And work is fulfilling." He grabbed his jacket off the coat rack by the door.

"*Fulfilling* doesn't mean the same thing as *full* or *filling* separately. Your heart needs filling. You need someone special to make your life feel full. To make a home with."

"Chanda, you're like a sister to me and I appreciate your concern, but my life is full. I don't need anyone else in it. I can't think of anything better than a good day on shift, one of your amazing meals, then going home to my dog."

"My amazing meals? Are you calling me an enabler?"

"Totally." Carlos laughed as he opened the door. The cool air swirled into the cozy room and Chanda pulled her sweater across her chest. "But truth be told, if I ever did let someone mess with my head the way Eve seems to mess with Jordan's without even meaning to, it wouldn't be for their cooking or cleaning abilities. That's not what makes a home or a relationship. I mean, like I said, I'm not looking for a relationship and I already have my home. I'm just saying. Since you brought it up."

"Of course. I get it. You're happy as you are. That's commendable. A good thing." She patted him on the shoulder as he stepped outside. Was she agreeing with him? Or placating him? He scowled back at her, only half meaning it, and she gave him a cheeky smile.

"Enough already," he said. "Focus your need to matchmake on your brother."

The corners of her smile softened into something wistful and sad.

"He's not ready. I push a little, but I know he's not. He can't seem to shed the pain. To trust again."

Carlos braced his hands on his hips and stood there staring at a divot in the wood floor in silence. He understood the pain. He'd trusted someone with his heart, only to have her leave when he needed her most. Jordan had suffered a breakup as well, but in many ways, it had cut deeper than Carlos's. It had struck a nerve so deep that it had to have tangled in his soul. He'd tried talking to Jordan many times, but the guy resisted. Joked off any attempt at bringing up dating again. Chanda was right about that.

"Eve would never hurt him the way Mary did."

"No, she wouldn't. There's more love in that girl than I've ever seen. More love in each of them than I've ever seen, for that matter. Both givers, yet afraid to give to each other. I think that's why he helps around so much. He has so much to give and needs to give it in a way that keeps his heart protected. I like Eve a lot. I truly believe those two are meant to be together. But Mary seemed nice too before her family became involved."

Carlos nodded. Mary had been a decent person. But she hadn't been strong enough to stand up to her family's pressure to leave the relationship because they didn't approve. As far as Carlos was concerned, that made her complicit. Or weak. Or she just didn't love Jordan enough to fight for him. Whichever it was, she didn't deserve him. Real love was unconditional and pushed through barriers and distance like a powerful wave destined… aching…to reach the sandy shore. Everyone deserved that kind of love. It was the only kind worth diving in deep for. But not everyone was meant to find it in their lifetime. He'd nearly drowned taking that risk. He'd survived because of his friends in Turtleback, but he'd never risk his heart again.

Jordan was younger, though. Carlos had eight years on him and had made a personal commitment to care for the town…and whatever dog entered his life. That's all he needed. Jordan hadn't carved his path yet. Two years on the force, after spending several at a desk job and hating it, but no definite goals beyond that. Carlos could see his deputy filling his boots someday. He'd make a superb sheriff. But Jordan probably couldn't envision that yet. His confidence had taken a beating. As a man, Carlos knew that took time to rebuild.

"A word of advice, Chanda?"

"What's that?"

"Don't take it the wrong way. It's a reminder to myself too. We can't push him too hard. The fastest way to scare those two apart is to let them think we're shoving them together.

Sometimes a guy likes to think he's figuring it out on his own. Even when he's not."

"I know. It's a pride thing. We women have it too by the way. It's all tied up with self-respect and choice. That said, I know they each have their reasons for taking things slow, but there's slow and there's plain stuck. Nothing wrong with a nudge now and then."

"Hey, I'm with you on that. I'd hate to see Eve find someone else before he gets the courage to let her know how he feels. And vice versa."

"I just don't want him being a lonely bachelor the rest of his life. And I wouldn't mind nieces and nephews to play with."

A bachelor. Like he was. Only he wasn't lonely. He was just fine. A soft image of Faye flicked ever so briefly in his mind. Not with the suspicious darkness in her eyes when she first met him, but the way she'd looked up at him while petting Pepper, with the sun making the crystal blue of her eyes shimmer like the sea at sunrise. He gave his eyes a quick rub and inhaled deeply. He wasn't taking it slow. He wasn't even trying to go anywhere with anyone at all. Least of all Faye. She clearly had baggage of her own and he wasn't getting involved…other than to help her out if needed.

Then why are you thinking of her?

Heck if he knew. No. He did. It was because she needed help. Protection. And so did the town from whomever she was running from. It was his duty. His moral compass kept pointing him toward her. That's all. Wasn't it? Was that why Natalie had been a part of his life? Because he'd wanted to protect her after hearing about her past? Protection and duty and love were different things. He'd loved Natalie, but had it been the kind of love his parents had had? The kind that even death couldn't end? The kind nothing could come between?

The moment Nat had told him she was leaving came back to him. The look in her eyes. The way she had tipped her chin up in resolve. There were no tears. Only resolve. Strength. Defense. It was in that moment that he realized she'd never really let him in. She had never jumped in with both feet, trusting him to catch her. His mother had told him that true love was when a person could let themselves free-fall, knowing and trusting that the other would be there to catch them. *Trust.*

He scratched his Adam's apple and hurried down the front steps. He needed to leave. He didn't have the time or patience for all this relationship talk. It was getting to him. Opening old wounds. Messing with his head. He needed to escape.

"Thank you for having me over. Sorry to eat and run, but—"

"No worries." Chanda patted his back. "You go do your thing. Text me if you see Jordan working on that door."

Okay, guess she wasn't going to take his advice. He waved without answering as he turned and headed off. He could hear her sigh. She knew full well he had better things to do than to report back on his friend and colleague's love life. And he knew she meant well.

Only he wasn't sure if that sigh was over her brother's lack of a love life...or his own. As far as he was concerned, Chanda needed to focus on her brother's...or *her* own, for that matter. Carlos didn't need anyone but the town and his friends. These people were his family. They *trusted* him to provide a safe place to live. Maybe he didn't have a great track record with relationships, but taking care of people? That he could do.

Which was why Eve's friend being in town was on his mind. If her abusive past was behind her, as it had been with Natalie, then maybe she'd realize that staying in Turtleback was an option. She already had a friend here in Eve. Turtleback was a safe haven. A good place to raise a kid like Nim. If her past was still haunting her, in the sense that her ex was still a threat, then it would be his duty to protect both her and the townsfolk. If she needed a place to put down new roots, they'd welcome her here, though he knew a small town like this wasn't for everyone. Most enjoyed the place as a temporary escape. A vacation. Not a permanent home. Natalie surely hadn't.

But if Faye wasn't in danger…if she was keeping darker secrets…an agenda that would endanger anyone in this town…he needed to find out about it. As an officer, there were rules about looking into people's pasts. Background checks weren't supposed to be done for personal reasons. That would be breaking rules, and Carlos practiced what he preached. He stuck to the law. There was a line between respecting a person's privacy and invading it, but if she was in danger he might have to. If he was going to be able to do his job right, either Faye could trust him enough to give him more information herself or he'd have to dig up that information himself. *Trust*. A single action that could either build or destroy it.

CHAPTER FIVE

FAYE TUCKED HER hair behind her ears and sat cross-legged in one of two beanbags Eve had in the Castaway Books children's nook. She scooped Nim up and nestled her into her lap, as six other kids sprawled on the throw rug in front of Eve's wingback chair. They were already waiting for the story to start by the time she'd arrived with Nim. Boy, did leaving a house take twice as long with a little one in tow, or what? She had always respected her sister, but now she was in complete awe of how Clara had handled motherhood…and everything else…with apparent ease. Of course, she now knew how deceiving looks could be. All those couples coming through her business, so blissful, as though they'd stepped out of a commercial for the one real estate company that would find you a house with a magic front door to happily-ever-after. How many of those couples had been putting on a front? How many happily-ever-afters really existed?

She adjusted her position a little and glanced about the room. Some of the kids sat with their legs crisscrossed like hers, some lay on their bellies with elbows in front and two practically clung to Laddie, the rough collie she'd been told about. That dog was absolutely gorgeous, with flowing sable hair, a white mane and blaze on his muzzle and a kind, knowing expression on his face. Every so often, he'd "mother" the two kids at his sides with a gentle nuzzle, just to make sure they understood he was their nanny for the hour. Faye had never had a rough collie come through her business, but she'd read up and watched instructional videos on how to groom them, just in case. She desperately wanted to run her hands through that coat and plant a kiss on Laddie's head, but she didn't want to disturb Eve's foray into some imaginary wilderness where trees could talk and birds loved math. Not exactly Valentine's fare, but the first three books she'd read had covered the season with various themes of love, from showing it to Mother Earth, to making everyone in school feel included on

the playground, to caring for pets…to how
love can make a family in a million ways,
including chosen or adoptive ones.

She held Nim a little tighter and pressed her
nose to her red hair. She could still smell the
henna, though the scent was fading slightly
beneath the classic perfume of baby shampoo.
She hoped no one else noticed it. If something bad did happen to her sister, would she
become Nim's only family? She'd promised
Clara she wouldn't let Jim have her. But he
was her legal parent. Faye wasn't. Unless she
could somehow prove he was unfit.

A snort escaped her, but luckily it coin-
cided with something funny Eve had read and
blended into the giggles around her. Prove Jim
was unfit? He was the lawyer with connections. Not her. And she was the kidnapper. It
didn't bode well. *You have to be okay, Clara.
I'll figure something out. I'll find you.* She
had no idea how. Nim had to be her priority.
She couldn't stay under the radar with Nim
while still searching for Clara. She closed her
eyes and lowered her chin. It all seemed so
impossible. So frustrating and unfathomable.
As soon as reading time was over and the
place cleared, she'd let Eve know that she'd

be leaving tomorrow. She'd come up with a reason. Another lie. A made-up relative she needed to visit or something.

She took a deep breath and absentmindedly clapped along with the others when Eve snapped the book shut with an elfish grin on her face. Reading to kids...running this place...really put a sparkle in her eyes and a glow in her cheeks. She was a natural with children. She would make a great mother someday, if she wanted to be one. Of course, being great with kids didn't necessarily mean that a person had to have kids of their own. But the opposite happened all too often. Awful parents who didn't deserve the gifts life had given them. Parents who failed miserably at parenting.

Faye was a natural with dogs, yet she had never had one of her own. *Because you might fail at that too.* It had been ingrained in her. The fear of failing anyone who'd put their faith in her, including a pet. She released one hand from Nim's finger grip and tried to smooth the knot tightening at the bridge of her nose. *Stop cutting yourself down. You hate it when Clara does and now you're doing it. So you don't own a dog. Not everyone does.*

Her parents' exact words. *Not everyone does.* They'd said it so many times over the course of her childhood and teen years, the phrase grated her skin. The assumption that the twins weren't responsible enough to take on a pet of their own always made its way into the conversation too. Their mom once used the analogy of them being drawn to glitter, but not able to handle the cleanup. For some reason, that comment stuck with her. Like glitter. It was a lot easier to care for someone else's pets. They were eventually sent home, just like grandkids, or kids at a day care, or even a reading group. The level of responsibility and risk of failure was different when the kid or pet wasn't your own. Wasn't it? She looked at Nim. It didn't feel different right now. She was an aunt, not a parent, yet she knew without a doubt that she'd risk her life to save Nim. No question about it. She was learning as she went when it came to Nim. God help her, she was finding herself having to search online to find out when car seats could face forward or what foods toddlers could eat, but she loved her niece. She loved her sister. And they were counting on her. They'd put their trust in her. That's what it all came down to. Didn't it? Love. Being there for someone when they needed you the most.

She thought of Pepper. That was the dog's name, wasn't it? Yes. Yes, it was. She could hear Carlos Ryker's timber-like voice saying the name in her mind, as clearly as if he were standing next to her. Pepper, an elderly dog who'd been abandoned. A sweet soul who might have spent the rest of her life without a permanent home or the love she deserved. Carlos had taken her in. Given her shelter, love and protection. Working full-time had been Faye's ongoing excuse whenever people—including clients—asked if she had a dog. But was it a good enough reason or was it a cop-out? No pun intended. She'd hidden behind the excuse.

For the amount of time she spent with dogs and for as much as she loved them, all she could really show for it was the money she earned for grooming and training them. Not that that was bad in and of itself. She ran a business. A service. Her clients needed and appreciated her. They knew she was dedicated to their dogs and loved and cared for them as if they were her own. Working with dogs was her passion. It was just that she'd never been able to take that next step. She held back out of fear. Self-doubt. What if she ended up being a better dog trainer and groomer than she was a dog parent? What if she failed at it or didn't have the time and energy to dedicate to her pets after a long day at work? Just because other people with careers owned dogs, did that mean she had to? Just because she loved them, did it mean she could handle one of her own? That fear of failure that her parents had pounded into her had kept her from getting a dog as soon as she was living on her own. The residual influence parents' words could have on a kid was a powerful thing.

Her parents had a way of spinning every wish she or Clara made into something they wanted only because others had it. The projection of all projections. Mom and Dad never did look in a mirror and see how *their* choices and decisions had been based on what friends and colleagues in their social circle had or were doing. And they assumed their twins were cut from the same cloth.

Story time ended and Nim squirmed out of her lap and headed for Laddie, yanking off the small quilt another child had covered the pooch with.

Kids shared mere threads with their parents. They weren't the same swatch of material. They didn't have the exact same pattern, no matter how carefully a parent tried to stitch one. Her parents had threaded every needle with the utmost care—what schools they went to, what outfits they wore and what got packed in their lunches, lest a teacher judge them for it.

Eve made eye contact with her and cocked her head inquisitively. Had she been frowning? She smiled widely. Maybe too widely.

"I loved that story, Eve. You're so good at reading with expression. You had the children mesmerized. Me too, I must say."

Eve's expression flitted from concern to joy as swiftly as a butterfly unfolding its wings and taking flight.

"It's so much fun. Seeing their eyes open wide tickles my heart. Give me a sec," she said, leaping up and stopping a six-year-old from scaling a ceiling-high bookshelf. She lifted him down just as his father entered the shop and gave the kid a look that scolded without words. The boy ran over and hugged his dad's leg, then looked up with a cheeky grin. Faye had a feeling it wasn't his first climbing adventure. The dad left, just as a mother entered, followed by a few others, including, from the hellos she overheard, the vet, Grayson Zale.

Nim had started playing with a large, square, wooden box that had puzzles and mazes built onto it. Faye had seen a similar one at her sister's house in Mia's room. She'd been told it was good for fine motor skills. She really had a lot to learn. She needed to see if the local grocers had any small developmental toys in the baby aisle. She couldn't lug the poor kid from state to state with nothing to stimulate her mind or help her to be happy and forget anything negative she'd witnessed between her parents.

Laddie sniffed and licked Nim's ear. *The henna.* Faye held her breath until Dr. Zale said a quick hello, then proceeded to greet others who were picking up kids. Faye had nothing to add to all the small talk about Valentine's Day and the local news.

All these people knew each other. Faye and Nim were outsiders. She felt even more out of place considering no one here knew her truth. A happy, close-knit town… And here she was, a criminal, marring their lives by hiding out among them. Lying to her old friend. Lying—for Pete's sake—to the town sheriff.

Faye tried to look interested in browsing books as Eve took care of customers. Dr. Zale and Laddie left pretty quickly. She could only assume he had other animals awaiting his care. A few parents lingered. One mother purchased a book titled *365 Ways to Be Romantic*. Was she buying it for herself or her spouse? If the gift was for her spouse, that probably said more to Eve than the poor woman probably realized, but Eve didn't flinch or ask. She simply rang up the book and had it bagged with streamlined efficiency.

"That was busy for a bit," Eve said, slathering on some hand lotion and coming around the counter. "I'm happy you came. What did you think?"

"It was wonderful. I can tell you love what you do," Faye said.

"I really do." She hesitated. "Do you have a minute? I'd love for you to stay longer and talk. I have a coffee maker and tea in the back."

"Yes, actually. I was hoping to talk to you about something too."

The shell-and-bell chime announced another visitor. Eve turned and something shifted in her face at the sight of a very handsome man in jeans, a red cable-knit sweater and down jacket. He quickly shut the cold outside, jiggling the loose door handle briefly, then turned and stood a little taller. His warm brown eyes were completely on Eve.

"Hey, Eve."

Goodness, that voice. Deep and firm, yet there was hesitation…a softness in the way he said her name…as if whispered on a final breath. So, he knew Eve. Of course he did. This was Turtleback. What did Faye expect?

"Jordan." Eve gathered herself before turning to Faye. "Oh, Faye, this is Deputy Jordan. He works with Carlos…the sheriff you met. Jordan, Faye's a friend staying over at my place."

"Nice to meet you."

"You too," Faye said.

A deputy. She looked over her shoulder to check on Nim, even if she could hear her flipping pages in the corner nook. She tried to look calm but her insides skittered frantically. She needed to stop getting so jittery at the mention or sight of cops or someone was bound to get suspicious. Why was Eve's store such a magnet for cops? Were they onto her?

Eve cleared her throat and a small cough escaped. On second thought, how could a pretty woman like Eve not be a magnet for single men?

"Returning, donating or consigning?" Eve glanced at the books he carried. "Is romance not your thing?"

"What?" Jordan shuffled on the spot, then glanced Faye's way. Faye immediately looked away, not out of fear this time, but because she didn't want him thinking she was eavesdropping. Although she was. Hard not to. The poor guy seemed flustered and at a loss for words. What was it about the word *romance* that threw so many guys off-kilter?

"The books," Eve said. "They're romance novels." She cocked her head, splayed her hands and waited a beat. He only blushed more, then dropped the books on the counter and took an extra step away from them for safe measure. Faye bit her lower lip to keep from laughing. Eve shook her head and picked up the books.

"I was kidding, Jordan," she said. "I know these were Chanda's. She bought them here. Returning them so soon? Didn't she like them?" She flipped to the page where a bookmark was, seemed to note how far along it was in the storyline, then removed the bookmark and added it to a basket with others for the taking. Faye had noticed earlier that whenever a customer made a purchase, she told them they could pick a free bookmark. Bookmark recycling. Kids loved looking through the basket. No sugary lollipops needed.

Jordan rubbed the back of his neck, glanced back at the door, then at Eve.

"Oh. Um. I have no idea. She asked me to drop them off. That's all. Maybe you should call her to sort it all out. I'm just the messenger."

"Okay, then. I'll give her a call in a bit."

"Okay. That works." He didn't turn to leave. Eve stood expectantly, rocking on her heels a few times. She tucked her hair behind her ear.

"Did you want to browse around?" she finally asked.

"Oh. No, no," Jordan said, apparently waking up from his Eve-induced trance. "I'll see you around."

Faye could tell by the way he fidgeted with his jacket, the guy wanted to say more. He didn't want to leave just yet. Her nerves fired up. What if she was misreading him? What if it wasn't Eve he was interested in? What if the sheriff had sent him over to spy on the stranger with a kid in town?

If there's a search out for you, this deputy wouldn't be dawdling. The sheriff would be here too. You'd be on your way in for questioning already.

She took a deep breath and tried to focus on Nim at the bookshelf. The man was clearly interested in Eve. He was here for her. Not Faye or Nim. She dared a side-peek over at the two. Yep. Eve wasn't acting the way she did around other customers…super cheerful. She had toned it down a notch or two. Seemed a bit more controlled. Or maybe unsure of herself?

"Yeah, see you later," Eve said, nibbling on her bottom lip as he headed for the door.

He turned the handle once, opened the door, then turned the handle again and inspected the latch on the door frame. He wiped his palm across his jaw.

"I, uh, know you probably plan to fix this yourself, but if you need any help—I mean, not because you can't do it yourself—I know you can—but…what I mean is, if you're busy with the store or customers…" He nodded in Faye's direction "…I'm happy to tighten it up for you. I have twenty minutes before I need to report back into work. I have tools in my—"

"I have a toolbox."

"Yes. Of course. I was only offering. I know you're handy." He started to leave.

"Eve, sorry to interrupt, but I'd love some help picking books out for my daughter," Faye interjected. She wasn't sure why or where the impulse had come from, but it seemed like the right thing to do. Get Eve to let Prince Charming give her a hand. Eve crinkled her nose at her.

"Sure. I'll be right there, Faye."

"I feel bad for taking up so much of your time with my visit. Eve, you should have told me you had so much to do around here. Like fixing the door. I can get out of your way. Or help out," Faye said.

"You're not in the way," Eve insisted, looking a little perplexed.

"Like I said," Jordan jumped in. "I can lend a hand, if you like. I was impressed with all the repairs you did yourself after the last hurricane. But I get that sometimes life can get busy and hard to keep up with."

"I keep up fine," Eve said, then immediately looked at her feet and gave her head a shake. "You were?"

"Yes. That was a lot of work. Made me think of those do-it-yourself shows on TV. You could've been on one with all you did around here," he said, smiling sheepishly.

"Thanks." Eve seemed at a loss for words. This was interesting, Faye thought. "I'm sorry if I sounded rude. I usually do keep up, but if you're offering, I have my toolbox under here. You don't have to go out to get yours."

She pulled a toolbox from under the counter. It was one of those standard red ones, only she'd painted it with a trail of carpenter ants, going from tiny to extra-large, around the perimeter and a sun and flowers on top. All with smiley faces.

"Right." Jordan eyed the box skeptically. Eve held it out closer to him.

Faye picked up Nim and rubbed noses with her as a cover-up, just so she could let out the chuckles she was holding back.

"These are good-quality tools," Eve promised. "They used to be my father's. He loved fixing things around the house. Or trying to, at least. It didn't always work out as intended."

"He was an artist too," Jordan deadpanned.

"I painted the box after saving it from a box of garage sale items after he died. Carpenter ants because carpentry was his thing and he was a hard worker. I used to tell him that his spirit animal had to be an ant. He humored me. Nothing fazed him. He used to tell me that I shouldn't let anything or anyone ruffle me up either. My mom didn't realize how much it meant to me, I guess." Her voice lowered with the last words. She set the box on the countertop and ran her hand over the top. "I don't want anything in it getting lost or disorganized. If it's too girlie for you, then use your own. But don't expect a second chance with it. I rarely let anyone else use it."

Second chance? Was she talking about the box or herself? Was there a history between these two? Jordan frowned slightly, then grasped the box's handle.

"Nothing's too girlie for a real man. And if you can't trust a cop with your valuables, who can you trust? I'll get this done while you see to your friend."

If you can't trust a cop, who can you trust? Faye swallowed hard. Her sister hadn't been able to count on the police where she lived.

He set the toolbox by the door and got to work. Eve's eyes lingered on him a few seconds, then she lifted her chin, smiled and strode over to Nim.

"I hear giggles over here."

"I'm hearing a lot going on between the lines," Faye whispered.

"Shh! You're imagining things," Eve said in an even quieter voice. She shook her head and gave Faye a brief scowl. Fine. She wouldn't say anything, especially not within earshot, but something was definitely going on there.

"Ants, huh? If I believed in spirit animals and had to guess what yours was, I suppose it would be a bookworm," Jordan called out as he worked.

"Very funny," Eve said, as she began reshelving books in the children's area.

Faye bounced Nim on her hip. What would hers be? A turtle hiding in its shell? No, wait. A chameleon or any other animal adept at camouflage. Eve stuck a couple of fantasy books an older child had been looking through back in their spots on a higher shelf. Did shape-shifters count? Not that she had to shape-shift all that much in order to look like her twin.

"How many guesses do I get?" Jordan asked as he pulled out a Phillips screwdriver from the box.

"Maybe I don't have one."

"Dragonfly," Jordan said.

Eve's lips parted and she folded her arms. The corner of his mouth lifted. He shrugged. Oh, the flirting.

"How'd you know?" Eve asked.

He waved the tool around the room at the various dragonflies she had included in the decor: a stained-glass dragonfly hanging in the window, origami ones dangling from the ceiling, watercolors of the insects hovering over ponds. Then Jordan pointed the tool he held at her neck. Her fingers covered the pendant she wore.

"You noticed this tiny thing?" she asked.

The necklace was quite small. Silver with amethyst eyes.

"I notice a lot of things," Jordan said, then his face flushed and he turned his back on them as he finished the repair. "What I mean is, I *have* to. I'm trained to. The power of observation is crucial in my line of work."

Eve's shoulders sank a fraction of an inch. She brushed her hands together and started straightening puppets on the shelf behind her.

"That makes sense. What about you, Faye? What's your animal?" Eve said, clearly deflecting the conversation away from herself.

"Me?" She wasn't about to mention chameleons, lest they ask why. "I don't know."

"Well, is there an animal that plays a big role in your life? That represents something for you? A sort of guide," Eve explained.

Faye let Nim run off and tumble onto the beanbag. It was good to see her acting more normal and not crying so much. She missed her mother. Faye missed home and her work. *Your work.*

"Dogs, I suppose." Yes. Dogs. They were all about unconditional love and loyal friendship. They had appeared in her life, not just in passing but as a work opportunity, back when she had needed it the most. Back when she felt that her parents' love had been weighed down with too many conditions. Back when she and Eve had graduated college and she no longer had her nearby as a friend…and Clara had met Jim. And now she'd had to leave the dogs in her life behind because, well, because of love and loyalty for her sister. She'd gotten the spirit animal message. Was that a sign that she'd never see her business again? That dogs wouldn't be a part of her life anymore?

Jordan looked over his shoulder, his face lit up.

"You have a dog? What kind?" he asked, before turning back to the door.

"Actually, she—"

"No," Faye said, interrupting Eve and giving her a pleading look and small head shake. "No dogs."

Eve knew from social media that Faye owned Dog Galaxy. Darn it. She'd asked her not to mention her real hair color, and had completely forgotten to tell her not to mention her work. She needed to step out of this conversation. She was digging a hole for herself big enough to put a beagle to shame. A hole that would open her up to questions. That would only lead her to reveal too much and risk potential inconsistencies in her answers. Eve frowned but gave her a nod. Good. No doubt her friend would ask questions later. Maybe she figured Faye didn't want her business mentioned for the same fake reason she'd given earlier—to keep her in-laws at bay.

"I'm about to get one," Jordan said. Oblivious to the signals that had passed between Eve and Faye, he grinned and stood, closing up the box and setting it back on the counter. Job done. "I'm on my way to adopt a Newfoundland pup. A rescue, mind you. Not from a breeder."

"Really?" Faye asked, walking over to where Eve stood. The image of her last, mud-caked grooming customer and the defeated look on his owner's face came to mind. "You're going to have your hands full. All that slobber. The hair. And let me tell you, they're like ducks when it comes to finding water. They'll turn a dewdrop into a swimming pool. Or a mud bath."

"You know a lot for never having owned a dog," Eve said.

"Oh." *Shoot.* "A friend once had one. Used

to vent all the time." Faye swallowed but her mouth still felt dry.

"Over a hundred pounds of love and fun. That's how I see it," Jordan said. "I can handle it."

"You have a full-time job." Eve tucked the toolbox back in its hiding place.

"I'll figure it out. I'm sure my sister can help once in a while. In fact… You let Gray bring Laddie around for story time, don't you? I bet the kids would love a puppy hanging—"

"No!" Eve and Faye jumped in simultaneously. Jordan held up his palms in defense.

"Sorry for going there."

"Jordan, there's just no way," Eve explained. "I love puppies like nobody's business, but here at the bookstore? I don't think so. They piddle and chew. I have books that would turn into chew toys and wallpaper. And your puppy—not the story I'm reading— would get all the kid attention. I'll admit, probably mine, as well."

"She's right, you know. Like I said, I've heard some wild stories from friends," Faye added, to ward off more questions. "I bet they're as much work as a toddler, and I can tell you Nim keeps me on my feet."

As if on cue, the sound of ripping paper caught their attention. Nim stared in wonder at the book in her hands, apparently relishing the sound and feeling of accomplishment. She took out another page.

"Oh, no! I'm so sorry, Eve. I'll pay for it." Faye ran over to rescue what was left of the fairy tale. The last pages that had been torn out. Forget a happy ending. There would be no ending. Was this some sort of omen? Or just an indicator at how inept Faye was at taking care of a child. She was failing miserably at it. She should have been keeping a closer watch.

"It's alright. I can tape the pages back in and discount it. No big deal," Eve said.

"It is a big deal. I'm so sorry."

"Hey, it really is okay," Eve said, gathering the book and pages as Faye carried Nim away from the crime scene. "Take this as a lesson, Jordan. Puppies are like toddlers. Never a dull moment."

"I'm getting this puppy. There's no talking me out of it."

"We're not trying to. I'm just saying make

arrangements that don't include me. I have my hands full." Eve waved a puppet in the air for emphasis.

"I've got this. The crate for training is set up. I have the supplies. More toys than I had planned to spend on, but have you seen the pet aisle at the store? I couldn't decide on just one. Besides, the poor thing needs a loving home. I'm telling you. I've got this. I'm all in."

The man was in love. There was no doubting it.

The crate and supplies. Toys. A leash. Faye's energy spiked and her pulse picked up. She needed money. A job that wouldn't require a lie detector test or ID or references. One that she definitely knew how to do.

"I've heard that puppies, or any dogs, that get a lot of exercise are less likely to chew things up or cause trouble. I used to walk my neighbor's dog when I was a kid. I could be available for dog walking."

"That's perfect," Eve said. "I bet there are others who could use dog sitting or walking. Carlos for one. Or even taking Laddie to Gray after reading time so he doesn't have to take off work to pick him up."

"You'd be willing to do that?" Jordan asked.

"Well, I don't know." She had intended to tell Eve that she'd be leaving tomorrow. She didn't necessarily want to publicize those plans to a cop who worked with the sheriff. But it also wouldn't be fair to Jordan to make a dog-walking commitment then disappear.

"Oh, come on. Just try it a few times while you're here," Eve said. Her friend was really trying to get her to stick around. She didn't know that Faye had hoped to be gone in less than twenty-four hours. She needed to think. She wanted to leave to keep Jim off her trail and because the sheriff lived too close for comfort, but she needed money too. If she was going to go nomadic with Nim, she'd require cash for motels and gas and food. Staying just a little longer and walking dogs would allow her to earn enough to get by.

Maybe she could survive here a week or two without being discovered. She'd bought a carrier when she got the playpen. One that indicated it would work for Nim's size—which was small for her age, according to Clara. Clara used a carrier for walks all the time. Faye had figured it would feel familiar to Nim and comforting. Faye was quite fit and had plenty of upper-body strength, considering all the dogs she worked with and often had to lift onto grooming tables. Carrying Nim around would be worth the try. If it proved to be too much, well, then she'd call it off and move on. She didn't think pushing a stroller with more than one dog tagging along would be doable. Nor did she want to have dogs whose temperaments she didn't know walking near Nim at face level. Eve raised her brows.

"Who can say no to time with a puppy?" Eve added for good measure.

"Fine. I don't think I would be able to walk the older dogs with your puppy. I heard once that puppies shouldn't go on walks that are too long, until they're a little older, but I could help with potty training. Taking him or her out when you're on duty. And play with all the toys you bought. I could take the older dogs separately."

She almost took her offer back. What if the sheriff really did want her to walk his dog, Pepper? She had intended to keep him at bay. It was bad enough that he lived just down the street from the cottage. She could end up having to talk to him more often than was safe.

But at the same time, maybe it would show him that she wasn't a threat. If Jim got to him through his police contacts, maybe Carlos would give her the benefit of the doubt, which would buy her just enough time to disappear again…or get him to listen to her instead of Jim.

"I can have word out within the hour," Eve said. "Jordan, could you have Chanda post a sign at the clinic when she goes into work? I could put one here. Dog sitting and walking available. Faye, do you have a cell you want to put on it?" Faye didn't answer right away and tension must have shown on her face because Eve didn't wait. "Come to think of it, put the Castaway Books number down," Eve told Jordan. "Town residents will recognize it and ask me for details. You'll have to figure out what to charge. People may not trust their pets to someone they don't know. But don't worry, Faye. A friend to one of us is a friend to all, so once I get word out you can help with pets, you may have more leashes offered than you can handle."

"Your number, then," Jordan said. "I'll talk to you later. About compensating you and all. First, I need to get to the vet clinic before someone else gets first dibs on the puppies."

"Thanks for fixing the door!" Eve called out as he rushed off.

Faye wasn't sure if he heard the thanks or not. Or if he cared.

"He seemed nice." Faye let Nim grab her index finger and helped her toddle closer to the door. "Interested."

"What? You have the wrong idea. Jordan is like that. He helps everyone. All the time. Trust me. It's just his thing."

"He seemed determined to help you. Miss Dragonfly." Faye fluttered her lashes at her friend. Eve swatted her arm and chuckled. But her nose did tinge pink.

"No, really. It had nothing to do with me. In fact, he hasn't offered help around here in a long time. Maybe he was interested in the town's pretty newcomer."

"Ha. You're hilarious. Anyway, thank you for helping me get word out about dog walking."

"It's all a ploy to convince you to stick around longer. If you make commitments and money, you'll be less likely to leave." Eve gave her a loving smirk.

"You're a good friend. With that, I need to head out too. Nim will get cranky soon. It's almost time for a snack and nap. Thanks for the reading hour."

"Don't leave yet. We were about to have coffee when Jordan walked in. There's something I want to ask you. Talk about."

"I know. I'm so sorry. I'll clean up whatever I missed when I get back to your place."

"Faye. I haven't been home since this morning. Clean up what?" She glanced over to where Nim had torn up the book. "Never mind. But whatever it is, it's fine. That's not what I want to talk about. I caught on that you didn't want your Dog Galaxy business mentioned. You made it clear when you got here that you were lying low. But there's more, isn't there? What's going on? Really?"

Faye's cheeks suddenly felt cold and clammy.

"Going on? You lost me." She secured Nim on her hip again and grimaced as she freed a lock of hair Nim was trying to pull out by the roots.

"That." Eve gently touched the marks on her wrist where her sleeve had hiked up. "Who did that to you? Is that why you're here? Why you left him? Was your husband abusing you? Faye. You know you can trust me. That I can help hide you. I think that's why you came here. To Turtleback."

"That's not what you think. I got nipped by a cranky Chihuahua who—"

"The truth, Faye. Look around here. Between my work helping abused women and children escape back in college and the number of suspense thrillers I've read, it's not hard to see the clues. The hair henna. I know the smell. The story about not wanting your ex's family to find you. The marks on your arm. The way your face went white when Carlos first came in here this morning and then again when I told you Jordan was his deputy. Was your husband a bad cop? I read a novel based on that scenario. It was made into a movie too. Every profession has its villains. You can count on me. You can trust Carlos and Jordan and others at the station here."

Faye's brain wouldn't stop spinning. She closed her eyes to get her bearings. Regain her equilibrium. She had to keep her facts straight and her lies straighter. She pinched the bridge of her nose with her left hand and held on to Nim with her right. *No cops. Don't trust anyone.* She couldn't get Clara's warning out of her head. She felt like someone was ripping her in half. Her gut told her she could trust her friend, but whom was she going to be loyal to? Her sister who'd asked her to keep Mia safe and not to trust a soul? Or her friend who'd once trusted her with what she did in secret because she had needed Faye to lie for her just once, in the name of saving someone. Only now she was lying to Eve. She needed to trust someone. She couldn't do this alone. But what if she told Eve the truth and word got out and something bad happened to Clara or Mia because of it? What if taking the risk put them in worse danger?

She tried to say something but her throat stuck. What if the others had noticed the same clues already?

"Not a word. Promise. This is between the two of us. Nothing about the marks or my ex."

Half-truth. For now, at least. *Forgive me, Eve.*

"I'll keep anything you tell me between us, but I have to be honest, Carlos is the one who came to me about the marks on your wrist. He was worried and didn't want to scare you off by saying anything himself."

"Oh, no." Faye shuffled over to the wing-back chair and collapsed in it, still clinging to Nim. Thank goodness the kid wasn't a hyper one. Her quietness was a concern, but at the moment, Faye wasn't sure she could handle more than the ripped book and pulled hair. She covered her face, took a deep breath, then pressed her fist against her lips. Her marks were mere scratches. They weren't anything like the bruises she'd seen on Clara. The ones her sister had always had an explanation for. Faye hated herself right now. Why had she not put the clues together sooner, like Eve had? Why hadn't she been more insistent with her sister? But would Clara have listened? Or would she have pushed back harder, covering up for her marriage?

Eve knelt before her and laid her hand gently on Faye's knee.

"Listen to me. I wouldn't tell you that you can trust him unless I *knew* you could. Stay here. Consider Turtleback your safe haven. He—we—won't let anything happen to you or Nim."

Faye shook her head but needed a minute to formulate her answer. She was rocking on the edge of a cliff. One misstep and she'd pull everyone down with her.

Eve couldn't understand. She didn't know about Clara. Yes, she had been aware that Faye had a twin. They'd never met, since Clara wasn't at the same college. In fact, they'd deliberately gone to different schools, wanting to separate socially for a while so that they could nurture their differences without people constantly assuming they were identical in personality and intellect too. Come to think of it, she wasn't sure if Eve knew they were identical.

"No. I can't talk to him. At least not yet. He can think what he wants about my wrist, but please don't elaborate. Just tell him I'll be fine. If he asks. I'm not putting my personal life on display. Please keep it to yourself."

"But you could press charges."

"It has been tried. Trust me." It wasn't a lie. Not the way she'd phrased it. She'd tried taking Clara to the station. Look where it got her. It had fueled Jim's anger, proving he could get away with murder.

"Is your ex a cop?"

"No, but close enough. Let it go. Please."

"But—"

"Eve."

Her friend stood up, paced twice, then stopped.

"Okay, fine. But promise you'll let me know if you need something. Protection."

Faye got up, tugged Nim's jacket on her and slung the cotton bag she'd borrowed from Eve for kid supplies onto her other shoulder.

"Promise."

Only that *was* a lie. Jim had manipulated her sister. He'd manipulated authorities. No way would she let him get away with it again. He wasn't going to put Faye in jail and take his daughter away. She'd never be able to find Clara and protect Mia from a cell. If she so much as suspected that Jim or the police were on to her, she'd run. She'd leave this town and never come back. Safe haven? Homes were supposed to be safe havens. Clara's wasn't. Faye no longer had hers. Hiding out here was only a temporary solution. She was beginning to believe that safe havens didn't really exist. That the word *safe* was nothing more than a platitude, the same as when grown-ups told kids that everything would be okay, even if they knew it might not be.

Faye had no idea what would happen a few

hours from now or tomorrow or the next day. The only thing she knew for sure was that her days here were numbered. She feared her sister's days might be numbered too, if Jim hadn't done something horrible to her already.

CHAPTER SIX

CARLOS WAITED HIS turn at The Saltwater
Sweetery. Standing there, enveloped by the
aroma of freshly baked goods and Darla's secret recipe for saltwater taffy, was a special
kind of heaven. Darla had acknowledged him
with a smile when he first walked in, as she
helped Joel Burkitt, the town lawyer, select
his wife's favorite flavors of taffy. From what
Carlos could overhear, Joel didn't have a clue,
but Darla had an uncanny ability to mem-
orize her customers' favorites. She guided
Joel, adding his choices to a heart-shaped
box embossed with the shop's logo in spar-
kly white lettering. She'd told Carlos once
that she chose the white sparkles because they
looked like both salt and sugar, two ingredi-
ents she depended upon, as the bakery's name
suggested.

There were two other customers ahead of
him and, although he knew Darla wouldn't

hesitate to pack up his usual, hand it over and let him pay later, he'd signaled with a wave of the hand to let her know he'd wait. He was against using his position to cut in line or pass folks on the road—unless there was an emergency, of course.

Her assistant, one of the high schoolers who worked weekends, came through the double doors from the kitchen with a tray of heart-shaped cookies, each frosted in white with either pink or red lettering spelling out words like *forever, love* or *soul mate.* He grimaced at the last one. They were gingerly placed next to rows of Darla's famous "crab claws"—her version of bear claws with a seaside twist—frosted in red with similar inscriptions, and "sea turtle" clusters, made with melted chocolate, nuts and nougat. His stomach rumbled and he rubbed his hand against it. The guy in front of him turned his head.

"Mine's doing the same thing. I need one of those doughnuts like there's no tomorrow. And a cup of her double-shot, double-cream espresso."

"Guess I'm not the only one here for myself and not for Valentine's gifts," Carlos said, sort of relieved.

"Having to head to the gift shop for my wife is exactly why I need the sugar and caffeine first. It'll help me think more clearly. Calm my nerves. The pressure cooker I got her for Christmas didn't go over so well."

Carlos nodded without comment. Even he had more of a sense of self-preservation than that. The guy—Roger's cousin, who had his own gas station up in Corolla—smacked the air with his hand.

"I tell ya, she talked about nothing but having one of those for months. Said it would save her so much time. Went on and on about how if she didn't have to spend half her day in front of the stove cooking for our five kids, her back wouldn't hurt so much and she'd have more time to herself."

Carlos stretched his neck and put his hands in the pockets of his khaki uniform.

"So, you bought her a pressure cooker instead of a massage and day at a spa."

The man pressed his thumb and fingers against his eyes.

"I may need to make that a triple espresso shot. Maybe the gift shop isn't where I should be heading," he said.

"My two cents? Let Darla here help you

pick out a box of sweets, then head to the gift shop and then book a spa treatment. That may make up for Christmas."

"You're right, Sheriff. Thanks, man. I think you might have just saved my life."

"All in the line of duty." Carlos grinned at Darla as the guy went up to the counter for his turn.

The rush of air from The Saltwater Sweetery's door made him glance over his shoulder, but the sight of Faye with Nim in a chest carrier had him doing a double take. Her red hair was peeking out from under an off-white, crocheted beanie hat he'd seen Eve wear before. She had on a matching scarf, jeans and hiking boots. All Eve's.

The lift he felt in his chest when she walked in sank at the realization that she must have packed very light. People did that when they had to leave a situation fast. He wondered if Eve had spoken to her yesterday or last night.

"Hi." He gave a terse nod.

"Hi," she said, hesitating before proceeding to enter. She took her place in line behind him.

He tried to think of what to say next. That was so unlike him. He was used to starting conversations with townsfolk. Communication was an important skill in his profession. He rocked on his heels, then took his hands out of his pockets and motioned ahead of him.

"You're more than welcome to go first. You have a kid with you and all," he explained, as Nim pulled her thumb out of her mouth and grabbed Faye's cheek.

"I'm good. I can wait," she insisted, wiping her cheek and giving Nim her sunglasses to play with. That wasn't such a good—

The little girl snapped one of the arms off and threw it to the ground. Pretty brutal for such a quiet child.

"No, Nim. No. Don't do that." Faye took the surviving parts and put them in her pocket. Carlos picked the temple off the floor to save Faye from trying to stoop down with Nim strapped to her.

"Thanks," she said, taking the broken part. "I should have known better." He didn't comment. "I forgot her toys at the cottage," she added, sucking in her bottom lip and shifting her stance.

A few seconds of silence passed.

"How's—" They both jumped in at the same time. He didn't have anything important to say. He was just going to ask how she'd fared on her first night at Eve's.

"You first," Carlos said.

She wet her lips and placed her hand on the back of Nim's carrier.

"How's Pepper?"

"Good. She's fine. Thanks… Are you sure you don't want to go ahead of me?"

"No, no. Thanks for offering but I'll wait. I need to decide what I want first… What's good here?"

"Everything. I usually get the cinnamon pecan muffin. My personal favorite. But you can't go wrong with anything. Darla, the owner, is magical when it comes to baked goods."

Another pause. Faye looked around the place, then inhaled deeply.

"It smells good in here," she said.

"Always does. Planning anything in particular today? Sightseeing? Is Eve taking you around?"

"Dog walking. I suppose I'll see the town in the process."

"Dog walking?"

"It wasn't planned. Just happened. I met one of your deputies, Jordan."

"Good guy."

"Yes. He was very nice. And apparently the father of a new puppy. I offered to help out with potty breaks and training. And then, somehow, by this morning, I found myself with a list of three other dogs in need of daily walks. I'm grabbing a quick breakfast before I pick the first one up. Laddie, at the vet clinic. We already met. And one named—" she pulled a small piece of paper out from her pocket and read through the notes she'd jotted down "—Bison."

"We all know Bison around here. A bulldog who thinks he's a vacuum cleaner. Not so good in the listening department and can pull hard."

She didn't look bothered.

"The other is Casanova. Hmm. Guess that name speaks for itself."

"Let's just say it's a very good thing that Dr. Zale makes sure dogs and cats around here get spayed and neutered."

"Good thing dogs don't know about Valentine's Day," Faye muttered as she stuffed the paper back in her pocket.

"That one does."

A small laugh escaped her. Light and airy.

As if for a fraction of a second, her guard came down and she could breathe. He thought about seeing if she'd help with Pepper, but snuffed out the idea. He wasn't sure she could even handle the group she'd already taken on.

A frown creased the smooth spot between her brows.

"I was told by each of the owners that their dogs are safe with kids. As in not biting."

"True. They can be difficult—except for Laddie—but not dangerous. Unless you get dragged. Don't hang on. Especially not with Nim on you."

"I know. Thanks."

"Hey, Darla," Carlos said, stepping up for his turn.

"Thanks for waiting. I have yours ready." Darla started to ring it up.

"Hold up. Add hers to the tab."

"What?" Faye said, realizing what he was doing. "You don't have to do that. There's no reason to."

"Consider it a gesture of welcome to our town and a thank-you for working some of the energy out of Casanova. Besides, it'll make the line go faster," he said. He figured that would keep her from arguing. Everyone had their pride and she didn't know he knew what she was going through, but hopefully the gesture would buy him some of her trust. If she was borrowing Eve's clothes and walking dogs during a supposed vacation, she didn't need to spend whatever little cash she had on breakfast. It wasn't much, but maybe it would help, if only to alleviate some pressure. His mother used to say that there was no greater gift than that of giving someone peace of mind. Maybe, if she did alright with dog walking today, he'd go ahead and see if she could add Pepper to the roster. Help her earn a few more bucks and add to the reasons she'd have for staying in Turtleback. She glanced behind her at the people who'd come into the shop shortly after her. Nervous? "Maybe Nim would like a treat or something tastier than sunglasses."

He wished he could rephrase that but it was too late. He had meant to put her at ease, not imply that she wasn't feeding her child enough. He hoped she didn't take it that way.

"Thank you. I, um—"

Carlos held up a finger as a message came through on his shoulder radio. Some tourist was trying to surf despite a warning not to.

One of Damon's water rescue crews was on it but the individual was giving them trouble. He was needed on the scene.

"Sorry about that," he said, apologizing for stopping her midsentence. "Don't think anything of it. Darla, could you just put it all on a tab for me and I'll take care of it later? I need to head out."

"No problem," Darla said, handing him his bag. "I'll take good care of her for you. You have such a cutie there!" She turned her attention to Faye and Nim. Faye's cheeks had turned about as rosy as the frosting on the strawberry cake sitting in the glass case under the counter. Carlos ducked outside before the heat in his own cheeks showed through.

Man, he really did hope his paying for her purchase hadn't been taken the wrong way. Not just by Faye, but Darla. Take good care of her for you? That implied...something. He wasn't sure what, but Faye wasn't his. He was simply trying to be kind. He had acted out of concern. That's all.

He rubbed the back of his neck and stomped over to his vehicle.

Then why had he actually considered lin-

gering at the bakery with her, before the call
came through?

"You're just taking your job seriously. Way
too seriously."

TWENTY-FOUR HOURS. The longest day and
night of her life and she'd already started
today on the wrong foot. Why in the world
had Carlos Ryker paid for her bakery order?
Had Eve said something to him? She'd promised she wouldn't. Even if she didn't, she'd
said that the sheriff had noted the marks on
her wrist. He probably felt sorry for her. Paid
for her breakfast out of pity. She hated that.
She didn't want anyone taking pity on her.
She was strong and capable. She was trying
to do the best that she could. She didn't need
to depend on anyone. She could hold her own.
That's why she was working to make a few
bucks. Work. Not a hand-me-down.

"What can I get you? Faye, right?" Darla
asked.

"Wow. How'd you know my name?" The
hairs on Faye's back prickled. Carlos hadn't
mentioned it while he was in here.

"It's a small town." Darla's smile was genuine and kind. She flipped her thick, blond

French braid over her shoulder as she bent down to get a new pastry box. Faye liked the way she'd braided in a red ribbon. It would be forever before her own hair was long enough to style like that. Darla popped the flat pastry box open. "Eve was in earlier for an herbal tea to go. I have a blend that's good for sore throats. She mentioned that her best friend was in town and that she'd send you over to try something. It's nice to meet you."

"You too." She felt a little better. At least Darla hadn't seen her name on the news or plastered with a rough sketch on street posts. Eve hadn't mentioned a sore throat. Though she did hear her sneezing three times before she left the house early this morning.

"What would you like?"

"Anything filling. Oh, gosh. Are those cream cheese pastries?"

"Yep. We have blueberry-topped cream cheese ones too."

"I'll take one of those and a black coffee to go. And one of those sugar cookies. You can just put it on a napkin and save the box. It won't last long. Thanks." She figured sugar cookies were soft enough for Nim to enjoy. She hoped she was right. Darla didn't show any hesitation or disapproval, so it was probably okay. Except for the sugar, maybe.

"Would she like a milk with the cookie?" Darla suggested.

"Oh. Yes. Sure. Thanks." Why hadn't she thought of that? *She's not judging you. She just suggested a drink. It goes with running a food business.*

She pulled out a tip and added it to a glass jar shaped like a gull with its beak open. A tip was the least she could do, even if Carlos had insisted on paying.

"Are you coming to the Valentine's bonfire tomorrow?" Darla asked.

"I don't think so. This little one will probably be asleep. Fingers crossed. She's been up on and off since three this morning."

"Poor thing. Maybe she's teething."

"Maybe." Faye made a mental note to look into that possibility. She had no clue about kids' developmental timelines. "Thanks." She took the pastry and coffee and slipped outside. One bite and she was in heaven. Nim had eaten her breakfast before they left this morning, but Faye had been too busy seeing to the baby's needs to realize just how hungry she was until she had caught the aroma from the bakery wafting down the street.

A chilly gust of wind snapped at her face, then died down to a breeze. She set her goodies on an iron bistro table outside the shop long enough to secure the snap that kept the hood of Nim's winter jacket shielding both her head and neck.

"Mi!" She tried undoing it.

"Nim, leave it alone. I might work up a sweat walking dogs, but you won't. Here." She dug in her jacket pocket and pulled out the rubber dolphin key chain Eve had given her to use for the spare key. It was big enough not to choke on. "Play with this instead. We need to hurry up before we're late."

The dolphin went straight into Nim's mouth.

"Well, that's one way to go swimming."

She ate her pastry in less than a minute, tossed the napkin in a trash bin by the store and headed down the street in the direction Eve had pointed out earlier. Not hard to figure out, since the only other direction to go in would have led them straight to the boardwalk and beach.

She was supposed to pick up Bison first,

then Casanova, then swing by the vet clinic to get Laddie. They'd all go back in the reverse order. She could do this. She felt at home doing it. Grounded. In control. The pack leader, for what it was worth. Most important, she'd be able to make enough to pay for things like filling her gas tank. She needed to have it full just in case. Whatever cash she had on her would be rationed for Nim's needs. Diapers, food and any clothes she might outgrow. Faye had no idea how long they'd be in hiding.

She also needed to try to find Clara without getting tracked. Could calling cards be tracked? Place of purchase and call? She took a deep breath of cold air and tried to center her thoughts. Yeah. They probably could. Maybe not by Jim himself, but if he initiated an Amber Alert, no doubt the authorities would be able to track any calls put through to anywhere associated with her sister, like friends, cell phones, hospitals. Or he could hire a private investigator. *Where are you, Clara?*

What if her computer searches had been traced? Her calls from Eve's place? No. She was overthinking. It wasn't her laptop. She'd used Eve's. Eve wasn't a suspect. Faye was pretty sure he had no idea where she was. But he was looking. If he'd gone to the police, Carlos would have identified her already. Jim was waiting. He was hoping to get to Faye first. That meant he had something to hide. He didn't want an investigation. He knew Faye wouldn't hurt Mia, so he wasn't worried about that. It bought him time. Although he'd eventually have to come up with a valid reason for not reporting a missing child sooner, if Faye didn't make contact.

But what was he hiding? His history of abuse? If he was abusive and domineering at home, she wouldn't be surprised if he was the same at work. Were there other women he controlled? With the whole #MeToo movement, maybe he was extra worried about his career. There might be other women besides Clara whom he had mistreated who could speak out. Clara had mentioned once that he had been having a lot of meetings with various congressmen and local delegates. Was he considering public office? Was that why he needed to keep Clara from reporting his spousal abuse? Maybe even create sympathy for himself in the process? Wife with mental health issues and Jim trying to raise his child without her?

Faye tossed her coffee cup in the next bin she passed and muttered a curse. She quickly covered Nim's ears.

"You didn't hear that. Do. Not. Repeat."

"Da—"

"Nope." She touched her fingertip to Nim's lips. She had no idea if Nim was about to repeat the curse word or if she was trying to say "Dada"…or which was worse at the moment. "Don't say that. Look! Birdie!" She pointed to a swarm of swallows that gracefully traced the edges of incoming clouds as they dipped and dived in the sky above them. Nim pointed toward the flock, thankfully forgetting whatever she'd been trying to say.

They passed a doctor's office and headed four shops down where the sign read Krinks' Hardware. Easy enough. She entered and was immediately faced with an overweight, slobbery dog. He barked, just once, then lay down on the spot, letting her know walks weren't his thing and not his idea of how to spend his Saturday.

"You must be Faye. People around here just call me Krinks." He offered his hand and gave hers a firm shake. Krinks was a large man with more facial hair than head hair. He had a toothy smile, wind-chapped lips and rounded cheeks that all came together in a way that made her wonder if he posed as the town Santa each year.

"Nice to meet you. I take it Bison isn't fond of walks?"

"What gave it away? The way he's trying to disappear into the floor or his weight? He's on a special diet Dr. Zale prescribed last summer, but he knows how to sniff out the lunches my staff keeps in the back work and storage room."

It was a hardware store. He had a wall of locks to her left next to one of those machines for making key copies. She wondered why he didn't put a lock on the backroom door, but she didn't say anything. It was her first dog walk. She didn't need it ending before it started on account of insulting the owner.

"Perhaps he'll find he likes them when friends are involved. The energy and motivation of a pack."

"I hope you're right. I'll get his leash." He handed it over, then clapped his hands and called to Bison. The dog gave him a dirty look and stood reluctantly, but didn't approach.

"Could I purchase these first?" She chose a pair of sunglasses off a rack by the door and set them on the counter. She didn't bother trying them on. They looked big enough to keep anyone she didn't want from recognizing her.

"Sure thing," Krinks said.

She pulled out a ten from her pocket and handed it over. Krinks rang up the purchase, then grabbed a leash that had been dangling from a hook near a short hall at the side of the store that led to a restroom. He hooked it onto Bison and gave her the handle.

"And who's this little one?" he said, giving the top of Nim's hat a gentle pat. He seemed taller the closer he stood. Bigger. *Chill. Eve wouldn't have suggested walking his dog if he wasn't a nice person.* But people thought Jim was nice too. Appearances could be deceiving. Nim clung tighter to the dolphin key chain and buried her face against Faye's chest.

"My daughter. Nim," she added. It wasn't like she was giving a toddler's name to a stranger. It was a fake name. If anyone asked him if he knew of a girl named Mia, he'd be able to answer no. Besides, if she didn't tell him, he'd find out anyway. The whole small-town thing. "Sorry. She's shy."

"No worries. I have a granddaughter up in Nags Head about that age and she's the same way. Cute as a button. Even when she scowls at her grandpa for telling her not to feed Bison her cookies."

"I bet he loves visiting her."

"Does he ever. Anyway, I need to get back to work. Do you want me to pay you per walk or per week?"

"Is per walk okay with you?"

"Sure thing. I'll have it ready when you get back. Oh, and keep an eye. He's an indiscriminate eater. If he starts sniffing where he shouldn't… You know."

"I'll keep an eye out. Thanks for trusting me with your best friend."

Krinks stood a little taller and looked fondly at Bison.

"That, he is."

Faye put on her sunglasses, tucked her hand in her pocket, then held it out—empty—for Bison to sniff. The dog wagged and followed her without trouble.

"How'd you do that?"

"I have a small baggie with cheese in it in my pocket. Works every time."

She kept a straight face, though she wished she could take back the *every time* part. Darn it. She needed to think thrice before talking. Thinking twice wasn't cutting it. Luckily, Krinks didn't know enough to question her comment.

"Well, I'll be. I'll admit. I'm not the best at training. I get so busy that I'm just happy to have him around. The company. You know? Enjoy your walk."

She had Casanova added to the pack within ten minutes and made her way to just beyond the edge of town where the veterinary clinic stood. There were several cars in the parking lot and a fenced area off to one side. She could see someone in scrubs taking a dog wearing a cone out to relieve himself. A woman came out with Laddie bounding right along beside her.

"Faye?"

For crying out loud. Everyone here knew her by name before she even met them. It was a little disconcerting. She let the dogs greet one another but maintained control of the leashes.

"The pack must have given me away."

"All of these dogs have been patients here and I've never seen them so well behaved and under control. You're a heck of a pack leader. I'm Chanda by the way. The office manager and receptionist all in one. Dr. Z is in the middle of surgery and told me you'd be by for Laddie."

"Nice to meet you. I didn't bring an extra leash. I thought he'd have one."

"Laddie doesn't need one. He won't leave your side unless you tell him to. Unless he decides he has to for the greater good. He's a town hero. Helped save Dr. Z and my friend Mandi, his wife, not too long ago. He'll help keep the others in line too. And this must be Nim. I've heard all about you, sweetheart." Chanda rubbed the back of Nim's hand with her finger and Nim actually reached out to her.

"She likes you."

"I love kids. Don't have any of my own—I was told I'd never be able to, but that's another story—though I helped raise my brother. I'm hoping he has a bunch someday. He would have good-looking kids too. But I doubt anyone could be as pretty as you are, sweetie pie," she said, directing her attention to Nim once again.

"Thank you. I think she's pretty too. And sweet. When she's not crying all night."

"Chamomile tea in a bottle and refrigerated teething rings. No kids, but I've done my share of babysitting," Chanda explained. "There's always children's acetaminophen if she develops a fever or the pain gets too much for her, but I always like to try natural ways first."

Faye was beginning to feel like Dorothy in the *Wizard of Oz*, following the yellow brick road and meeting helpful friends along the way. All the while knowing that the evil witch and her monkeys were hunting her down. In this case, the evil one being Jim and anyone he had under his thumb. Would that make Eve the good witch of the north? She really needed more sleep. Or to stop browsing through children's books.

"Got it. Thanks for the suggestions. I bet Eve has chamomile at her place. And aspirin."

"Oh, no, honey. Not aspirin. Not with a child her age. Too dangerous. Most pediatricians warn new parents about that," she said, frowning.

No aspirin for kids. She didn't know that either. Thank goodness she hadn't tried any already. Chanda was going to think she was an idiot. A bad mother. Or maybe she'd suspect something was off.

"Of course. I meant aspirin for me. All the crying and lack of sleep has been giving me headaches. I'll try the chamomile and iced teething ring for Nim."

"Hon, you could probably use that tea to relax, as well. And a break. If you ever need a babysitter while you're here, give me a call," Chanda said, her shoulders relaxing.

"Thanks. I should get going." Faye motioned her chin toward the dogs.

"I need to get back inside, myself. I'll be here when you return. It was nice to meet you, Faye. Help her out, Laddie."

Laddie wagged his tail, happy to have a job to do.

Faye led the way back along the path she'd come from, then veered right down a trail that took them behind the main road through town and toward the beach. Tall reeds danced whenever the wind picked up, waving them along the sandy path and over a short dune that opened up onto an endless stretch of pristine beach. The town's boardwalk lay a quarter of a mile to her right and beyond it were beach cottages, spread far and wide. She could see a blue one that had to be Eve's from the backside, if she had her bearings right. To the north of her a short distance away, a black-and-white lighthouse stood like a sentinel, watching over several more beach houses that sat beyond it. Short fences made of what looked like reeds or bamboo marked off a couple of areas. She led the dogs past one marked with a sign that read Turtle Nesting Ground. Do Not Disturb.

Wow. She'd read articles about sea turtle nesting habits and rescue efforts in the nature magazines she subscribed to and had sitting in the reception area of her business. It was amazing to see them in person. If only she wasn't hiding—like a turtle in its shell—in this place. What she wouldn't give to be able to stick around long enough to witness a hatching and watch baby turtles scrambling for the water. Nim would probably love it.

"Ah. No." She gave Casanova's leash a gentle tug and Laddie trotted up to his side to make sure he didn't cross the barrier. That

Laddie really was amazing. It was as if he spoke English. Or could mind-read.

They hit the main part of the beach and picked up their pace. White-tipped waves rolled in and fizzled against the shoreline. Gulls squawked and eyed them as they flew by. This place really felt like an escape. Surely it was busier during the summer months, but right now, it was as though she'd crossed a bridge to heaven. Nim had fallen asleep against her chest. She was glad she'd chosen to have Nim face inward when she'd read the instructions on the toddler carrier. Her first thought had been to protect her face if need be, but right now, Nim's cheek against her chest felt as comforting to her as it seemed to be for Nim. The rhythm of the walk probably helped lull the kiddo back to sleep too, though all this catching up would mean another sleepless night for both of them. She'd have to find a way for Nim to burn some energy before bedtime. Maybe dancing to music in Eve's living room? Her parents used to do that. Her mom would play songs for Clara and Faye to dance to until they had burned up any energy left from the day. She mentioned years later, while reminiscing through photo albums after Mia's birth, that the dancing used to work like a charm. Without it, getting the twins to sleep simultaneously had been a challenge, with one constantly waking the other up for entertainment. Clara and Faye had definitely not been as mellow as Nim.

Faye closed her eyes and let the pack's pace and tension on the leashes guide her. She was giving up a touch of control, yes, but the seconds of letting them lead felt like an eternity. She felt free and careless, yet still in charge.

The sound of the waves crashing and wind in her ears was hypnotizing. Mesmerizing. Meditative. She began humming the same tune she always sang while grooming or walking dogs as part of their training sessions. It was a calming melody, much like the sounds about her right now. There was something about being on a beach so far away from the rest of the world that washed away worry and stress. Even if she knew they still existed and could be tossed back on shore at any moment.

She added in the words, pretending the wind was the harmony Clara would have sung. It had been their favorite as kids. An old Irish song that they'd performed once for a talent show in the fifth grade. She wondered if Clara still sang it as often as Faye did. If she'd ever shared it with her baby. She opened her eyes and scanned the horizon, her peace gone as swiftly as it had come.

"Come on. Time to head back."

She turned the group around and made for the same reed-lined path over the dune and into town that they'd come from, this time with a draining fatigue that clawed at her muscles as she trudged through the sand. Bison and Casanova barked and pulled toward a kite someone was flying farther down the beach. Laddie circled around, his herding genes kicking in until the other dogs gave up on the kite and beachgoer.

The sight of a police SUV in the parking lot of the vet clinic had both her feet and pulse tripping. They were on to her. They'd questioned Krinks and Chanda and everyone else and knew her walking route. She looked behind her and back at the handful of leashes. Laddie wagged and went straight for the clinic door. Casanova barked. Bison grumbled. Nim started to whimper and rub her eyes. There was no running. She'd never get away. She'd be endangering Nim in the process. *Think. Think, Faye.*

Chanda stepped outside, let Laddie in and waved as she walked over to Faye with cash in hand. She was smiling and about to pay her. That made no sense. Or maybe it was a good sign. Perhaps the vehicle was Carlos's and he'd brought Pepper here for some reason. Oh, jeez. Now she was worried about the old dog.

"Hi. Laddie was a big help. Wonderful dog. Kept the group together." Her voice sounded hoarse. Almost squeaky. She took a deep breath. Nim started to cry and the sound rattled her nerves even more. She took a pacifier out from the pocket opposite the cheese and offered it to her. Thank goodness the child took it. Her eyes stared ahead in that groggy half asleep, half awake liminal zone a person found themselves in after a nap.

"Good to hear. Zale asked me to give this to you and thank you. It has been a busy day or he'd come out himself. He said he'd love to take you up on walks or dropping off or picking up Laddie for reading hours."

Her eyes flicked over to the SUV. Did that mean no one was after her? Yet?

"Excellent. Is Pepper okay?"

"Pepper?" Chanda followed Faye's line of sight and something shifted in her face. The corners of her mouth lifted and her brown eyes caught the sunlight. "Oh, you mean Carlos's Pepper. Hon, that's not his car. That's my brother's. He's a deputy."

The dots connected and Faye threw her head back in relief.

"Jordan, by any chance? I met him at Castaway Books. He said something about adopting a puppy."

"The one and only."

The clinic door swung open and Jordan stepped out with a not-so-small bundle of pup in his arms.

"It's all good," he called out. "I changed her food too quickly last night. Upset her stomach. That's all. Hi, Faye. I see folks wasted no time in taking advantage of you."

"Maybe I'm the one taking advantage. Good company on my daily walk."

And possibly good protection, come to think of it.

"Watch out. He'll try to coax you into puppy sitting. He already tried it on me," his sister said, planting a kiss on his puppy's head.

"He already has. Had to really twist my elbow because who wants to spend time with an adorable puppy?" Faye teased. "Congratulations, by the way. Did you pick a name?"

"Shamu. She's going to be big and her breed loves to swim, so I figured name her after a whale."

"Creative. I like it. Hey, Shamu." Faye reached over and scratched behind the pup's ear and then under her chin. Shamu licked at her hand. "Goodness, so much puppy love. If you ever come home and don't find her, you'll know who kidnapped her," Faye teased. Her heart stopped the second she realized what she'd just said. What was wrong with her? "Uh, so I should get these other pooches back to their homes. I'll see you two around."

She waved and turned on her heels, almost tangling the two leads. She put distance between her and the clinic as quickly as she could. She was a numbskull. An idiot. She shook her head and took a comforting whiff of Nim's baby scent. Perhaps she wasn't that bad. She was talking freely. Acting like her normal self. That was akin to hiding in plain sight, wasn't it? Wouldn't choosing her words a bit too carefully come off as fake and raise even more suspicion? Or was she just trying to make herself feel better?

She wasted no time in dropping off Casanova and hurried over to Krinks' Hardware.

"How'd it go?" Mr. Krinks asked, as he finished hanging a supply of shovels.

"Beautifully. He burned calories and enough energy that hopefully he won't go about eating your merchandise."

"He did chew up a roll of duct tape once, but mostly it's the trash or things that fall on the floor by accident." He laughed, knelt down slowly, holding the edge of the counter to give his knee support, and gave Bison some love. "Good boy. Missed me?"

Bison licked his face, then went over to a spot by the window and settled down for a nap.

"See. All tired out," Faye said, searching her pockets for her keys. She was so ready to get back to the cottage. She needed a nap too. Only Nim had already had hers. No wonder parents of babies and toddlers were always exhausted. One little thing like not syncing sleep time and things went downhill from there. This was like that lesson in abstinence the teachers taught in middle school, where they made kids carry around dolls that needed to be fed and changed. Only Nim wasn't a doll and her well-being was at stake.

Speaking of dolls, she'd given the rubber dolphin to her to play with. The key chain. Nim didn't have anything in her hands but the pacifier she'd pulled out of her mouth. Oh, man. She'd probably dropped it during the walk and Faye hadn't noticed. She'd have to backtrack the whole way. What if it had been on the beach and by now it was buried or washed away? A loud burp and whine came from Bison. *Oh, no.* She turned slowly and looked at him. Whining, tired, grumbling. Stomachache? Obstruction? She pressed her hands to her face. *Oh, God.* She was making a dog sick on her first outing. Possibly endangering his life. She rushed over to him and tried to coax him up.

"I swear I'll cover his vet expenses. Maybe he didn't eat it, but I'll get him over there and see if they can do an emergency X-ray before I look anywhere else. He comes first. I'm so sorry. I had him with me the entire time. He never got away. But Nim was holding my keys and she must have dropped them when she fell asleep. I know you warned me about Bison eating everything and—"

"These here?" Mr. Krinks dangled the dolphin key chain in one hand and held her payment in the other. The air swooshed out her lungs. She slapped a hand to her forehead.

"You have them."

"I think she dropped them before you left the store. I figured you wouldn't need them until after the walk and that you'd be back with Bison. You thought he ate them?" Krinks belted a laugh. "I wouldn't be surprised if he had."

Bison farted. The odor was brow raising. Faye waved the air in front of her as she accepted the keys and money.

"Thanks. I'm sorry I overreacted."

"I'm sorry for his gassiness. It's always coming out one end or the other. I'm told it's a breed thing. The snoring too." Bison was already in dreamland.

"No worries." She caught herself this time. She had been close to saying that she was used to it. She had several gassy dogs as customers back home. She kept that detail to herself. "Enjoy the rest of your day."

A really bad headache was brewing. The

sunglasses helped a little, but she hoped the mass of clouds over the ocean would hurry up and mask the glare. Sometimes a person needed a day to crawl under the covers, listen to rain and not do anything else.

"Banna. Mi banna."

"Are you hungry? You're probably hungry." She crossed the street and headed for the only intersection. "I know you're getting stir-crazy. I'll get you out of this contraption in a few minutes. As soon as we're at the house. Trust me, my back is aching. You're not as light as you look."

"Banna." This time Nim added a wail and kicked her legs around. Faye held on to Nim's shoes to keep from getting knocked.

"Are you hungry for banana? You want a banana?"

Nim nodded and simmered down.

"Okay. There's some at Auntie Eve's. We're going to get it right now and you can gobble it up. How about singing 'Five Little Lemurs Jumping on a Bed'?"

She started the rhyme, reciting it to the beat of each step she took, hoping it would buy her time before Nim cried again. Next time, she'd remember to bring along a snack for her. She stopped at the intersection before taking a left toward the cottage and looked to her right. The sheriff stepped out from the side of the law office and looked right in her direction, before moving on. Had he been watching her this whole time? Standing where he had a clear view of most of the town and the beach beyond? Goose bumps trailed up her arms and down her back. Carlos Ryker knew more than he was letting on. What she couldn't figure out was why he didn't just arrest her on the spot. She needed to keep her distance. If anything, she needed to pray that Carlos wouldn't ask her to walk his dog too. She needed the money, but taking care of Pepper would put him much too close for comfort.

CHAPTER SEVEN

"You have to go. Come on. We won't stay long. Actually, I'm feeling run-down so we really won't stay too late, but it's part of town tradition. You'll get to meet more people," Eve insisted, wiping her nose with a tissue. Meeting more people, having to deal with small talk, was what Faye wanted to avoid.

"I already walked the dogs today and took Shamu out for two separate potty breaks. I'm tired. Nim's tired from all the teething. You go and we'll hold down the fort." She was beginning to see the cottage as just that—her fort or castle. If it weren't for bridges, boats and planes, the waters surrounding the barrier reef would serve as her old-fashioned moat. A barrier to potential invaders...like Jim. If she was living a couple of hundred years in the past, she wouldn't be worrying about getting tracked online or through computerized police systems.

"This will help you relax. It's a gorgeous evening."

That much was true. Yesterday's winds had died down and the temps had warmed up a few degrees. Without a wind chill, it had felt downright balmy for mid-February. Then again, she was farther south than she was used to.

"I don't know. I could sit on your back deck and watch from here."

"All you'd see is a flicker from the bonfire. Where's the fun in that? Besides, I didn't write up all these cards for nothing, so I have to go. I always hand them out, especially to singles. I even have generic ones in case I miss someone or there's someone from out of town. In fact, I'll give you yours now."

She held out a giant, handmade envelope made from photocopies of old black-and-white pictures.

"These are of us," Faye said, dumbfounded. She angled the envelope and took a closer look. A few were from a carnival photo booth. One was from a party. Another looked like it had been taken in a restaurant.

"I don't have a color printer here, hence the

black and white, but I think it makes the red card inside stand out."

Faye pulled it out.

Faye,
Happy Valentine's Day to an incredible friend and mother. You deserve the best, always. You deserve to love and be loved. May your future bring you happiness.
Here for you always,
Eve

Tears ran down her cheeks. *Mother?* Eve believed she was a mother. One who'd suffered. When in fact, it was Clara who deserved this card and this kind of friendship.

"I didn't mean to make you cry."

"It's okay. It's the nicest card I've ever gotten. I'm sorry that I didn't make you one."

"I didn't expect you to. I'm the one trying to convince you that Valentine's Day can be more than just about romance. Love makes the world go round. I'm trying to spread it."

"You're such a hippie. And I love you back for it. You have at least four peace signs inte-

grated into the decor of this one room alone."
Faye grinned.

"This is for Nim." She handed over a board
book from her shop that told a story about a
mother's love. "I noticed she liked it when
she was playing around there."

"Thank you so much. Again, I feel bad for
being empty-handed."

"Nonsense. Your being here is the best
thing I could ask for." Eve narrowed her
eyes. "But if you really want me to guilt you,
there's this bonfire going on at the beach…"

"Alright, alright. I'll go for a bit. But I'm
heading back if Nim gets restless."

"It's a deal."

Faye nodded, putting the card back in its
envelope. Clara had gone to a different college than she had. Eve had never met her.
Surely, Faye must have told her at some point
that she was a twin. Friends did that. Shared
tidbits about family, but it didn't mean the
details were remembered. Faye remembered
Eve once mentioning that she was an only
child, but she couldn't recall details about her
parents. Maybe Eve didn't remember much
about Faye's sister…or that she had a twin. Or
that they were identical. She would have said

something, wouldn't she? The question was how long would it take for Eve to remember?

CARLOS STOOD AT the edge of the shadows where the firelight began to fade. He wasn't on duty tonight as planned—schedule changes—but that didn't matter. He was responsible for the town and everyone's safety. That meant he was never really off the clock. At least not in his mind. He took a sip of his hot chocolate and patted Pepper's shoulder. The girl seemed content. He wasn't sure if the crowd would make her nervous or not, but she was doing just fine. She wasn't the only dog. A few other people had brought theirs along…about three or four total. So long as they picked up after them, he didn't mind. No one wanted their evening ruined by stepping in poop.

"You can't roast marshmallows from here," Jordan said as he joined him. He had Shamu with him. Pepper immediately sniffed the pup and began wagging her tail.

"I'm good."

They both raised their cups to Damon as he approached.

"What's up?" Damon asked, putting the last bite of a hot dog in his mouth. He brushed off his hands. "You guys look pitiful standing over here alone. It *is* a social event, in case you missed the memo."

"We're trying to help you out. If we were mingling you wouldn't stand a chance," Carlos said.

Damon laughed and Suzie from the jewelry shop glanced over from her spot by the fire and smiled.

"See. The mere sound of my voice breaks hearts," he said.

"You're delusional. She was looking my way. It's called puppy power," Jordan said.

"So that's the real reason you got Shamu?" Carlos said. "To pick up women? Need I remind you that by the time summer hits and the beaches are full, that dog isn't going to look like a puppy anymore." Carlos crouched down and gave Shamu a belly rub. "Where's her mama, Damon? We could have had a family reunion."

"I left her at home. She still needs more training. She kept dragging a rookie I was training out of the water before he could paddle out more than two feet. If I brought her tonight, I'd be trying to keep her out of the surf the whole time. Still trying to teach her commands."

"You do know Suzie's allergic to dogs, don't you?" Carlos pointed out.

"First off, I never said I was interested in her. Secondly, how would you know that?"

"I drink hot chocolate and I know things." He lifted his cup in salute.

"That's not how the quote goes and you haven't even watched one episode of *Game of Thrones*," Damon said.

"Some of us don't have time for shows."

"Is this going to turn into another Turtle-back Water Rescue versus the Sheriff's Department challenge? We all know who won that one." Jordan patted his chest.

"You tricked us," Damon quipped.

"No, I didn't. I used psychology. Technically, your own mind tricked you."

Carlos took another drink to mask his amusement.

"And here I thought the party was by the fire," Gray said, joining the group. They fist bumped him one by one. Laddie and Pepper started sniffing each other and touching noses. "Looks like it's a night for the dogs, too. Happy Heart Day to my bros."

"Love you, man, but you're sounding mushier than a roasted marshmallow," Damon said.

"I'm trying." Gray toasted with his cocoa.

"Emphasis on the *roasted*. That's what marriage will do to you. I bet you broke the bank buying jewelry," Jordan said.

"Nope. Mandi's not like that. I mean she likes jewelry, usually the locally made artisan type, though. But it happens to be our six-month wedding anniversary, so I wanted to do something special. I dedicated the side wing at the clinic to her grandmother. That's where we keep and treat any injured wildlife that's brought in until we can get them to the right refuge. Rescuing wildlife—especially the sea turtles and nesting grounds along this beach—meant the world to Nana. She brought us together even after she'd passed on, so it seemed right. She meant a lot to me too. She was like family. I had a plaque made that says 'Nana's Critters' followed by her name and a memorial. Don't say anything. Mandi hasn't seen it yet. I'm taking her by the clinic after we spend a little time here."

Carlos, Jordan and Damon just stared at him for a moment.

"Man, you're good," Jordan finally said.

"Careful. This might be contagious. I'm going to get more to eat before I catch it," Damon said. He smirked and gave them a thumbs-up as he walked off to mingle. Carlos noticed he went to the opposite side of the gathering from Suzie. So maybe the guy really wasn't interested.

"There you are. All bunched over here like you're outside the window looking in." Eve practically skipped over to them. How anyone skipped on sand beat him, but either she'd had too much sugar or she was floating. She reached into a woven bag she'd slung over her shoulder and handed them each a card with their name on it. "Happy Valentine's Day!"

"Thanks, Eve." Carlos reached over and gave her a quick hug. "Everything okay?" he whispered. He knew she'd know what she meant.

"Yup. Under control." She motioned with her eyes toward the crowd. He couldn't see Faye. Apparently, she was here. Gavin, one of the vet techs, and his fiancée were in the crowd. He also spotted Darla, who'd supplied a boatload of cookies for the event, with Nora, Gray's other veterinary assistant. But not Faye. Someone had to be blocking his view.

"Gray, I gave yours to Mandi. I made it out to the both of you. She's somewhere over there gushing over Nim."

"Now babies *are* contagious, I hear." Carlos chuckled. Gray paled and excused himself to go find her.

Eve had a good heart. Did this every year without fail. Brenda at the post office told him in confidence that Eve had brought in a box full of them to be sent to troops overseas. Yet, he wasn't sure if she ever got a Valentine herself. She wasn't dating. He was certain Jordan had never made a move.

She handed one to Jordan. It was way smaller than anyone else's. He simply pressed his lips together and nodded his thanks. No hug. Nothing verbal. Very smooth. He needed a few lessons from Gray.

"Okay. I have more to hand out. You guys need to make like moths and head toward the fire. You'll stand out less if that's the intention." She sneezed. "It's the smoke. I'm sure."

Carlos waited until she was out of earshot.

"She handed you a card and you froze?" Carlos let out an exaggerated sigh.

"I didn't freeze."

"Popsicle. Iceberg. Glacier. You name it."

"I get the idea. But it's not true. I was being civilized."

"Civilized? You didn't even say thank you. I think you hurt her feelings."

"No, I didn't. Look at her. She's laughing over there. She gives these to everyone. It's not like she was only giving one to me. It's nothing special. And, I'll point out, mine's like a quarter the size of yours and the others."

Carlos pointed a finger at him.

"Every card she makes is special. Don't take it for granted. She's a good person. Don't take her for granted either. She's not like—"

Jordan held up his palm.

"Don't go there. Eve gives out cards. I can tell you, mine says Happy V Day and that's it. You give a person a small card when you don't want to have to write a lot in it. Strategy, man. It's not like she's passing me a love note in class. Maybe you should watch more TV for entertainment. Temper that imagination of yours."

"It's the gesture that counts. Anyway. Maybe she wrote more in yours this year."

"She didn't."

"You haven't opened it."

"I get the same card every year."

Interesting. Eve was known for going all out with each card, but she kept Jordan's simple. She didn't know what to say to him. Just like he clammed up around her.

"I think she wrote something different this year."

"How would you know?"

"I drink hot chocolate and I know things." Carlos couldn't stifle his grin.

"You are too much. You're lucky I think of you as a brother, else I'd tell Chanda to kick you to the curb."

"Not a chance. You're too nice. And you like having your job."

A flicker of red had him stopping his cup halfway to his mouth.

"I see how it is," Jordan said. "She's nice. Pretty. Has. A. Kid."

"Now it's your imagination gone wild. I thought I saw the flames getting too high."

"You weren't looking at the fire. Well, that fiery hair, maybe. Go talk to her before she thinks you're just staring. That's creepy."

"I'm not staring. I'm keeping an eye on things. On the bonfire gathering," he added, before Jordan twisted his words.

"On her."

"She's new in town. If I've spoken to her, it was to be welcoming."

"You're not the mayor."

"The mayor's out of town."

"Pepper. Help your poor human out," Jordan said.

Someone called out, asking him to bring his puppy over for them to see. He saluted Carlos, picked up Shamu and left him standing alone.

Faye caught his gaze and the heat of the fire seemed to take to her cheeks. She had Nim on her hip. Several people were talking to her and cooing over the kid. The dark liner around her blue eyes only made them sparkle more in the fire. Mysterious. Exotic. Beautiful. Embers popped and danced up between them, then faded into the night like fireworks in midsummer.

A single mother, he reminded himself.

She was like family. Gray's words about Nana echoed in his mind. *Family.* His friend was right. Family wasn't about who you were born to, though Carlos was lucky to have had a loving mother. It was about the people who cared about you, who stood by you through tough times and celebrated the good ones. Chanda and Jordan had become his family when he had no blood family left. Nana and Mandi had become Gray's when he'd landed in town under the witness protection program and couldn't tell anyone who he really was. He scanned all the faces gathered around for the Valentine's celebration. Heck. He knew every one of them. They all knew each other. Most of them did, at least. Everyone here formed a family. Turtleback Beach was their home. Eve was right when it came to handing out those cards. Today wasn't just about celebrating romance. It was about love. Family. People who mattered.

What didn't count as family was anyone who caused others to suffer abuse, verbal or otherwise. Whomever Faye had been married to didn't count as family. He didn't deserve one. It killed him to imagine what Faye must have endured. The thought that Nim, at her innocent age, might have witnessed or overheard whatever went on gouged him out. It was so wrong it was beyond words. No one deserved that. He could see the constant fear in Faye's eyes. He wanted to erase it. To let her know she'd be safe here. He'd make sure of it.

He crumpled his cup, tossed it in a bin for recycling and clicked his tongue to get Pepper to stand back up. Eve wanted him to join the crowd? Make like a moth, she'd said? Fine. He'd go mingle a little. He'd talk to Faye. But for some reason, his gut was telling him that he wasn't just heading toward the fire. He was going to get burned.

FAYE TRIED TO stop chewing the inside of her cheek, but catching Carlos Ryker watching her made her incredibly nervous. This time there was something different in his eyes. Not the serious, focused look he'd worn earlier, but…she wasn't sure…kindness? She didn't know, but she had to stop herself from looking back at him. It had been hard not to. He wasn't in uniform. He looked really good in jeans, a pullover sweater and bomber jacket. Ruggedly good.

She whipped the beanie off her head and stuffed it into her jacket pocket. It was getting awfully warm. She wasn't standing that close to the fire and temps were cool out. She ruffled her hair so she wouldn't have a hat-head, excused herself and moved a few feet back from the fire so that she could set Nim down safely. Her arm ached. Her back ached. Her—

"Enjoying the celebration?"

Her nerves ached.

She looked up, then straightened as much as she could without letting go of Nim's little hand.

"Sheriff. I haven't been here long, but it's nice."

"Please, call me Carlos. Everyone here does unless there's something official going on. This—" he motioned around "—isn't work. People here are like family. And friends."

So, he considered her a friend? She was so confused.

"Carlos, then."

"There's popcorn, hot dogs, marshmallows and drinks over there." He pointed toward a foldout table covered in a red cloth. "Your hands are empty. The hot chocolate's good."

"My hands were full a second ago," she explained, tilting her head toward Nim. "I'm okay. Honestly. We ate plenty at Eve's earlier." Truth be told, she didn't have much of an appetite at dinner, despite all that walking, but Nim had eaten well.

"Are you sure? You've got to try one of Darla's cookies, at least. Consider it dessert. Here, come with me."

The touch of his hand on her shoulder, gently guiding her, felt warm and safe. But that wasn't right, was it? He wasn't to be trusted. Or was he? Why did a part of her want to tell him the truth and have faith that he'd make things right? That he wouldn't end up being like the cops Jim "knew"? Because Eve said she could? Her friend couldn't make that call. Not given that she didn't know the whole story.

He walked slowly alongside her and Nim, letting her "daughter" set the pace. Nim had her free hand on Pepper's back and the dog looked like she was smiling and happy to guide the little one. They worked their way toward the refreshment table and Darla, whom Faye recognized from the bakery, waved them over. Eve was there as well, handing Darla and another young woman with dark hair and a pretty face their cards.

"Hey, guys. Come try these cookies. She

won't tell me her secret ingredient, but it's so good. Marzipan?" Eve guessed.

"Nope, but close," Darla said. "No more guessing. I'm not telling."

"Darla, I think you met Faye and Nim," Carlos said, turning to the other woman. "Faye, this is Nora Nazari. She's one of Gray's vet techs."

Nora shook Faye's hand.

"It's nice to meet you. I've heard a lot about you already. Word at the clinic is that you are magical. Chanda said she's never seen Casanova not acting spastic on a leash."

Faye chuckled.

"I seem to have a way with dogs…that I didn't know about," she added. "But it really was all about cheese and that Laddie. Good herding instincts and he knows how to give the pack that look only parents and principals are masters of."

"Are you two enjoying the party? Or too busy organizing the food?" Carlos asked.

"Best night ever," Nora said, eyeing Darla. She raised her brows slightly. "Should we tell them?"

"Tell us what?" Eve asked. "The secret ingredient?"

"You wish," Darla laughed. "The real secret ingredient in everything here tonight is love. That said…" She put her arm around Nora's waist and Nora reciprocated. "We just got engaged."

"No kidding!" Eve squealed. "Congratulations! Next year I'll get to make one card for both of you, instead of two. Hugs!" She ran around the table and gave them both hugs.

"Come here, you two. Congrats. I'm happy for you." Carlos gave hugs, as well. The man was a hugger. Who knew the sheriff who looked so serious in uniform, had a soft spot?

Faye couldn't stop grinning. The joy was viral.

"Congrats from me too," she said. She held back, wanting to join in but feeling like an outsider at the same time.

"Oh, come here. Hugs for all today," Darla teased. Darla came around and gave her a big squeeze, then squatted and gave Nim a gentle one. Then Nora followed suit.

"Thank you. We hope you're liking Turtleback and if you visit again in the summer, consider yourself invited to the wedding. On the beach like Gray and Mandi's. They inspired us," Nora said.

"It sounds lovely." She had no clue where she'd be by next summer. With Clara? Nim? In jail? Or worse. The hugs felt good. She didn't realize how desperately she needed to be held. To feel that kind of comfort.

Carlos took two cookies from the table and handed her one, which she accepted because she didn't want to be rude. He took a bite out of the other.

"Can she have any?" he asked, regarding Nim.

"Caca!" Nim called out, earning a few laughs. She made a break for the table but lost her footing in the sand. Faye righted her up.

"Sweetheart, if only you knew what caca really means. We'll get you a cookie. Just one," she told Nim. "I was hoping to actually sleep tonight. I've found that sugar wires her up, but I don't have the heart to say no with all these on display."

"It's a party. Let her enjoy it. There's always tomorrow for sleep," Carlos said.

Tomorrow is never guaranteed.

Someone switched the music to something slow and nostalgic and several people strolled away from the fire to the cool sand closer to the shoreline and began dancing.

"Can I join in? Is this the free-hug table?" Jordan asked.

"You bet," Nora said, opening her arms.

"I overheard. Congrats to you both." Jordan held Shamu with one arm and hugged the happy couple.

"We love this song. You guys help yourselves," Darla said, heading off to the designated dance area.

Dancing with sand beneath your feet and stars above and the sizzling sound from both fire and surf filling the air. Incredible.

"It's a good song," Jordan hedged, glancing over at Eve. "Did—"

"We can leave whenever you want," Eve said, looking at Faye. "I've passed out all of my cards." She rubbed her temples. "I want to stay longer but have a headache coming on."

Ouch. Poor Jordan. He pulled back visibly.

"Yeah. I was about to say the same thing. I need to get Shamu home. I'm Chanda's ride, as well. You all enjoy yourselves." He waved and headed toward the wooden path that cut through the sand near the boardwalk and led to the main street.

Eve sneezed again.

"I hope I'm not getting sick."

"So do I. You just hugged how many people?" Faye said.

"But hugs are good for the immune system. They cancel out the virus." Eve tugged her jacket tighter around her.

"That's not how it works when it comes to spreading germs," Faye said.

"I know. I know. Don't make me feel guilty. Carlos, use your powers and send out a town memo to take extra vitamins."

"You just go home and rest," he said. "I can make sure Faye gets back safely if she wants to stay longer."

Was he trying to spend time with her? Like…*time* with her? If she lingered longer, would they end up dancing like everyone else? No. How could she let her mind go there? He was holding on to Pepper's leash and she was holding on to her niece. Daughter.

"Oh. Um, I need to get Nim back and I'm feeling rather tired. But thanks." She finished off the cookie, then rubbed the small of her back with her free hand.

"Alright, then. Do you need a ride?" he asked, directing the question at both Eve and Faye, but he looked pointedly at Eve.

"We'll be fine. It's not that long of a walk," Eve said.

"You're not feeling well and Faye would have to carry Nim the whole way. Plus, it's dark and cold out. I'll drop you off. I'm taking Pepper home, then I'll swing back around here to make sure no one needs anything. I insist."

With that, he handed Faye Pepper's leash—which she took without realizing why he'd given it to her—then he picked Nim up for her. *He was listening. Noticing. Your backache.* She was at a loss for words. Nim patted his cheeks and didn't freak out. Didn't they say the two best judges of character were dogs and kids? Maybe that's why her track record with guys was so bad. She needed a dog or kid to screen them for her.

Eve looked between the two of them. Faye hoped she could hear her telepathically screaming that nothing was going on here.

"You win. Let's go. I'm too drained to argue," Eve said.

Carlos bounced Nim twice and she giggled hysterically.

"Let's go, kiddo," he said.

Faye's eyes burned and she swallowed hard

to keep tears from spilling over. She wasn't sure why. Only that she wished Nim's father was more like the man she was looking at right now. The kind of man her sister should have met before promising her life to Jim. A man she'd only just met herself, yet had been wishing for her whole life. And yet, if he knew the truth about her, as sheriff he'd have to arrest her, or at the very least take Nim away from her and into custody. A sick twist of fate that promised one thing—her wish could never come true.

CHAPTER EIGHT

THE SUN WAS brilliant this morning. Too much so. Faye shivered as she closed the blinds and curtains over Eve's French doors that led to her deck. She couldn't stop shivering.

Eve was curled up on one end of the sofa with a tissue box tucked in the curve of her body. She had an essential oil diffuser blowing out vapors that she said would help their sinuses. Faye was game for anything. She was miserable. Feverish.

Nim sat in her playpen with toys and books. The television was also set to a show that was supposed to be mentally stimulating for kids her age, according to Eve. Yes, Faye was already succumbing to the television babysitter, but being sick had to be a good excuse.

She curled up in the armchair next to the couch and pulled a blanket around her.

"What about the shop?" Faye asked.

"I called Darla and asked her to stick a note

on the door letting people know I'm closed for the day."

"This town really is like one big family."

"It really is. Unfortunately, in big happy families when one person gets sick, it makes its way through everyone."

"Mine came on so suddenly. And the stuff I took only took the edge off the fever. I still feel cold and achy."

"You've been stressed out. Running on adrenaline. The second you were able to relax, your immune system crashed."

"Guess it's not all your fault for giving it to me, then?"

"You'll survive and be stronger for it." She let out a moan. "I wish I could breathe."

"I wish I could stop shaking. And I hope Nim doesn't get it."

"The essential oils in the air will help."

"Whatever you say."

"I need to fall asleep again. You should tell me a bedtime story. Like what was happening between you and Carlos last night? I thought you didn't trust him."

"There's no story. Unless you have one. Did you tell him anything? I told you not to."

She couldn't talk. She just wanted to sleep. Her brain felt all fuzzy.

"No. But like I said, he noticed enough on his own."

"I felt sorry for Jordan."

"Why?"

"Oh, come on. You can't tell me you didn't know he was mustering up the nerve to ask you to dance. And you said you had a headache."

"But I did. It wasn't an excuse. Look at me. And he wasn't about to do any such thing. He had his pup to look after. He didn't even say anything when I gave him his card—probably threw it in his kitchen trash without opening it—and you think he wanted to dance? You don't know Jordan like I do."

"Nothing like a little irritation to clear your sinuses and give you a burst of energy."

"I'm not irritated or energized."

"You sound like you are."

Eve whimpered and blew her nose again.

"I'm not. Not at you." She threw her afghan off and sat up slowly. "We need soup. I'll look and see if I have any cans I can warm up."

Nim stood at the side of the playpen and started bouncing and repeating "Fa" over and over. The sound ricocheted against Faye's skull. Eve put a pillow on her head.

"Bless her tiny voice that's not sounding so tiny right now," Eve said.

"I'm sorry. I'll fix her lunch." She tried to get up and felt off. Weak and dizzy. "We're quite a pair today."

She remembered the time Clara had the flu, Jim was on a business trip and Faye had back-to-back customers and couldn't pick up groceries for her until evening. How had she managed with a baby in the house? Guilt cut right through her bones and the relentless ache she'd felt since early morning spiked. If only she'd known how hard motherhood was, she'd have gone out of her way to do more. To be there for her sis. To put her needs first.

"I have these vitamins and herbs that'll help. I sip a tea made with oregano, thyme and astragalus all winter. Maybe that's why I don't have a fever like you do. It shortens a cold. I'll make you some. Give me a moment, though. I'm moving in slow mo."

There was a knock on the door and Faye stiffened. Nim squealed and she and Eve both covered their ears in pain.

"Shh!" Faye stumbled, half-disoriented,

over to the pen to give Nim attention and keep her from yelling. What if this was it? The FBI or child protective services at the door? "Shh, baby. Quiet."

"Stay put. I'll get it." Eve dragged herself over to the door and looked through the peephole. She let out a breath and looked over her shoulder back at Faye. "It's the police."

CARLOS GRIMACED AS Jordan made his way up Eve's steps with a reusable grocery bag that looked weighted down with something heavy. He hadn't intended to get caught in the act. The last thing he needed was to be given a hard time.

"Whatchya got there?" he asked, trying to look nonchalant. As if he wasn't standing at Eve's door carrying a giant pot with gloves on because the darned thing was still hot.

Jordan frowned up at him.

"Soup. Chanda made it and insisted I bring it over. She heard from Nora who heard from Darla who had a call from Eve this morning about not opening up shop because she's sick. Her and Faye. What about you?"

Carlos glanced down at the pot he was carrying.

"Soup. I made it myself."

"You did not."

"I did." Carlos stood a little taller.

"Since when can you cook? You have my sister feeling sorry for you and making you come over all the time for a home-cooked meal."

"I never told her I couldn't cook. She assumed I couldn't—the whole bachelor stereotype—and when I told her about the recipes I have from my mother, she insisted that I didn't have *time* to cook. Face it. Chanda likes to feed people and nothing'll stop her."

"That's for sure." He looked at Carlos's giant pot, then down at his bag. "Are you really going to one-up me in there? Can't we just pretend I made this?"

"Man, I love your sister's cooking but this is my mother's chicken tortilla soup—with extra cilantro and lemon for the vitamin C. I'd be one-upping you regardless."

"Not everyone likes cilantro."

"They'll like it. Or they'll be too congested to care. Besides, they'd eventually find out you lied about making yours and you'd never hear the end of it. From your sister, that is."

"You're right. Wait a minute. She could've

brought this here herself. She's off work today." So were the two of them.

Carlos cleared his throat and curled his lips in to stop from laughing.

"She could've."

The door opened before Jordan could answer and they both straightened up ready to impress...sort of...then slumped at the sight of Eve.

"You look awful," Jordan said. Carlos rolled his eyes and didn't say a word.

"Why, thank you. That's the nicest thing anyone's ever said to me, Jordan." Eve sounded like a frog. Talk about role reversal. Maybe if Jordan gave in and kissed her, she'd turn into his princess. Eve looked at what they were carrying. "What's all this?"

"Soup," they responded simultaneously.

"You've both earned a lifetime pass for forgiveness. Come in. If you dare. You've been warned." She held the door wide open.

Faye was crouched next to the playpen, hanging her arm on its rim and leaning her head against it. She looked terrible. But he had the sense not to say so. She also looked different...beautiful.

She wasn't wearing any makeup. And see-

ing her there with her little girl tightened his
chest and made it harder to breathe. He eased
his way inside, afraid to disturb them. Not
sure if she'd want his offering.

"I made soup," he said.

Her lips parted and she looked at him
bleary eyed, as if his making soup was that
hard to believe.

"Thank you."

He didn't like how weak she sounded.

"I'll put it on the stove and get some bowls.
Eve, you okay with us taking over your
kitchen?"

She closed the door behind Jordan, who'd
clearly never seen her place before. He stood
there, holding his bag with the soup contain-
ers Chanda had sent over, taking in the scent
of aromatherapy and earthy style.

"Go for it." She held out her arm to let Jordan know he was welcome to follow Carlos
into the small kitchen, then she went back to
the sofa and snagged three tissues from the
box she had on the coffee table. Faye held
her hand out and Eve passed her the tissue
box. She took out the last one. Jordan pulled
out another from the bag he'd brought and
handed it to Eve.

"I thought of that myself," he said in a low voice as he passed Carlos in the kitchen. Carlos grinned. He didn't know what he'd do without the brotherly sparring with Jordan. He enjoyed it too much. And he knew Jordan saw the humor in it, as well. Life needed a little humor. It was the only way to cope with all that was ugly in it.

They ladled soup into bowls and took them over to the living room. Carlos set Faye's on the table, then went over, helped her to her feet.

"Come sit and eat a few bites. Jordan and I can take care of Nim. You both just eat and sleep."

"Have you ever changed a diaper before?" Eve asked. Both guys froze.

"She's not potty trained yet?" Carlos asked.

"No, not yet. Just tell me if you think she needs changing and I'll get up," Faye said.

He walked Faye over to the armchair, touched the back of his hand to her forehead and went back to the kitchen for a wet cloth.

"We'll manage. Just rest," Carlos said.

"Maybe we should give the doctor a call. Make sure it's not the flu," Jordan said, propping a pillow behind Eve and setting a bowl of soup in her hands.

"It's not the flu," Eve said. "I'm sure it's just a cold. No doctor. I can get better on my own."

"If you insist, but at least eat a little or drink the broth part," Jordan said. "Can I get you anything else? Water? Tea?"

"I made herbal tea in a pot earlier. Faye should have some too. I can get it." She started to set her bowl down. Jordan put his hand on her shoulder.

"I'll get it. Sometimes it's okay to let others help, Eve. This is one of those times."

She nibbled the corner of her mouth and slumped back, letting him take over.

Carlos placed a cool cloth on Faye's forehead. She lifted her hand to hold it in place. The look on her face expressed gratitude without words.

"Did you take anything for the fever?"

"Yes. I think it's starting to kick in. I'll try the soup in a minute. Thanks so much for that."

"Just get well."

He reached into the playpen and picked up Nim.

"How about we get you some lunch?" he said, poking her playfully in the belly. She grabbed his nose.

"Da da."

Dada. No one had ever called him that before. It rocked the ground under his feet. Caught him off guard. He avoided eye contact with Faye and took Nim to the kitchen. He wasn't her father, but as soon as he found the man who was, he'd make sure the guy never hurt any woman or child again.

JIM POURED HOT water into the mug and dipped the tea bag several times. He loved this cabin. Not so much a cabin as a lodge, really. It had been worth the investment. Well built. Surrounded by western Pennsylvania's trees and streams. Isolated.

This was the only place where life slowed down for him. The one place where he could recalibrate. Reset. Think.

He took the steaming mug over to where Clara sat, staring aimlessly outside the two-story window of the A-frame sanctuary. *Sanctuary.* That was the word that described it for him.

"Here you go, darling."

She didn't shift her gaze. He had to admit the scenery…snow-capped evergreens that stretched for miles beneath their cliff-side vantage point…was mesmerizing. He picked up her hand, kissed her knuckles and set the mug in her grasp. She complied, finally. It would have spilled, burning hot, onto her lap if she hadn't.

"No thanks?" he asked.

"Thank you."

There. She'd spoken. She always did come around. Two words. Then after a while, five. Then ten. Then everything would be back to normal. She always forgave. Wasn't that the meaning of unconditional love? The point of having wedding vows?

"Can I get you anything else?" he offered. Because he was a generous man. He'd given her so much. He was asking for so little in return.

"I want to go home. I want to hold my baby."

"You know it's too soon, honey." He brushed his fingers lightly across her cheek and she flinched. The bruise was fading nicely. "I'm so sorry I lost my temper. Please, forgive me. You know how much I love you. Everything I do, I do to make you happy. To make our lives better and build a legacy for our child. Perhaps...someday...children."

She cradled the mug with both hands now. He could see the movement in her slender neck as she swallowed. He brushed her long hair back over her shoulder. She almost cut it short once. Thank God he had seen the salon appointment in her phone reminders and asked her about it before the damage was done. He had been furious with her. Just thinking about the fact that he'd come that close to returning home from work to find her hair all cut off made his insides coil.

He kissed her temple so as not to touch the tender area. She'd heal. His Clara would be okay.

"A little longer. When the bruise fades, we'll talk. You don't like the public eye, remember? I'm doing this for you. Things are going well at work and there will be reporters, articles, news about my candidacy. I don't think you can handle that stress right now. A person has to be strong, mentally stable, for all that. You know you haven't been. Your depression. Anxiety. Clara, darling, being here away from it all is better for you. You should be grateful that I didn't go the route of checking you into a facility."

"I'm not crazy. I want Mia. Let me talk to my sister. My parents, even."

Not her parents, for sure. Her parents and their political connections were half the reason he'd had his eye on her in the first place. Her parents liked him. Praised him. Would be his number one supporters as he ran for office. He chewed at the inside of his cheek until the coppery taste of blood assaulted his tongue. Now, see what she'd made him do?

"Clara, sweetheart. What did your mother tell you the last time you tried complaining about me to her?"

She didn't answer.

"Say it. Right now. I heard every word of it when I walked into her kitchen, but remind us both."

"That I should be patient with you because you have a stressful job."

"What else?"

"That men handle stress differently than women and that I need to be there for you."

"Exactly. You should listen to your mother."

Clara's mother was better than his had been. More loving and supportive. That's why he had gone out of his way that day, in her kitchen, to compliment her pie and insist on taking over doing the dishes. He had shown her parents that they weren't wrong about him by doing little things that mattered, like putting his arm around Clara and kissing her temple, holding her coat for her and the car door when it was time to leave and sending them a handwritten thank-you note for a lovely dinner. Because he was civilized and educated and if a person like him wanted respect, they had to behave in a manner that demanded it. That showed people he deserved it.

He put his hand on Clara's thigh.

"And Faye? Your sister hasn't even asked about you. You know she's always been jealous of what we have. But she's not good with kids. Can't handle them. You know that. You shouldn't have trusted her. You've only put her in trouble. The minute she found out the authorities were after her, she baled. I found Mia on our doorstep, and your sister? Gone. Ran off to save herself. Don't worry about Mia. I hired a nanny with excellent references. She's in good hands. I told you, darling, I'm the only person you can really trust. I've got your back. We're in this together. We can make this right. Put the past behind us, fix the situation and move forward."

He watched her face closely to gauge her reaction. She didn't move. Not a lash. He combed his fingers through her hair again. It didn't matter. He was in control. Faye was under his thumb whether she knew it or not. They both were. And if Clara tried anything stupid…well… It was easy for an accident to happen out here. Very easy.

CHAPTER NINE

Two days later and she was feeling so much better. Faye sat on the bottom step outside the cottage and let the sun warm her face. She was still too tired to dog walk, but told everyone she'd get back to it tomorrow. Nim was napping and Faye was relieved that she hadn't shown signs of catching the cold. Yet. Chanda had come around yesterday to help out, since Carlos and Jordan had helped the day before.

Whether it was Eve's magical tea, Carlos's family soup or his attentiveness that helped her and Eve get well quickly, she didn't know. But it worked. And she had to admit that feeling his hand on her forehead every hour and watching him tend to Mia had made her forget the aches and pains. Leave it to a man like Carlos Ryker to give a woman's immune system a boost. He was better than vitamins. And she suspected having Jordan around had had the same effect on Eve. Though her friend was too stubborn to admit it.

She inhaled the cool, fresh air, and a small cough escaped as a result. More tea would help clear her chest. Eve had made another pot this morning and took half in a thermos for herself. She'd taken her laptop with her too, stating that she needed it to do some inventory and payments, but that if Faye wanted to get online, she could use it tomorrow. She had warned her to be careful and to resist checking emails or answering any from her ex or his lawyer without consulting with her first. Little did Eve know that Jim wasn't her ex, but he *was* a lawyer.

A glint of light flashed from down the road. It was Carlos opening and closing his car door and backing out of his driveway. He slowed as he approached the cottage, pulled up and rolled down his window.

"Feeling better?"

"Much. Thank you for everything. The soup. Watching over Nim. I can't thank you enough." Her cheeks felt warm again but she knew full well it wasn't a fever this time. At least not the viral kind.

"No problem. Glad to help. Take it easy today."

"I plan on it. No dog walking until tomorrow."

He adjusted his hat, looked down the road, then back at her.

"Speaking of dog walks, I could use help with Pepper."

Faye rubbed her upper arms. What happened to keeping her distance from the sheriff? He and Jordan taking care of her and Eve had kind of ruined that plan. Not that she was complaining. She was grateful. She was really beginning to like Carlos, though, and that was a whole different kind of complication. It was getting personal and she had thought about that early on…about how if he got to know her, he'd understand that she wasn't a threat. But she hadn't been thinking about anything more than friendship at the time. Whatever she sensed was happening between the two of them didn't feel like plain friendship. She needed to be careful for entirely different reasons now. Carlos didn't know the whole truth, for one thing. Then there was the part about his life being here and the reality that she could have to pack up and leave tomorrow.

It wasn't fair to lead him on. It wasn't her intention, but acting too cold after all he'd done for her wouldn't be right either.

"I do owe you a favor for the soup," she finally said.

"You don't owe me a thing. I'm hoping you can take on another paying customer. Pepper doesn't need walking so much, but if you think you have enough energy to stop by and give her some attention midday, maybe a few rounds of fetch in my fenced yard, I know she'd love it. It would help me on days I can't get back here and it'd make her feel more secure."

"Of course. I can do that. In fact, I'd love to play with her."

"Great. The house is locked up and I don't have a spare key, but she has a doggie door, so if you enter the yard's gate and call out to her, she'll come. She's met you before, so I'm not worried about her getting defensive."

"I've got it. Don't worry about her. I'll go over there today after Nim wakes up from her nap and eats lunch."

"Perfect. Thanks."

"You bet." She returned his wave as he drove off.

Life could be so strange. She was going to be taking care of the sheriff's dog. The one man who might see her face come up on his computer at work at any given moment and slap cuffs on her wrists the next.

And he'd seen her without makeup. No eyeliner or lipstick. Just plain Faye, the way she'd always been before. Her morning routine had consisted of washing her face and pulling her hair back. She wore a touch of mascara, but nothing heavy, and sometimes lip balm if the weather was bitter cold, but that was about it. Now, she had to remind herself every morning to lay it on thick enough to feel safe. Unrecognizable.

Would he recognize her, now that he'd seen her face naked, if a warrant for her arrest circulated? She rubbed her temples and went back inside.

"Take each day at a time," she muttered. "Deal with it if it happens."

She began tidying up around the place. She didn't want Eve to get tired of their being around. It was enough that she'd opened up her home.

The landline rang and she looked at the number. It was the bookstore.

"Hey, Eve. You holding up?"

"Yes. But I feel so behind."

"You only missed a couple of days."

"Two days too many. Listen. I forgot to ask this morning. I'll be passing by the grocers on the way home. If you let me know what you need for Nim, I can add it to the list."

"Are you sure? I'll pay you back."

"I'm sure."

She glanced around what was left of kid food and checked on the dwindling stack of diapers and wipes, then rattled off a few items before thanking her again and hanging up.

She started putting used mugs and bowls in the sink, trying not to wake Nim with the clinking and clanking. She'd disinfect every surface too. She really didn't want that kid coming in contact with germs, especially with how much she stuck her fingers in her mouth.

A creaking sounded from the front of the cottage. She froze with a plate in hand, then set it down super softly on a nearby dish towel. The wooden landing outside the door creaked again, then a bump and rustle. Carlos had left. And Eve was at Castaway Books. Any other visitor would knock or ring the bell.

She looked around for something to use in self-defense if necessary and grabbed a four-foot-long, heavy rain stick that was leaning against the corner wall. She kept it vertical so the beads inside wouldn't shift and give her away. She tiptoed to the front door and looked through the peephole. That kid from the bakery. She recognized him as one of Darla's employees.

Her lungs collapsed and she cracked the door open, still holding the rain stick behind it.

"Hi. I thought I heard someone out here."

The kid fumbled with his cell phone and stuck it back in his pocket. He was balancing a pastry box in the other hand.

"Oh, hey. Sorry. I was about to knock but I almost dropped the box. Caught it against the door, luckily. Darla said to bring this over to you. Croissants. They're still warm. She said she hopes you're feeling better."

He held out the box, this time holding it sensibly with two hands. There was no end to cell phone distractions. They even put baked goods in danger. She took the box. Even with her slightly stuffy sinuses, the aroma filled her senses.

"This is so thoughtful. Please thank her for me. I'll stop in the bakery soon."

"I'll let her know. See ya."

He bounded down the steps and took off in his hatchback. Hopefully, his phone remained in his pocket.

She closed the door and stood with her back to it for a second. A simple delivery had rattled her nerves that much? How was she going to hold up if she saw her face on the news or if Jim found her himself?

"Fa!" Nim started crying from the bedroom, where Faye had moved her playpen. She padded in her socked feet down the short hall and went up to her niece with arms outstretched.

"Ma. Ma." She had to get her to say it. It's what kids her age called their moms. She recalled Nim saying "Dada" to Carlos. She'd been feverish and half-asleep, but she'd heard it. Unless the fever had been talking. But why had Nim said that to him? Was she remembering? Missing her dad?

"Fa fa."

"No, sweetie. I'm Mama."

Nim scowled at her. Faye lifted her out of the pen and got a whiff of her diaper. Maybe she did need to read up on potty training. Had Clara been potty training Nim? Come to think of it, she'd mentioned it a few times, and she did have one of those plastic kid potties in one of their bathrooms, but as far as Faye knew, Nim wasn't trained yet. Was that related to emotional distress too? Like not talking as much as peers? Or was she just too young? In any case, potty training was the last thing on Faye's mind.

"Girl, you do not smell like an ocean breeze. Let's get you changed. And then we'll find out if I'm as good at potty training kids as I am with puppies."

She had her changed and fed and in the umbrella stroller within an hour. She didn't think she had it in her to carry Nim's weight around in the carrier yet. The cold was still working its way out of her chest. She also didn't think that Nim had it in her to walk over to Carlos's place and then into town. Faye didn't want to use the car since Carlos had pointed out the registration needed renewal. He hadn't mentioned it again, which kind of surprised her. But maybe it was because she hadn't driven it. Leaving the car parked here also seemed like a safer bet, just in case Jim managed to track her to the town where she'd bought it. Cash or not.

"There you go. Let's get you some sunshine and fresh air." She slipped Nim's hat on. "Do you want to go see Pepper?"

Nim swung her legs excitedly and clapped her hands.

"Pepe."

It sounded like she had said "pee pee." Good thing Pepper probably wouldn't notice or care.

Carlos's yard was simple and neat. The left side of his beach house had a wooden fence that wrapped around a side yard that was about as big as her apartment times three back home. She opened the gate and pushed the stroller in, then closed it behind her. The yard wasn't landscaped. There was a small grassy area flanked with ornamental grasses that had browned over the winter and a short deck that was a weathered gray. A round charcoal grill sat on the deck with a table and four chairs. There wasn't even a tree for shade in the summer. Maybe it didn't matter to him if he spent more time at work than hanging around in his yard.

"Pepper?"

She bent down to unbuckle Nim and set her free. Pepper came rushing through the doggy door panting as if her visitors were the best surprise ever. Faye lunged to grab Nim, who was headed for the dog, before they collided. A swear word escaped her and she immediately regretted it. Small ears. She also should have known better than to release Nim from the stroller before letting Pepper settle down. She knew that much about dogs. She had been trying to be careful on walks. Whether it was having been sick or getting too comfortable with her surroundings, she'd let her guard down and that was dangerous. Kids were scary. Unpredictable. Helpless. And she'd nearly failed in her role of protector.

"Goodness that was close. Kiddo, hang on a sec and let Pepper calm down. Then you can stand and pet her."

She gave Pepper a good rub and kissed the top of her head. The dog sniffed at her pocket.

"Not yet. Treats are earned. Let's find your toys."

Pepper wasn't a puppy but her hips were doing fine, from what Faye had observed. A few ball tosses would do her good.

Nim wriggled free from Faye's grasp and

wrapped her arms around Pepper's chest. Pepper licked Nim's hat right off and Nim started laughing uncontrollably. The kind that brought on hiccups and made everything okay. Pepper, encouraged, picked up the hat and flung it, then licked at Nim's belly. Nim fell onto her bottom and laughed even harder as Pepper waited for her new "puppy" to go fetch the hat.

Now *that* was sweet love. Faye wished she had her cell phone to capture the moment. She wanted…hoped…to share it with Clara in the near future. But all she could do was cherish the moment and hope that the memory of it would never fade.

CARLOS WAITED UNTIL Jordan and Greg left to do rounds and the rest of the office staff had retreated to their desks and stations. He was supposed to be clocking out and heading home, but he'd been waiting for a private moment to do some searching. Faye's past had been nagging him ever since Nim had called him Dada. Who was the guy? Who had done this to them? He itched to use every bit of the law he could to punish the man. Checking Faye's background wasn't his intention. Finding the guy was…even if he never confronted him. He just felt better knowing where the threat to Faye was coming from.

He technically had no legal reason to check on her background. Well, she did start helping with Pepper yesterday, but that was different. He had no intention of telling her he required a background check for walking his dog, when she was living under Eve's roof. That would constitute manipulating the situation. He wasn't trying to scare her. He wanted to help her…without breaking rules. Yet here he was in front of his computer trying to justify looking into her past. Her ex's past. And he was running on assumptions when it came to her ex. Faye hadn't pressed charges or filed a restraining order. Getting info on the man—even with the intention of protecting her—crossed a line. And he had to admit, despite the fact that he had a right to protect the town if he thought there was anything criminal going on—and abuse was unequivocally criminal—his interest was becoming personal. He cared, not just about doing what was right, but about Faye and her little girl.

When he'd discovered her car was bought by a Donovan and not a Potter, he had reason to look into it. The whole registration expiration. But looking at her records to find out who her husband was? That wasn't exactly kosher police protocol. The way she'd reacted to him when they'd first met made him wonder if the guy was a cop. Wouldn't she just love it if he ended up being yet another law-breaking cop in her life?

He put "Faye Donovan" into the system but deleted it before hitting enter.

"Sheriff, you have a memo that just came through. A Jane Doe was found washed up off Ocracoke. They're notifying everyone in case she matches a missing person's report." Margie, one of his newer officers, set a printout on his desk. The report would be in the system but he liked keeping a print copy up on the bulletin board. Out of sight out of mind. He preferred visual reminders for his team to see day in and day out. Especially when it came to wanted or missing persons.

Ocracoke was farther south than Turtleback. They hadn't received any reports on missing persons as of yet. He logged out of his search page and turned his attention to the memo. Suspected riptide drowning. He cursed under his breath. He hated this part of his job. Knowing he was protecting people, that part he loved. But seeing cases where protection failed. That killed him. And a case like Faye's where his hands were tied unless she gave him the green light? Forget six feet. It made him feel like he was twelve feet under. Buried alive at that.

It couldn't get more personal.

Neck and neck with the emotions he'd dealt with as a ten-year-old, when his father died. He had been killed in a freak accident...or that's what it was called. A case of mistaken identity. Bull. His jaw cramped and he cranked his neck to loosen his shoulders. His father had been stereotyped. Killed by friendly fire. Not at war either. He was an off-duty officer on vacation with his wife and kid and he had tried to do what was right. He had gone inside a gas station to pay, leaving Carlos and his mom in their car. His father had jumped into action to save the clerk when two masked men entered and held the woman behind the register at gunpoint. Local police responded to the 10-31. The robbers escaped. The cops, arriving on scene as Carlos's father was running for his car to make sure his wife and kid were alright, shot him.

He had fit a profile. His mom tried to pursue it legally, but the case fell through. The cop who'd shot him was inexperienced. He had been following procedure, according to the investigation. His father was running away from a crime scene toward a potential getaway car. That's how it stood. A reasonable sounding defense, but the situation had been more complicated than that. The officer claimed there had been no racial profiling involved. His mother never believed it. Nor did he.

His father had been killed while trying to protect not only the clerk, but his wife and kid.

Faye and Nim.

He rubbed his face and pushed away from his desk. He wasn't going to cut corners and break rules. He was nothing if he didn't abide by the laws he upheld. He'd avoided following in his father's footsteps for so long. He'd gone into the air force instead. But after he'd returned home for his mother, she had encouraged him to join the police force. To run for sheriff. To be one of the good ones—and the vast majority of cops were just that. Putting their lives on the line for others. Every day.

Those who knew his father had poured in their support, as did others from many states. Some had even come to his mother's funeral so many years later.

Be one of the good ones. Make a difference. He could hear his mother like she was standing in front of him. He couldn't let her down. He couldn't betray Faye, then expect her to trust him.

"Margie, I'll see you tomorrow." He took his jacket off the back of his chair and put it on.

"See ya, Sheriff. Be good," she teased, as she always did.

He shook a finger at her.

"I'll think about it."

Thunder rumbled as he stepped outside and the wind picked up. Dark, rolling clouds loomed over Turtleback, moving fast enough for a passing rain but slow enough to drench. It looked like a heck of a storm. If he hurried, he'd make it home before it hit. Pepper didn't like the sound of thunder. She was really going to hate it when the bolder spring storms started coming through in a few weeks. And then there would be the summer hurricane season to reckon with. She hadn't been with him during the last one.

Several drops hit his windshield by the time he reached the intersection. A slew of them followed hard and fast once he turned onto his road. He flicked on his windshield wipers, his headlights already set to automatic, and navigated the one area where he knew the side of the road flooded easily.

"Aw, man."

Faye was up ahead on the left side of the road, pushing Nim's stroller hard and fast. She would never make it to the house before getting drenched and she'd barely gotten over being sick. And Nim would be soaked. Temperatures had already dropped five degrees with the front. He pulled up a few feet ahead of them, noticing the way Faye jolted but recovered when she realized who it was. He leaped out of the driver's seat and was unbuckling Nim within seconds. "Quick. Grab her and get in. I'll get this." She shielded Nim against her chest as she ducked her head and climbed into the back seat. He folded the stroller and put it across the foot area and got back behind the wheel. "You okay?" He called out over Nim, who'd started bawling. He couldn't blame her.

"Yeah, thanks. Wet, but okay. The weather was fine around lunchtime, when we went to play with Pepper, so after Nim had her afternoon nap, I thought we'd take a short walk for fresh air and to build my stamina back up before tomorrow's dog rounds. I started back as soon as I saw that cloud rolling in." She shivered and her teeth chattered as she spoke. It was strange seeing her in the back seat of his vehicle where people he'd arrested had sat, but it had been the closest door to her.

"Let's get you two home." It was only three more minutes by car, but in a rain like this on foot while pushing a buggy? It would have felt like forever. She started searching through the bag she had strapped across her chest. He headed straight for Eve's place.

"I can't find the keys." She wiped a hand across her face to dry her eyes and her makeup smeared along her upper cheeks. "I swear they were in here. I didn't let Nim play with them this time." She kept digging frantically. Lightning flashed, followed five seconds later by a deafening clap of thunder. He couldn't leave her at her doorstep in this. Eve wasn't home yet. He had seen the light still on at Castaway Books on his way home. He didn't normally take anyone to his place. He glanced at her in the rearview mirror again. She clung to Nim with one hand and covered her eyes with the other for a moment before she resumed rummaging. A diaper fell out onto the seat. Nim was crying louder than the last boom and Faye… She looked like the last drop of rain that hit her had been the last straw. He'd begun to slow as he approached Eve's cottage, but passed it instead.

"Don't worry about it. You can wait out the storm at my place."

Faye looked up, full lips parted and smeared face just sad. And slightly emo. Her shoulders sank and she gave up on finding her keys, rocking Nim against her chest instead. Or maybe she was soothing herself just as much. She nodded reluctantly.

He parked as close as he could to his front door, making sure the side she was on was closest to it, then jumped out and ran around to help her.

"Here, give me Nim. Leave the stroller. We'll get it later." He carried Nim and was at his door in several long strides. Faye followed, running to keep up. He'd have carried her too if he could. He shook the rain off his face. Where had that thought come from? He unlocked his door and stepped in before holding it open for Faye. Getting Nim under his roof had to come first. He was sure Faye felt the same way. He closed the door behind her, still holding a crying Nim. Faye reached out for her as Pepper, whining louder than the little girl, tried gluing herself to the three of them. His entryway wasn't big enough.

He took off his wet jacket, hung it on the hook behind the door and took Faye's from her. She sank to her knees and began slipping off Nim's. Pepper was all over them.

"Come here, girl. You're alright." Carlos led his dog a few feet away and rubbed her down. She calmed somewhat. "I'll get you something dry to wear. You'll swim in whatever I have, but at least you won't be soaked through. We can toss your stuff and Nim's in the dryer."

"It's okay. I'm sure the rain will let up any second. Thank you for this. I'm so sorry we're intruding. I could have sworn I dropped the keys into this bag after locking the door when we left earlier. They're on a dolphin key chain. Hard to miss."

"They'll turn up. But you can't stand there all wet like that. You'll end up with pneumonia. You still have a cough from the cold and you're shivering. I'll get some towels and a blanket we can wrap Nim in while her clothes are drying. I can watch her while you change. Sit, Pepper." The dog sat but stamped her paws nervously.

"Hey, Pepper, it's okay. Just a bit of rain," Faye said, drawing her in and scratching her muzzle and behind her ears. Pepper nudged Nim, who almost immediately stopped crying and began patting her.

Carlos disappeared into his bedroom and came back with a sweatshirt, drawstring sweatpants, a stack of towels and a throw.

Faye had Pepper lying down with Nim resting the back of her head against the dog as Faye undressed her. She had them all settled down that fast. He stopped in his tracks and took in the scene. Dog. Mother. Child. In his house. Doing regular stuff like coming in from a rain.

He swallowed hard and refocused on the stack of towels.

"Here you go. I'd offer you the shower to warm up, but it's not safe in a thunderstorm like this. I have some leftover soup I can heat. That'll help." He set the stack next to her on a chair and stepped back. "This will keep Nim warm. My mother made it years ago."

She took the green-and-yellow blanket from his hands.

"It's pretty. And soft," she said, setting it down next to her and taking the plastic bag of clean diapers and a container of wipes out of her oversize purse. "I don't believe it." She pulled out a set of keys dangling from a dolphin and held them up. "I swear I looked and felt around the bottom of the purse."

"Don't worry about it. You're here now. It's not worth going back out there until the storm passes."

Faye finished putting a dry diaper on Nim, stood her up and wrapped the blanket around her, tucking it in place near her armpit so it looked like a toga.

"Does your mom knit a lot?"

"She passed away years ago. Cancer."

"I'm sorry."

"Thank you. She'd be happy knowing it's being put to good use." He kicked off his boots, reached past her and picked Nim up. "Come here, Pepper." The dog followed him to the couch and sat next to him. He nestled Nim between them and turned on the television. "The bathroom's the first door on the left. We'll start the clothes dryer and brew some coffee or tea when you're done. Assuming we don't lose power."

She took off her sneakers and picked up the towels.

"Thanks. You've been rescuing us a lot lately."

He looked over at her and their eyes locked for seconds too long. Something passed between them. He wasn't sure what or how. Just that his world had shifted. He cleared his throat and put his arm across the back of the couch where Pepper and Nim sat.

"It's nothing. Go on. We'll be right here."

Him rescuing them? He fingered Nim's red hair, then swiped her cheek playfully. The image of her and Faye with Pepper had him scrubbing his hand across his face. Why, then, did he get the nagging feeling that Faye and Nim were rescuing him?

FAYE TOOK ONE look in the bathroom mirror and was mortified. He'd seen her like this?

She wasn't sure which was worse, Carlos bearing witness to what she looked like when she was sick, or now. She resembled a fallen angel with black eyeliner dripping down her cheeks and hair plastered to the sides of her face. Forget thunder. She was likely the reason Nim and Pepper had been crying. She looked like she'd stepped off the set of a horror movie.

She ran the water in the sink until it warmed, washed her face and patted it dry before even bothering with her wet clothes. She didn't have any makeup on her, but he'd already seen her without. She piled up her wet clothes, dried herself and put on Carlos's sweats. They were way too big on her, and cozy...and much too personal. She drew the waist tie as taut as she could and rolled up the bottoms to her ankles. She looked in the mirror one last time.

Much better. She looked like herself. But she didn't feel like herself. She was standing in Carlos Ryker's bathroom, surrounded by the musky scent of his lingering aftershave and personal items like his toothbrush and sunscreen. And she was wearing his sweats. She closed her eyes and wrapped her hands around her waist. It felt good and safe being here, yet at the same time she knew she was standing in the eye of the storm. The calm before everything would be swept away.

She took the towel she'd used and bundled her wet pile in it.

When she headed back out to the living room, Carlos was hiding a crumpled-up piece of paper in his palm and playing "Which hand?" with Nim. The wide-screen that sat on a pine TV cabinet was turned off. The room was comfortable. Simple as his yard, but not empty or uncared for. Most of the furniture was pine, except for the denim colored sofa and leather recliner. A long piece of driftwood hung over the sofa and a painting of a lighthouse and a boat sailing on the waters beyond it hung on the wall by the entry. The only two items on the end table, other than an iron lamp, were a framed photo of an older couple and one that was a close-up of the woman.

"I let Eve know you're okay."

"Are those your parents?"

"Yes," he said, hiding the paper in his hands behind his back then holding his closed fists out for Nim.

"Your mother was beautiful. Is your father—"

"He passed away many years before her. She essentially raised me on her own. With the help of friends."

"I don't know where your dryer is."

"I'll get those." He jumped up, then realized that maybe leaving Nim on the couch wasn't a good idea. He put the paper on the coffee table and picked her up. "The satellite went out, so we improvised."

"I see. You're good with kids. Younger siblings?" She was glad that he was carrying Nim. She wasn't about to give him her pile of laundry. Not with her bra in it. That would definitely be too personal. He led her to a closet at the end of the hall and opened the accordion-style door. A stacked washer and dryer stood behind it. He opened the dryer with his free hand, took out a pair of jeans and threw them onto the bed in the room right next door.

"Nope. Just me. But I've been around enough of Turtleback's youngsters. Especially during the summer when they're all running about."

She put her stuff inside the dryer, then went

to the entryway to gather Nim's items before starting it. The hall was rather crowded with Pepper, who insisted on standing there with them. Carlos held Nim over Pepper's back and let her pretend she was riding a horse all the way back to the living room. The guy was a natural.

"Mo!"

"More? Well, you have to ask Pepper," he said. The dog barked. Carlos took Nim on another ride, keeping her supported so her weight wouldn't bother Pepper.

Both child and dog seemed to forget about the storm outside. An entirely different kind of storm was brewing inside Faye. She wasn't a real mother or a dog owner, yet watching Carlos's horseplay stirred something primal at her core. Instinct, maybe. An urge to have more. Family…children…love? She'd always been content—truly happy—with her independent single life. Until this very moment.

He set Nim on her feet after the second time around the living room and braced his hand on his hips.

"Tea or coffee?"

"Tea, if you don't mind."

He went into the kitchen that opened into

the living room and watched the dog and kid as he set water to boil.

"I don't think I've ever seen Pepper so relaxed and playful. Those two were made for each other."

"Nim's going to be a fellow animal lover. Dogs, for sure. She had a good time with her earlier today."

"Did that go well? That reminds me, I need to pay you."

She needed money, but mention of payment hit her the wrong way. A jerk to reality. He'd hired her. This whole being here with him and his dog was a result of his sense of duty. Nothing more.

"You brought us here in a storm and you're making tea. Forget about the payment."

"We had a deal."

"Let the deal start tomorrow. We'll call today a test run. I owe you that much."

"Like I said, you don't owe me a thing, but okay. If you insist."

"I do. By the way, can I ask you something?"

"Go for it."

"Is there history between Jordan and Eve? Like did they break up once or something?"

"There probably should be history but there isn't. Maybe it was in a past life. Everyone sees how perfect they are for each other, except the two of them. He's been hurt and is gun-shy."

"And she's independent and doesn't trust easily." She understood now. Eve had witnessed too many women escaping bad relationships. That had to have left a permanent mark on her.

"Maybe that puppy... What's her name? Shamu. Maybe Shamu will bring them together," he said.

"I don't know about that. She nearly jumped down his throat when he asked if Shamu could help at Castaway Books like Laddie does. We were discussing puppy-sitting arrangements. Oh, speaking of dogs, watch this." She went over to Pepper and told her to sit, then lie down, then stand, then shake. Pepper performed every command on cue, ending with the paw-to-hand shake.

"You trained her to do that? Between yesterday and today?"

"That saying about how you can't teach an old dog new tricks is a bunch of nonsense."

"But in just a few hours?"

"She's a smart one. Not all dogs learn that quickly. I discovered she'll do anything for an ear scratch. Some are food motivated. Not her."

"I'm impressed. Floored, actually. And you won't let me pay you? At least eat while you're here." He opened the fridge. "I have more of that soup, some leftover enchiladas—homemade using my mom's recipe—and some meat loaf and mashed potatoes that Chanda had packed up for me yesterday."

The man was good with dogs and kids, protected people for a living *and* he could cook.

She was doomed.

"I'll have whatever you're having. Nim too. She loved that soup and I bet she'd go for the meat loaf and potatoes if we give her bite-sized pieces. If you're sure it's no bother."

"Just remember you said you'd have what I'm having." He grinned as he pulled *everything* out of the fridge. The soup, enchiladas and Chanda's cooking. All of it.

"Let me rephrase. I'll *taste* everything you're having. That'll easily add up to a full meal for me."

She watched as Nim sat with Pepper on the area rug. She'd taken the crumpled paper and was placing it on the rug between her and the dog. Pepper put her paw on it, then uncovered it, and the two repeated the game over and over.

"Amazing. Those two. Everyone should grow up with a dog."

"Except for you?" He set a mug of tea for her on the table. One of those souvenir types she'd seen in the window of the gift shop. OBX was printed on the side—the accepted and popular abbreviation for the Outer Banks. She recognized it from all the T-shirts and bumper stickers, and the sweatshirt she had on, that sported the logo. She ran the pad of her thumb along the lighthouse on the other side of the mug.

"Except for me. My parents weren't into having pets. My mom didn't want the house smelly—her words—and my dad said it was an unnecessary expense. Neither believed we—*I*—could handle the responsibility."

She left out the part about having a twin. She hoped he didn't ask about siblings.

"Wow."

She shrugged. She couldn't argue with his reaction.

"Yeah. Wow."

He placed a dish in the microwave.

"And you didn't rebel? You didn't get one as soon as you left home?"

"Dogs weren't allowed in the college dorm."

"But after that?" he asked.

She pinched and fiddled with the material of her sweatpants. *His* sweatpants.

"I suppose I was convinced that I couldn't take on the responsibility. They'd said it so much, it had to have some truth to it. I'd worked hard to make good grades and prove to them I could accomplish things, but if I ever got a dog of my own and failed at managing the care and expenses, especially with getting a job and being out of the house, I'd have been proving them right."

"You chose the safe road. Don't try. Can't fail."

"I guess so."

"That's a shame. You have a way with dogs." He set a bowl of soup and a plate with samples of the other dishes in front of her, added his own in the spot at the table next to hers and sat down. "You can feed Nim after you eat. She's preoccupied with Pepper. Take advantage while you can." He took a bite of his own food, a sip of water, then leaned back.

He frowned and moved his food around, as if considering his next words very carefully. "If I didn't know better, I would have pictured you owning your own dog training business, surrounding yourself with four-legged friends in a win-win way. Not failing at being a good owner, while proving you can be successful. But, of course, you've never owned or worked with dogs. Your ability to control a whole pack of them and to train an old dog with ease is a natural, born-with-it gift."

Faye set her spoon down.

"How long have you known?"

"Not long. Since the night after bringing over soup."

How much did he know? Possible replies and their consequences shot through her mind. He was waiting. She needed to say something or he'd get suspicious.

"I really have never owned a dog. That's the truth. I do own a dog grooming and training place. Or did. It has been locked up since I left and I'll likely have lost all my customers to other businesses if I ever get back."

He leaned forward and lowered his voice.

"The truth. Both of us. I'll start. I know your last name isn't Potter. It's Donovan.

Faye, I had approached Eve after I noticed your wrist." He reached over and pushed back the sweatshirt cuff. The brush of his fingertips against her skin left a trail of warmth she wanted to hold on to. But all he was doing was revealing the marks Eve didn't believe were dog scratches. "Put 'Faye Donovan and dogs' into a search bar on any computer and guess what comes up? You're public. I knew I had the right Faye because your website has your photograph. Not with the burgundy bob, but definitely you without the makeup. And there were social media links. Very convenient. A person can glean a lot of info off social media alone, even when care is being taken not to divulge too much." He let go of her hand. "You don't have a cell phone or use credit cards. Nor have you made any effort to register your car. Faye. I know all about Eve's extracurricular activities in college. You came here for a reason. She has kept your confidence and has said nothing other than reassuring me that you'll be okay with her. But I'm not convinced that you feel safe."

"You've been running checks on me? Like a criminal?"

Oh, no. She closed her eyes and pushed her chair back.

"No. Nothing that wasn't public. Nothing anyone in town couldn't have looked up. And even then, only because I was worried about you. On my honor. But I'm asking you now to save me the time and effort. The truth, Faye."

She rubbed her eyes then held on to the edge of the table. *Truth? Or more lies?*

"There's nothing left."

"Are you divorced? I need to know the truth about that."

"Why?"

"Because... Because maybe I'm starting to care too much."

The room stilled. Even Pepper's ears perked and she looked up from her game with Nim. At least it seemed like it. It could have been the noise Faye's mug made when it slipped from her hand and hit the table too hard. What was he saying? He was interested? He liked her? That's why he'd looked her up? She pushed her hair back but couldn't bring herself to make eye contact.

"Yes." She knew for sure that she had not disclosed her marital status online. She was single either way.

"And he's still after you? Have you tried getting a restraining order?"

Think. Think.

"Yes and no."

"Why not? I can help you with that."

"No. You can't. It's complicated."

"I'm in law enforcement, Faye. I was in the Air Force. I've cooperated in cases with WITSEC and the FBI. There's nothing too complicated that I can't at least try and help with. Let me in," he pleaded.

"Carlos, you don't understand. He's... blackmailing me."

It wasn't the full truth, or a complete lie. He was manipulating her sister and her both. If he was straight-shooting, he'd have her face plastered everywhere by now. Nim would be in custody. And Carlos wouldn't be asking questions because he'd know Nim wasn't her daughter. She wasn't even her legal guardian. She needed to buy herself a little more time. If he knew the truth, he'd be obligated to arrest her and, whether he believed her or not about Jim, without proof, Nim would be put in the hands of her father. He'd have her in jail and her sister labeled as unstable, assuming he hadn't done something horrible to her. Nim would be lost to him. Raised by him. An abusive, arrogant, controlling, manipulative man.

"Is he in the police force? Is he using his connections and abusing his power? And you?"

"You could say that. He's not a cop, but is in law. A lawyer. With a lot of clout and connections. And many of them are police in high enough positions to smooth out and cover up anything he pays them to do."

She was piecing together bits and pieces of what she knew about Jim from her sister and from what she'd suspected about his character all along.

"Still, he lost custody in the divorce?"

She took a long sip of her tea and looked back at Nim, avoiding eye contact. *Just tell him the truth. Let him help you. No... Jim has too much reach. Clara said not to trust anyone.*

"The judge was sympathetic to mothers. Given her age and the fact that my hours were more flexible and accommodating, I got custody except for weekends. He was furious. He made that clear whenever I dropped her off. I told him I wasn't going to bring her over anymore and that I'd report him. He threatened to destroy me. Hunt me down. Use everything in his power to make my life miserable forever. I took her and ran. Tried to cover my tracks."

He got up, paced the kitchen, then pulled his chair out and put it right in front of hers. He moved her chair, with her in it, as if she were weightless, and sat to face her.

He took both of her hands in his and held on to them with a gentleness that tore her up inside and burned the rims of her eyes. She didn't want to lie to him. Couldn't. But was afraid to trust. Afraid of failing in the worst way possible. Failing her sister…her niece.

"I'm sorry for what happened to you. I don't ever want it to happen again. I'd do anything in my power to ensure that. I can keep you and your daughter safe. I can keep him from going anywhere near you. I just need you to trust me and give me permission. File a complaint and I'll run a check on him. With men like that, there are often others in their past whom they've abused as well. We'll find them. Maybe they'll testify. But even if you're the only one, I can—"

"Please, Carlos. We're fine here for now. Nim and I." She thought of Clara and what

Jim would do to her if he so much as got a hint that Faye was trying to bring him down. If Carlos went after him, Jim would take it out on her sister and then come after her. The image of Clara's bruised face and black eye came to her in full color. She shuddered at what Jim was capable of. "I don't want you to get involved. I don't want to deal with any of it. If he causes trouble, I'll let you know, but until then, I'd rather just be. He doesn't know where I am. Not yet."

"But Faye."

"No *buts*. If you really do care…" She'd started to refer to what he'd said about her earlier…that he cared too much. The words didn't come out. "If you care, then please just listen to me."

She let her hands turn in his. Let his fingers link through hers. Allowed herself to imagine…to feel…for a moment, what could be. She hated leading him on. Lying. Destroying any possibility of his feelings ever amounting to anything. She wanted more. Her hands in his felt right. It felt like home. Safe. But she had to keep Carlos out of it. His duty was to the law. She'd broken it. Her responsibility was to Clara and Mia. She couldn't lose them. But she knew…just knew…with every cell and every breath, that she was losing the only man she'd ever felt a connection like this with. A man she had an urge to bare her soul to, but couldn't. And most of all, she was losing a chance…at love.

CHAPTER TEN

YESTERDAY'S STORM PASSED. At least the weather-related one did. The one brewing in Carlos was driving him off the plank. And it wasn't all about worrying that anyone would harm Faye, who was safely at home with Eve right now. The turmoil he was dealing with was in his chest, not his gut. He'd felt this way once before, only this was different. This time it was deeper, stranger and more disconcerting than it had ever been with Natalie.

With Natalie, they had had a plan. Their relationship made sense. He *had* loved her and not because he wanted to protect her—they were dating long before he found out about her abusive past—but because she had a strength about her. She was determined. Fearless…until it came to the idea of getting pinned down in Turtleback. He'd been ready to marry her and he would have devoted himself to that marriage. Dutifully. That's how he ran his life.

But he knew love was about letting go, if that's what a person needed. He had thought, for the longest time, that Nat would change her mind and come back to him, realize that putting down roots didn't mean losing one's freedom. But he eventually accepted that wasn't going to happen. He'd learned his lesson. Their relationship had been easy, but it fell apart when things got complicated. When the going got tough, not everyone had the kind of strength it took to step up. To take a stance and stick around.

With Faye, everything had been complicated right off the bat. None of it made sense. She was a single mother. He'd never imagined starting a family and having kids until meeting her. He didn't even know if he was ready for one or if he'd be any good at it. All he knew was that that little girl had triggered some sort of paternal instinct in him that was hard to shake. Faye also came with the sort of emotional baggage she might never get past to let him in. Natalie hadn't loved him enough to be in it for the long haul. Faye was at a point in life where she probably couldn't see that far into the future. She was hiding out. Watching over her shoulder. Looking only as far as tomorrow and hoping things would be okay.

He didn't want to be drawn to her. He didn't want to care so much. But he did. That was pretty much the only simple thing about this mess. He cared beyond any sense of duty and that was that. It was as if their paths had been destined to cross. He couldn't stop thinking about her and it sure as heck wasn't because he felt sorry for her or was worried for her. Yes, when he saw her wrist, it had triggered a protective instinct and reminded him of all that Natalie had confided in him, but that was only initially. Things had changed since then. He wanted to be around her and Nim. When he was at work, he thought about going home and maybe stopping by Eve's to say hi. When he went to pick up groceries and dog food earlier, he found himself picking out a few items Nim could enjoy, just in case they ended up at his place again.

He used to go home after work and relish the alone time, feet up in front of the TV with his dog next to him. Since the storm yesterday, when he'd taken Faye and Nim to his place, his house felt empty. He already missed sitting down and playing "which hand" with Nim, while Faye had some time to herself. He missed sharing his dinner. He missed the tender look on her face when she'd stepped out of the bathroom and found him playing with Nim. And the truth was, he had no right to feel all this. He hadn't even known her that long.

If Natalie hadn't been ready for commitments, Faye certainly wasn't. He had to keep reminding himself that caring for someone was about giving them their freedom and fulfilling their wishes and needs, not one's own. Faye was on the run. Even if he managed to fix things so that her ex could never bother her again, she had her business to return to, several states away. She had no reason to stay in Turtleback Beach. And he couldn't forget the fact that his being a sheriff had really made her nervous, at least initially. Would she ever get over that and trust him? Could he trust her? Trust was crucial in a relationship and she still didn't trust him fully. Definitely not enough to let him do his job and protect her. Offering that protection and help didn't mean she couldn't take care of herself. Heck, she was incredible. The kind of inner strength and courage it took to escape an abuser, with a child in tow, no less, and face each day with the level of determination she did was incredible.

But Faye had something in common with Natalie. Turtleback wasn't her home and it didn't look like she planned on staying. He couldn't blame her. She had just escaped a bad relationship. Starting a new one was probably the last thing on her mind.

He rubbed the back of his neck, then went and rinsed his coffee mug out. He needed to wash away whatever feelings he was starting to have for Faye too.

Stick to protocol. Don't get personal with a case. You're already in too deep. Pull yourself out while you can. Before it's too late. Before you get hurt again.

He filled Pepper's water and food bowls and stuffed his keys in his pocket, then proceeded to lace up his boots.

Faye's keys. He smiled to himself. He was kinda glad she couldn't find them yesterday. Having her and Nim here for dinner and seeing how happy it made his dog had given him a taste of what his father must have felt whenever he came home from work.

He finished with the second boot and grabbed his jacket. He needed to get to work. He desperately needed to pick up a cinnamon pecan muffin at The Saltwater Sweetery first. Thinking about Faye triggered his cravings. Made him happy. Made him want more. He wanted to give her more. Make her see that life wasn't all bad. That there was beauty in it. Peace.

Peace. Show it to her. If she can only see as far as tomorrow, then give her a tomorrow she'll never forget.

He opened his door and the morning air breathed new life into him. Give her peace and an unforgettable tomorrow. He knew exactly how he would.

FAYE WAITED UNTIL Eve left for work and Nim went down for her midmorning nap before booting up the laptop. She drew the afghan around her shoulders and took the computer and a mug of tea outside to sit at the teak table and chairs on Eve's deck. The deck overlooked the Atlantic with its white-tipped waves and the endless stretch of sand that welcomed it. Stairs descended onto a wooden walkway that led through patches of wild grass and reeds, over a short sand dune onto the main beach. The beach and shore were in clear view from up here on the deck.

She had been up before dawn today with Nim. The sunrise had been the most breathtaking, brilliant blend of pinks and oranges she'd ever seen, but she didn't get to sit and enjoy it for long. If she were here in Turtleback under different circumstances, she would have a hard time leaving. She would never tire of waking up to a sunrise like the ones she had been witnessing on clear mornings. But Nim had woken up cranky and drooling like a Newfoundland with a bowl of food in front of him. No wonder puppies chewed everything in sight when they were teething.

It had to hurt. But all the tips she'd been given by people like Chanda, including a refrigerated teething ring and the more holistic amber one Eve had surprised her with, were helping. She had needed to resort to acetaminophen only one night, when the teething had given Nim a low-grade fever and the teething rings didn't seem to be soothing the pain, and they had both finally caught up on some lost sleep. Until this morning, when she'd resorted to giving medication again. At least it was working.

More than once, the town doctor had been suggested and she'd declined every time. She was grateful that Nim hadn't shown signs of coming down with the cold she and Eve had suffered—and if she did develop a high fever or severe symptoms of any kind, of course she'd take her in. But she wasn't going to a medical professional for minor ailments. Not when that involved records and signatures and past pediatric information, which she didn't have. It was too risky. Clara had kept up with all of it. She was an awesome mother. Completely taken for granted by her husband. But she had persevered. She'd been too tolerant, in Faye's opinion. Or too stoic. Things had to have gotten worse for her to have trusted Faye with the most precious thing in her life.

A massive bird that resembled a Pteranodon soared over the ocean, then dive-bombed the waves and came up with a beak overflowing with fish. It lifted its heavy cargo with graceful ease and disappeared over the cottage and in the direction of the sound side of the island. That bird didn't let the dangers that lurked beneath the waters stop it. It could fly despite the weight it carried. That's how it survived. She would too. She'd handle whatever life threw at her and whatever threats Jim shot her way because she had to be strong for Clara and Nim.

She wasn't sure that she could handle Carlos's confession. He cared about her. Too much. She tugged the wrap a little tighter. Why did this feel like she was leading him on? Was it, though, if she was beginning to really like him too? If things were different, she'd admit to more than just liking him. Life wasn't fair. It wasn't being fair to any of them.

A dog barked in the distance. She looked toward the northern end of the beach, toward the Turtleback Lighthouse, which she'd been told was under Gray and Mandi's care. She could see Laddie out for a jog with Gray. They were far enough not to notice her in the shade of the deck and overhang. The bark was answered by another that emanated down the road from the cottage. Pepper. She loved the way dogs communicated without technology to bridge distances.

Some friends were like that. The kind where even if years passed without any contact, within seconds of finally reconnecting, it was as if no time had been lost and the familiarity and comfort was still there. True friends were never strangers. In some ways, they could be stronger than family. Gold to be treasured. Like Eve.

Despite the fact that they touched base only with a hello or holiday greeting online a few times a year, Faye had known Eve was the one person she could go to in a time of need. She had felt safer reaching out to her than to her parents. Not that they didn't love her, but they didn't get it. They would have insisted on fixing things. On contacting Jim and saving the relationship. They wouldn't have been able to wrap the idea of a controlling, manipulative Jim around their heads. It wouldn't have fit the image they had of him or the image of the perfect marriage they needed to believe their daughter—at least one of them—had. Of course, she couldn't have gone to them for the added reason that it would have been the first place Jim or the authorities looked for her.

Jim. Carlos didn't even know his name. He had no idea how much power the man wielded or the status he held, but he wanted to go after him. And if he started digging, everything would get worse. She didn't know what exactly Carlos had seen online. What if he had held back information just to test her? To see if *she* was revealing everything to him? Wasn't that what cops did when questioning suspects? They did in all the police dramas she'd watched or thrillers she'd read. They kept the upper hand.

She rubbed her eyes, then her entire face, and pushed her hair back. What if Carlos didn't listen to her and he went after "her ex" despite her plea? He'd find out she was lying before she had a chance to defend herself. But what if he understood? Eve told her that she could trust him. She would know, wouldn't she? Faye was going to lose her mind. She wasn't sure what to do, and the fear of taking the wrong step and ending up making things worse for Clara and Nim scared her to death.

Stop. Think. Understand who you're dealing with. Get in their head. Just like you do with dog training. Understand their perspective.

Okay. She could at least figure out what Carlos had found out about her online. She knew in general, but she couldn't recall the details of old posts she'd put up or comments she might have made. She hadn't even checked her profile bio in a long time. Was there anything in there about her not having kids? Could she have posted about doing some activity on a time frame that would have clashed with her supposedly being pregnant and giving birth at the same time? Or being single? She needed to stalk herself online.

She threw the afghan off when the search screen finally loaded. Okay, so she had to be careful. She wouldn't log in anywhere. IP addresses could be tracked. She knew that. But Carlos had mentioned her website and social media. She'd be able to at least see public comments. She could also check news sites for missing person's reports. There had been nothing on television this morning— she had been checking the news at least three times a day since arriving in Turtleback— but sometimes the internet was ahead of the local news.

Was there a photo with her sister online? Clara and Jim, in fact, both had a policy of not posting pics of their child for safety reasons. It made sense, so Faye had respected that on her pages and website. Never even mentioned Mia by name. But Clara was a different matter. Faye couldn't recall if they were pictured together or not. Was he testing her? Waiting to see if she'd confirm what he'd seen? All it would take was a police background check to know she had an identical twin. But he said he hadn't done that. Yet.

She searched her name, Mia's, Clara's and missing persons sites. She didn't find any reports or alerts that fit her description. *Really, Jim? What are you up to?* She went to check comments on her social media pages and scrolled through. Several were asking what happened to her and if she'd be reopening soon because their pooch either needed a behavior lesson or haircut. A few gave get-well wishes, apparently assuming she was out because she'd gotten sick. Ooh…one angry one. She'd forgotten to cancel his appointment and he had waited in his car for thirty minutes with a bull mastiff who could fit only with his head sticking out the sunroof…and it started raining. She covered her mouth. Deep breath. Things like that happened. One had to admit that there was humor in the incident. Maybe her client would come to appreciate it in retrospect. It certainly made for a good story. Besides, she had worse things to worry about right now and there wasn't an iota of humor in any of it. Not even the dark kind.

She scrolled back up to the most recent comments and stopped. Her pulse hit rapid fire and pounded at the base of her throat. It was posted by *him*. Early this morning. The sound of his voice in her head as she read his words made her feel like sand fleas were crawling up her back. He must have realized that she was smart enough not to log in for fear of being tracked by one of his minions or a private investigator. Or the authorities, if he switched gears and reported his daughter as kidnapped. How could he be so sure she'd see this? Wouldn't his leaving a comment work against him if he ever tried to turn her in? Maybe not. He could always say he was trying to fish her out. Dangle a lure. Trap her.

She read the post a second time to be sure she caught everything between the lines.

We really appreciated the time you took care of our puppy so that my wife and I could get away for a few weeks. Unfortunately, she's not feeling very well and we need your help again. Her inability to care for our pup is stressing her, and eliminating stress is crit-

ical to her recovery. Looking forward to your return.

It was code, obviously. He knew she'd understand the threat to return. The pup he was referring to was his daughter. He was trying to scare Faye. She couldn't give in. She wouldn't play his game or come when called. The most important thing was that Clara *wasn't feeling well*. That meant she was alive. A sob escaped and Faye covered her mouth. She had sensed that her sister was alive. She didn't think Jim would be stupid enough to risk murder. He had been careful to inflict pain with his hands and words only in private, up until the black eye. That's what had worried her. What if he lost complete control? Not just his temper, but the kind of control that fed his manipulative tendencies and allowed him to walk that line between being a respected family man and respected professional in public and a wife abuser in private.

But knowing that Clara was alive for sure… Another sob escaped and she let the tension and stress that had built up since her disappearance release until there was nothing left in her.

How can I find you while I'm in hiding? How? He's baiting us both.

She was damned if she did and damned if she didn't. Stay hidden and she'd keep his daughter safely away from him. Go after him and his little girl would end up in his custody because he always won. That little girl in the hands of a man who might someday unleash his temper on her. She felt like a mother faced with being able to save only one of her children from drowning. An impossible, heart-wrenching choice.

I don't know what to do. Clara, I can't stand the thought of him hurting you, but I don't know how to find you. Help me. Give me a sign. A signal.

Faye stilled. Maybe she had. Was it possible? Clara had somehow managed to leave her a message once—the plea to take Nim away. What if she had tried calling Faye's cell? The one she had left behind so that she wouldn't be traced? What if Clara had managed to secretly access the internet and post a message online, as Jim had done?

Faye started to pull up her sister's account, but realized she wouldn't be able to check it without logging in herself for access. Faye had a public site because of her work. Clara didn't.

She slumped back in her chair. She'd never felt so lost in her life. So helpless. She was letting Clara down. Her sister, who was probably holding out hope that someone would find her. Unless... What if Jim didn't have her? What if he was bluffing? What if Clara had escaped and was in hiding on her own, but had no way of knowing where Faye and Nim were? If so, she would know that Jim would be looking for her and she'd never risk leading him to their daughter. If that were the case, Jim would be the one who was nervous. The one with more to lose if his wife managed to find a support system. People who didn't owe him anything.

Too many what-ifs. Zero facts.

She carried the laptop inside, nixed the tea in favor of ice-cold water and went to wash her face. Cold water, again. The cold would help her puffy eyes. She was supposed to resume dog walking in a couple of hours. Folks would probably attribute red eyes and nose to having had a cold—because no doubt by now every soul in Turtleback knew that she had been sick—but if Eve or Carlos saw her, they'd realize she was upset. She didn't need them freaking out and asking more questions.

CARLOS'S STRIDE GOT a little longer and lighter when he spotted Faye with Nim in her chest carrier and a pack of dogs at her side. She was headed back up from the beach, her sunglasses and hat on, but only a light jacket this time. The sun was feeling warmer today, teasing of spring around the corner. March would be here any day now, and he had promised Gray he'd do the Running of the Leprechauns event, though he hadn't been training like his friend. The one thing he wouldn't be able to back out of was the Turtleback Saint Patrick's Day Parade, since he was in it. Kids liked parades. He couldn't help but wonder—hope— that Faye and Nim would still be around to watch it.

He caught up to her, waving so she'd notice him and not be alarmed or taken by surprise.

"Hi," she said. The entire pack sat down the second she stopped walking. They looked up at her and waited patiently for her to give the green light. That woman was a dog whisperer.

"Hey. I can walk along with you so I don't hold up the pack," he said.

She resumed the walk and he fell in step, along with the dogs.

"You wouldn't want to do that. Hold up the pack."

"Wouldn't dare."

He tucked his hands in his pockets and judged her mood. Serious, despite the way she was trying to press her lips into a flat smile.

Give her a moment of peace.

"So, I was thinking," he said. "Chanda loves kids. Kids love puppies. Puppies bring people together and make them happy. And happy people...are a good thing." He gave himself a mental shake. What was he going to say? That happy people fell in love? Or that— as the popular saying went—happy people didn't kill their husbands?

Faye tilted her sunglasses down on her nose and gave him a look.

"You're talking about Shamu, aren't you? Jordan and Eve?" she asked, saving his blunder.

"I am. And Nim."

"If I didn't know better, I'd have thought you were trying to enlist my services and Nim's in matchmaking."

"Sort of. You got me there. But they wouldn't be the only ones spending time together. I checked the weather and tomorrow is going to be even nicer than today."

"Okay. You're losing me."

"I'd like to show you the Outer Banks. Chanda said she'd be willing to watch over Nim. Eve said she'd be willing to take Nim over to her first thing tomorrow morning so that you and I can leave early. She said she'd stay to help with her too. And Jordan said he'd be willing to take his puppy over there to help entertain Nim."

"Everyone is jumping in to help with Nim."

"Look at her." He gave Nim's chubby cheek a playful swipe. "Can you blame them?"

"And my instincts tell me that Eve doesn't know Jordan will be there with Shamu and vice versa. You're setting this whole thing up."

"Guilty, but in my defense, I only asked Chanda if she could babysit. I trust her completely. And I did ask Eve too, because she knows…about your ex… So, I thought you'd feel better leaving Nim behind if she was present. Chanda was the one to come up with the rest. She does that sort of thing. Matchmaking. Her brother is her new project. I must say, she's on the money with those two."

"I see."

Faye looked nervous. Tense. Not at all the reaction he'd hoped for.

"So?"

"So what?"

"So, are you game? You'll let me show you the beauty of this place?"

"I've seen the beauty. The beach. The wildlife. The sunrise. I read that the Outer Banks has a lot of famous lighthouses. Is that what we're doing? Climbing lighthouses so I can get a full view? We can take Nim along for that."

"Nope. I thought about doing that, but I think you need to give yourself more time after that bug to have the energy to make it to the top. The Turtleback Lighthouse alone has two hundred and eight steps and it's not even the biggest one we've got. You still have a cough. Even if I carried Nim, I don't think you'd be up to the climb yet. But stick around long enough and I'll take you to every one of them, including trips to Manteo to see the Lost Colony play, the Elizabethan Gardens, the Wright Brothers National Memorial,

Jockey's Ridge State Park with the amazing sand dunes at Nags Head. Water sports if you like when it warms up."

He wished he could take her parasailing over the ocean but it was still too cold for that and he had no idea if she was comfortable with dangling from a giant kite. There was nothing as quiet as floating up with the birds, too high up to hear anything but your thoughts.

"For now, I have something else in mind. Unfortunately, Nim would need to stay behind."

She stopped and looked left and right to see if anyone was nearby. No one was watching them but the dogs. Especially Laddie, who cocked his head to one side. She pressed her lips to the top of Nim's head, not as a kiss, but as though she needed the contact and couldn't part with her. Maybe his plans weren't such a good idea after all. He should have known she wouldn't be comfortable with leaving Nim behind, but he figured she trusted Eve enough and—

"Sheriff Ryker. Are you asking me out on a date?"

His neck warmed and he scratched his shoulder.

"I guess I am."

"You're not sure?"

"No. I mean, yes, I'm sure. Faye Donovan, I'm asking you out on a date." He held his breath. She stopped walking again but kept her eyes on her pack. She couldn't even bring herself to look at him. Maybe he'd been reading all the signs wrong. Maybe the chemistry had been one-way. "I just thought you'd enjoy a break. It wouldn't be anything fancy. No pressure or expectations," he quickly added. "Just a chance for you to enjoy yourself for a few hours."

She nibbled at her bottom lip, then finally glanced at him. The eye contact was brief. Barely long enough for him to catch the regret in her eyes. It was the same look Nat had in her eyes when she told him she couldn't stay. That she was leaving him. His chest suddenly felt hollow. Cold. He knew what Faye's answer was before she said it.

"I'm sorry, Carlos. I just can't." She glanced at him one more time, before taking off at a brisker pace with the dogs and leaving him standing…alone.

"WHAT DO YOU mean you said no?" Eve plopped down next to her and took over dicing up a banana for Nim.

"I couldn't say yes. You know that."

"I'm not sure that I do. I understand about not leaving Nim alone and not trusting anyone fully with her. I get it. My experience, remember? There were times when, in order to help a mother disappear, I—and others I worked with—had to separate the mother and her child or children in order to cover tracks and get them to their final destination. I was entrusted with their kids and never let them down. I wouldn't let you down either. I'm here for you. Why else do you think that I told Carlos I'd bring Nim to Chanda's and stay for the day? It was so that I could be there with Nim, in your place. I *knew* there was no way you'd leave her otherwise. But you do need a break. And I'm not going to lie. I love seeing the chemistry between you and Carlos. Two people I care about. Look, I'm certain nothing's going to happen in the few hours you're off with Carlos—and no, I'm not spoiling the surprise he had planned, so don't ask—but if anyone suspicious came into town or something showed up on the news, I'd take care of it. I'd keep Nim safe for you. You know it."

Nim squished banana pieces in her palm instead of eating them.

"Banna," she said, giggling. She was a happier child now than she was when they'd first arrived in Turtleback. She laughed more. She was still content to sit quietly and play on her own, but she was also trying to say more words and seemed less shy around others. She was thriving here, but that fact was bittersweet. Faye didn't want her forgetting her mother. Her real mother.

"I know you'd watch over her. I do trust you."

"Okay, then? You'll go?"

"No. I can't lead him on like that. It wouldn't be fair to anyone. Not him, or Nim. You should see them together, Eve. It breaks my heart because nothing can come of it and I can't stay in this town forever. You know that."

Eve pushed the sippy cup closer to Nim, then touched Faye's arm.

"It's one outing. Not a marriage proposal."

Well, that made her feel a bit silly. Eve was right. Maybe she was overthinking things.

"I don't know. It would feel irresponsible."

"Spoken like a true mother. Girl, you are such a good parent. It's totally natural to feel guilty about taking time to yourself, but the fact is that everyone needs to recharge. Moms especially. Why do you think my story time at the shop is so popular? Parents can drop off kids and take an hour to rest, do yoga, shop or even grab a quick lunch date together. A car can't run forever without having its gas tank refilled. Same philosophy. What good would you be to Nim if you got sick again—worse than last time—because you had drained yourself?"

She was a good mother? Eve's compliment stirred something in her. She was a good mother. Not really, but what her friend was saying without realizing it was that Faye hadn't let Nim or Clara down. She had been pulling through on her promise to her sister. Maybe she didn't know how to find and protect Clara, but she hadn't failed at caring for her niece. That was something. She took a deep breath and it seemed to fill her with a rush of confidence. Control. She had this. She'd made it this far. She'd figure things out a step at a time. Maybe time alone with Carlos would help her decide if she could trust him with the truth…or not.

FAYE HAD NO idea where they were headed when he picked her up at 5:00 a.m. It was still dark out, but she wasn't nervous. Not anymore. She knew Carlos wasn't tricking her. She wanted to spend time with him. She didn't want to leave Nim, but she knew Eve wouldn't let anything happen to her, and Chanda and Jordan were good, caring people. Even if Jordan heard about the truth from the station while they were gone, he'd never act on it without checking in with Carlos. And she'd be with Carlos. She'd be able to explain and convince him to listen. Besides, he assured her they'd be gone for only a couple of hours total. Three max, with driving time. And he had promised that they wouldn't be leaving the Outer Banks.

In a way, they had.

She looked outside the window of the Cessna. She'd thought she'd seen a beautiful sunrise but nothing compared to watching it unfold and feeling like she was a part of it. It was magical. Tangerine and melon hues slowly melted into gold with streaks of violet, filling the sky before them and above them. Reflecting off the ocean beneath them. They were enveloped by it.

She glanced over at Carlos as he piloted the four-seater back over the barrier reef. He looked so good in his old bomber jacket, sunglasses and headset. He didn't bother shaving this morning and she itched to run her palm along his face. She kept her hands on the edge of her seat. Every so often they hit a bit of turbulence, but she was in safe hands. He'd mentioned having been in the Air Force, but she had no idea he still flew. The plane wasn't his, but a buddy at the nearest airfield trusted him enough to let him have it for a few hours—a Cessna 172 or Skyhawk, his friend had explained with a good dose of pride. Some connections were good to have.

Carlos looked over at her and gave her a lopsided grin. The guy was in his element. Loving every second of this. So was she. From here, she could see the barrier reef's sound and marshes to the west and seaside to the east all at once. The lighthouses looked amazing from a bird's-eye view, and the beach houses dappling the shoreline reminded her of the dollhouses she and Clara used to play with.

"Over there."

She touched her headset reflexively when his voice came through, then followed the direction he was pointing in. The sky had already lightened considerably and she could see cars moving and people the size of ants walking about and starting a new day. He circled a lighthouse she knew wasn't the one at Turtleback. Its black-and-white bands were similar, but it was larger and the base had a red brick surround.

"That's the famous Cape Hatteras Lighthouse. We're flying over Buxton right now. That lighthouse has been there since 1870. The original one was damaged during the Civil War so this one was built to replace it."

He moved on and pointed out all the sites he told her he wanted to take her to on foot. Someday. Probably never, she realized, then banished the thought. She was going to live in the moment for the next hour. Up here, she had no control over anything that was happening below. She had to let go. She had to trust her friends to help with Nim. They were her friends. All of them. Not just Eve. She had to trust Carlos too.

She realized, at this moment, that she was flying like the pelican she'd watched outside Eve's place. Soaring.

"You've got to see this," he called out, turning back over the water.

A dark mass slithered beneath the water's surface and he took them down closer.

"A shark?" she asked, too loudly. She forgot that she had a Bluetooth and he'd hear her despite the loud hum of the engine.

"School of fish. And look over there."

She leaned toward the window. Shipwrecks. Entire remains of old ships still in their watery resting spots.

"Oh, wow."

"This coastline is referred to as The Graveyard of the Atlantic for a reason."

"I can see why. This is all so incredible."

"Glad you're enjoying it. If we're lucky, we might spot some wild mustangs on one of the beaches. Another thing we're known for."

She reached over and touched his arm.

"Thank you, Carlos. I needed this. And you knew I did. Thank you for that. This has been the best surprise…and date… I've ever had."

That wasn't a lie. High school didn't count. The one or two guys she had been out with to homecoming or prom hadn't been her type really. In retrospect, she had hung out with them because she knew they would pass muster with her parents. In college, she had dated only one guy seriously and he ended up dumping her when he got into a graduate program on the West Coast. The fact that she wasn't that upset when he left said something about their relationship. In all honesty, relationships were a two-way street and she had been holding back. Just like she was with Carlos. Only back then, it had been because she didn't want to follow the same path as her parents, ending up in a marriage that was all about shining on the outside while it was lackluster on the inside. Their marriage didn't involve abuse, but it wasn't all that warm and loving either. In a way, her sister had followed that path. A marriage that looked perfect on the outside. Granted, neither of Faye's parents were physically abusive.

She couldn't imagine Carlos ever being abusive. He was a good man. A good cop. But he believed in following rules and protocol, and that could backfire when it came to dealing with someone like Jim, who knew how to twist and turn rules to work for him.

"You're welcome. But it's not over yet. There's more when we land."

He thrilled her for a bit longer before taking them back down to the small airport where they had started. It took her a minute to feel steady on the ground when he helped her out of the plane. He guided her away as his friend took the plane into the hangar for a checkup and refueling.

"That was amazing," she said, hanging on his arm. "I'm not sure I can handle more. I'm still processing the feeling of being up there."

"I did say there'd be more. Didn't I?"

"You did. But honestly, Carlos, this was more than I could have dreamed of. You don't have to do anything else."

He led her around the corner of the hangar where no one could see them and stepped closer.

"I don't have to. But I really want to."

Her heart started racing. The anticipation. The hoping that what she thought was about to happen really would.

"You do?" She sounded breathless, or maybe the hum of the plane engine was still in her ears. She could hear his breathing too. She felt it. Closer.

"More than anything." He held her face, the rough pads of his thumbs caressing her cheeks. "Tell me I'm not imagining that you want this too. That there's something here neither of us can deny or ignore."

She couldn't deny anything. She wanted everything.

She grabbed his jacket, stood on her toes and kissed him before he could change his mind. He pulled her closer, holding on like he never wanted her to leave. Like he was afraid she would. The touch of his lips against hers made the earth beneath her go soft. It defied gravity and time. She had felt it…experienced it…in her dreams. It was a kiss from a past life, centuries old, or another universe. As if their paths had crossed time and time again, searching but always missing, destined but denied. She wrapped her hands around his neck and let him kiss her until they both had to catch their breath. He wiped the tears that had trailed down her cheeks…the release… emotions she couldn't hold in…then he kissed her eyelids one by one with a tenderness she'd never experienced. He kissed her forehead and the tip of her nose. Then, once more, a whisper of his lips against hers.

He rested his forehead against hers.

"Wow."

"Yeah. Wow," she said, still hanging on. Still waiting for the ground to turn solid again.

"That was…powerful."

She nodded and swallowed hard. There was no going back. No forgetting what had just happened. And here she didn't want to give him false hope or lead him on.

"We haven't known each other that long. It seems like forever. I don't know how that can be," Faye said.

"It's not about time. When it's right, it's right."

Love at first sight? Kismet? Fate? What if fate was playing a cruel trick on her?

"If we stayed like this for as long as I'd like to, they'd end up sending a search party after us," he said.

A search party. If only he knew. Reality started to set in.

"I guess we should go," she said, licking her lips. His taste still lingered and she wished she could kiss him again.

He linked his fingers in hers and stepped back, pulling her away from the wall.

"Let's go get Nim," he said, as if that little girl were as much his as hers. As if they were together in this. A pack.

He was right. The connection between them was intense. But she didn't know if it was strong enough for forgiveness...or powerful enough to keep him from walking away once he discovered the truth.

CHAPTER ELEVEN

"WE'LL TAKE A half a dozen croissants, a dozen of those salted caramel cupcakes and your orange cream cake." Carlos turned to Faye at his side. "You haven't lived until you've tried her chocolate cupcakes with a caramel in the center and salted caramel melted on top. Messy eating but worth it."

"I've lived a lifetime today," she whispered. He could feel the back of his neck warm. If Darla wasn't behind the counter, boxing his order, while trying very hard—from the look on her face—to pretend she hadn't heard a thing, he would have kissed Faye again right then and there.

"A lot of sweet going on here," Darla said. They both raised their brows at her. There was no looking innocent. "I'm referring to your order. Not that I'm complaining. I'm more than happy to make a sale," she teased.

He narrowed his eyes at her. It was pretty clear she wasn't referring to the baking.

"A lot of sugar. Right," Faye said. "It's not all for us. Chanda, Jordan and Eve were looking after Nim this morning, so I'm taking them some as a thank-you."

"Well, I hope it's all enjoyed. I like seeing smiles. I tried getting one to crack on Mr. Krinks before you got here. That man was in a bad mood for some reason. As in cranky Krinks."

"Hmm. Maybe his blood sugar was low," Carlos offered. Krinks was typically pleasant.

"Or perhaps Bison ate something he shouldn't have," Faye said.

"Now that's a good possibility. There you go." Darla set the boxes down and rang up the sale.

"Is it even possible not to enjoy anything you make, Darla?" Carlos asked, pulling out his wallet. Faye started to reach in her purse but he wouldn't let her. "I've got this."

"Thanks. I'll treat next time, then. I insist."

She said *next time.* He liked the sound of that.

"We'll see you around." Carlos picked up two of the boxes and Faye held on to a third.

"Good to see you again. Say hi to Nora for me," Faye said.

"I will. And bring little Nim by when you get the chance."

They left The Saltwater Sweetery and headed to Chanda's place. Carlos hated that Eve wasn't opening Castaway Books until this afternoon. He'd offered to pay for any lost revenue but she refused, telling him keeping Nim safe was important to her too and that seeing him look so happy around Faye was the best thing ever.

"I hope Nim didn't give them too much trouble."

"Are you kidding? I bet they're having a ball. Chanda has a cat, Sandy, adopted last summer when Mandi found an abandoned litter. She and Gray took home two and Chanda got the third. Between a cat, puppy and toddler, I'm thinking they'll be ready for all this carb reload."

"I can imagine." Faye laughed, as she followed him up to Chanda's door. It swung open before they could knock and Chanda had her finger to her lips to keep them quiet.

"Come see this. Warning. It may be more cute than you can handle," she whispered.

They followed her inside.

Well, I'll be.

Carlos jerked his head toward the living room and nudged Faye with his elbow. Her lips parted, either from shock or, as Chanda put it, cute overload. Chanda mouthed a thank-you when she saw the bakery logo on the boxes and took the one Faye was carrying to the kitchen. Carlos hurried after her, set his load on the table and returned to find Faye trying to get in for a closer look without waking anyone up.

Carlos took out his cell phone and snapped a photo. Not for posting or sharing online. Just to have it to show them after they woke up.

Jordan was lying on the couch with Nim, draped belly down, on his chest. He had one hand protectively on her back and the other arm hanging off the couch, his hand resting on Shamu, who was curled up in Eve's lap. Eve was on the floor, leaning back against the couch, with her head propped against Jordan's side. Chanda's eight-month-old tortoiseshell kitten was snoozing on the back of the couch right next to them. He wasn't sure if the purring sound was the cat or Jordan snoring. All of them were completely zonked out.

He tugged Faye's sleeve and they both went back to the kitchen, where Chanda was pulling a casserole out of the oven.

"You must be a happy big sister," he said, keeping his voice down so it wouldn't carry to the living room.

"Now, don't you go saying anything when they wake up," Chanda said. "It'll ruin it. They'll get all embarrassed and put their shields up again."

"They look so blissful. Like a family on a Saturday morning," Faye said.

Chanda paused while putting her pot holders back in a drawer.

"I love that analogy. That's exactly what I thought. They look right. Like family, whether they are or not. I mean, obviously, that's your little one in there, but oh boy did my heart melt when I saw them. I had come in here to cook and Eve was telling them all a story she was coming up with on the spot. I'm not sure if she ever made it to the end."

"I say we eat without them." Carlos leaned in and inhaled the aroma rising off the casserole. "I'm starving."

"If we eat now, those two will be left to eat together once they wake up. And we can find reasons to be in the living room and leave them alone in the kitchen." Faye gave Chanda a wink.

"I like you more and more every time we meet. See, Carlos? I'm not the only one with matchmaking skills."

"Hey, give me some credit. I started this whole thing by taking Faye out on a flight."

"How was it?" Chanda asked, directing her question at Faye, as they sat down to eat.

"Spectacular. Thank you for watching Nim."

"Anytime. Assuming I'm off work. Dr. Zale insisted that I use some of the vacation time that had carried over this year. He said too much work and no play makes for a bossy office manager."

"He called you bossy?" Faye asked.

"He was kidding." Chanda brushed the air with her hand. "He and I have this wicked banter we do. I've worked for him since he moved to Turtleback. We're all like family at that clinic. Like a bunch of siblings."

"This is delicious. Thanks for cooking." Carlos shoveled in another spoonful. He was starving.

"It really is," Faye agreed.

"Thanks to both of you for dessert. That's what I'm saving room for." Chanda only ate a few bites, then took her plate to the sink, rinsed it and loaded it into the dishwasher. "That orange cream cake is my favorite."

"I know." Carlos chuckled and drank some water.

"Hard to believe you're still single," Chanda said.

Was that a nudge directed at Faye? Faye's cheeks flushed and she took a very, very long drink of water.

A whimper sounded from behind them. They all turned and Shamu was standing in the kitchen entry.

"Someone woke up before everyone else. Come here, sweetie." Faye scooted her chair back and went over to pick up the pup. "I'll take her out for a potty break before she piddles. Be right back." She went out the front door as quietly as they'd come in.

"I like her," Chanda said. She was to the point and frank by nature. Didn't beat around the bush.

"I like her too," Carlos said without hesitation.

Chanda nodded, eyeing him as she sliced into the cake.

"So would your mother. Of that, I'm sure."

It was his turn to nod. His mom really would like Faye. He could picture them hanging out during the holidays, picnicking on the beach or giving a teenaged Nim advice. A wave of sadness coursed through his chest. He regretted that his mom and Faye would never know one another. Faye would have been there for him...for her. He could tell by the way she cared for her daughter. She would have done whatever she could to help. To be supportive. She wouldn't have skipped town because life was complicated or because the idea of settling down unsettled her. No... Faye wasn't Natalie. But life wasn't hypothetical. It was real and the fact was that Faye's life was unsettled and she was just as likely—if not more so—to move on from Turtleback.

"I think you could handle an instant family. You're a natural family man," Chanda added.

He got up, walked over to the entry and looked out the window. A family. One like his parents had built. A family that was full of heart until life stole it from him. The cop who killed his father. The cancer that killed his mother. He somehow sensed that fate was about to take Faye away from him too.

"Maybe. Her life's been a little complicated. I'm not so sure she's ready for that big of a step."

They switched topics as soon as the door opened. Shamu ran in, went straight for Eve and jumped into her lap, waking her up. Faye came in and closed the door. Eve looked at them bleary eyed, then peered around her. She scrambled to her feet, straightening her hair, when she realized how comfortably close she and Jordan had been napping.

"Hey," she said, hoarse from sleep. "When did you get back?"

"We already ate and there's dessert waiting in the kitchen," Faye said, glancing quickly at Carlos and stifling a smile.

Sandy the cat meowed and leaped off the couch and onto the floor. Shamu stopped and watched, curious and confused, as the cat stretched and arched. Jordan opened one eye and took in the situation.

"I fell asleep?" He looked at Nim on his chest and dropped his head back on the arm of the couch. "I was wide awake when we started putting her to sleep. I swear it."

"Eve's story must have been really boring," Carlos said, going over and sitting in the armchair across from them.

Eve threw a pillow at him. Nim stirred from all the movement and talk, then pushed up against Jordan's chest and looked at everyone. She immediately scrambled down and headed for Faye.

"It happens to me, so don't feel bad," Faye said, picking Nim up, planting a kiss on her cheek and hugging her tight. "Hey, sweetie pie." She nuzzled her again, then smiled at Jordan. "If I rock her while walking around, I'm okay. But if I lie down with her, all bets are off. It's like she secretes a sedative or something." Nim settled her cheek against Faye's shoulder, still in that half awake, half asleep zone.

Jordan sat up. He rubbed his eyes.

Chanda appeared from the kitchen.

"First, bringing that cake here was dangerous to my waistline. I've had two pieces already. I'm brewing a pot of coffee for anyone who needs it. Second, Eve and Jordan, the food's on the table and I don't want to put it away until you've eaten, so you two get over here." She disappeared again.

Eve's and Jordan's eyes met briefly. They broke eye contact faster than a camera flash.

"I'm going to go to the kitchen," Eve said.

"Me too. Sister's orders." Jordan followed her.

Carlos looked after him and did a double take. The edge of the tiny red Valentine's envelope Eve had given Jordan at the bonfire was sticking out of his back pocket.

Maybe fate wasn't always the bad guy after all.

JIM TAPPED THE end of his pen against his desk. He knew where Faye was.

Man, he loved money. There was nothing he couldn't get done because he had the means of doing it. Deep pockets made for deep connections, including the best private investigators. Ones who could hack website tracking programs and find out where "visitors" to a site were logging in from. When it came to a business like Faye's, customers were local, for the most part. Any online visitors from other places stood out. It narrowed things down beautifully. It wasn't hard for his PIs to connect more dots after that. Technology made it so easy and small towns meant shorter resident lists to go through. Lucky for him, it turned out that Faye happened to have gone to college with one such resident. Bingo.

He had warned Clara not to mess with him. To respect the privacy of their family unit. Talking about what went on between the walls of a person's home with others wasn't acceptable. It breached privacy. Caused people to judge what they didn't fully understand. It gave them power against you. Why couldn't she have simply listened to him? She was ungrateful. The way she took everything he provided her with for granted really ticked him off. Seriously.

He had accomplished more than his parents ever thought he could. The corner office. The sleek mahogany desk and oriental rug he'd won the high bid on at an estate auction. He didn't dare keep items like that at home. They weren't meant to have food and drink spilled on them. They were meant to impress people in high places that he needed favors from when they stepped into his office. His decor, down to the collectible pen he'd just used to sign on a high-profile client, set the stage. He was respected here. His in-laws respected and appreciated him, even if his parents—and his wife—didn't.

He loved being at work, whether in this office or addressing a jury in a courtroom. He loved the admiration and deference he received. Such an irritating contrast to how he was treated when he got home every evening. Being asked to take garbage out or help start dinner, his wife in an old T-shirt and no makeup on, the baby crying. What had she been doing all day? Spending his hard-earned money? Every week there was some sort of new knickknack lying around that she insisted would make life easier for her or Mia. How much did a kid Mia's age need beyond diapers and food?

He placed the papers on his desk, then lined up his pens with all the clips facing the same direction. It would be a couple of days before he returned, depending on the weather. It had been snowing heavily up at the cabin when he left Clara this morning. A blessing from the heavens. He had been locking her up in a comfortable room with plenty of food, drinks—even an espresso machine—whenever he had to go to the office or show up for a court case. He had to make sure she didn't wander off, even though the place was quite remote. But he'd be gone much longer to find Faye and get his daughter back. And for that, he was grateful for the snowstorm. It had been coming down hard enough that he knew he needed to make it back to town before the roads weren't passable. The unpaved one leading from the main road to the cabin couldn't be plowed.

Under normal circumstances, it would have annoyed him, but right now it was perfect. Just a little extra assurance that no other lost soul would find their way to the cabin. No deliveries. No mail. And with temperatures dropping and the early spring snowstorm blowing in, there was no way she'd make it anywhere on foot if she did get out. Not with her ankle as swollen as it was.

He dug his nails into his leather satchel. He hated when she made him do things like that. He didn't keep her in that room when he was around. He set her free, within the confines of the cabin. And he had warned her not to go outside. It wasn't his fault that she didn't listen—again—and she had tripped on a rock when he yanked her back toward the cabin. He wasn't to blame. He'd even carried her the rest of the way to the door. He'd given her an ice pack and wrapped it up for her. Kissed the injury to show her how tender and caring he could be. All she had to do was follow his rules. That's all. People who followed rules didn't get punished. That's how life worked. No standing in corners. No principal's offices. No getting grounded. And, as the people he prosecuted learned the hard way, no jail time.

He'd have everything under control again soon. He'd have his daughter home. He'd kindly explain to Faye how the numbers added up if she didn't fall in line. He could have her business go under in no time. The right inspector would have it shut down. A write-up on any violation that came to mind would ruin her forever. Maybe he'd add animal abuse to her list of crimes.

He already had an affidavit signed by Clara stating that her twin had always had it in for her. What he had to do to get her to sign it pained him. It really did. But she had eventually caved in. The injuries? Faye's doing. People would believe it. The woman was strong for her size. A result of handling all those big dogs. His excuse for not filing an Amber

Alert? Family. He was a forgiving, compassionate family man who chose to trust that his wife's twin would do the right thing. He had been giving her a chance, for the sake of her good parents. He was benevolent.

He could have her put away for such a long time for kidnapping and impersonation. Faye out of the way. That's when it would finally be safe to bring Clara back home. That's when she'd finally understand that he was the person she was supposed to be loyal to. Not her sister. *His* wife and child, by his side for his future campaign.

He locked his office door and headed down to his car. North Carolina's coast. He pulled a photo of his little girl out of his wallet and placed it on the console. He'd show it around if need be. He'd find her. He started the ignition and revved the engine because he needed to punch something hard.

"Mia, honey. You'll be home with Daddy really soon."

CHAPTER TWELVE

FAYE WALKED UP from the beach, Nim in her carrier, and Pepper on leash, toward Castaway Books. She had parted ways with Carlos after lunch at Chanda's. He had headed for the precinct and she had told him she'd take Pepper for a walk with Nim. That way, she could have Pepper back at his place before walking the other dogs later this afternoon. She also really wanted to see Eve. She needed someone to talk to about whatever was happening with Carlos. She still hadn't been upfront about Nim, so that might skew Eve's advice, but still. Faye didn't have anyone else. She tapped on the door and cracked it open, not wanting to take Pepper inside. Laddie was the only one who ever went in the store, as far as she knew. In fact, he was in there now, ears perked at the sight—or scent—of Pepper.

"Hey, Faye. Did you enjoy the beach?" Eve asked.

"Yeah. It was nice."

Laddie came to the door and touched noses with Pepper.

"We just finished story time. Gray can't get here for another thirty minutes to pick him up. He and Mandi had an appointment up at the hospital in Nag's Head and are on the way back. I told him you were busy today. Laddie likes them older, huh?" she teased.

"That or Pepper is a cougar."

Eve laughed.

"You can bring her in. The kids are all gone and the only people shopping are Chanda and Nora. They're upstairs in the science section looking for coffee table books with dogs and cats that they can put in the waiting room at the vet clinic. Slow day over there." Faye entered. The shell-and-bell chime jingled as the door closed and Eve pulled her behind the counter. "I'm so glad you stopped by. I need to ask you something about Jordan. I need advice," Eve whispered, pointing upstairs to remind Faye that his sister might overhear.

"Later, then?"

"It'll be after closing, but yes, we'll make it a girls' night. You, me and Nim. My sofa, chips and ice cream."

"I'm walking the pack later, but I can make some pasta for dinner and have it ready by the time you finish here," Faye said.

"Sounds great to me," Eve said. "Thank you."

The door chime tinkled again and she jumped, until she realized it was Jordan. She moved aside and let him in.

"Hi, Faye. Eve. Nim." He tapped his finger on Nim's nose, earned a smile, then stooped down and gave both Pepper and Laddie ear scratches.

"Hey."

"I was just leaving," Faye said, looking between the two of them.

"Please stay," Jordan said, shoving his hands in his pockets and shifting his weight side to side. "If I'm going to throw this out there, I might as well have witnesses. For my protection, because I'm not exactly sure how you'll react, Eve, but I want everyone to know how I feel. I'm all in or not. It has taken me all afternoon to get myself here, and Faye, don't let me go until I say what I came to say."

"Jordan—" Eve tried to point upstairs and warn him of the two women there, but he was fired up and kept going.

"It's like you wrote in the card," Jordan said. *"The smallest gesture can turn a single moment in time into forever.* It took fixing your door for you to let me in a little. And I'm hoping you let me stay. I like you, Eve. More than like you. Always have. I'd never hurt you. Never. And I promise to keep Shamu out of your shop if you'd let me into your life."

Eve looked like she was about to cry. She pressed her hands to her cheeks, then to her chest.

"Promise me you won't," she said.

"Won't? But I thought—"

"Promise you won't hurt me and you won't keep her out of here. I'm thinking she'd make a pretty great store mascot, at least until she's older and starts drooling. Wet books don't sell. Hopefully, we can count on Faye to help train her, for short visits."

"We," Jordan said. "Can I read into that?"

Eve had her arms around him in less than a second.

"Stay. Be a part of my life. I more than like you too. Have for a long time. I can't imagine a day without you. And I have a pretty great imagination," she added.

"I love that about you," Jordan said, wrapping his arms around her.

"You do, huh?"

"I do." He kissed her. "Is this what it feels like? A moment that's turning into forever?"

"I want every moment we spend together to be that special and magical."

"I promise." He kissed her again.

Laddie made a noise that sounded like he was trying to state his approval. Faye's eyes filled with tears. She was so happy for them. Genuinely happy. She only wished her sister could experience that kind of love. She prayed that when Nim grew up, she'd find someone who would love her unconditionally. Someone kind, gentle and with a pure heart.

"Hallelujah. Finally," Chanda said, appearing from the stairwell. "I need some orange cake to celebrate. Come on, Nora. Let's go raid Darla's stash."

"You heard all that? You were in here? Can't a guy get some privacy in this town?" Jordan asked.

Chanda just gave him a big sisterly hug and kiss, then did the same to Eve.

"I'll save you two some cake. Maybe."

"Caca," Nim chimed in, reaching her hand

toward Chanda. Chanda ruffled Nim's hair and chuckled.

"We really have to work on you saying 'cake' and 'cookies.' Until then, it won't be as sweet as you are, but I'll save you some cake too."

FAYE SAT CROSS-LEGGED in the sand, digging a moat around the castle she was building with Carlos and Nim. A moat like the one she wished she could build around Clara, Nim and herself. Maybe with a dragon to help protect them from Jim.

Pepper sat near them watching, the end of her leash next to Carlos, just in case she decided bird chasing was in her future. Or in case Laddie went out for a jog with Gray. Laddie and Pepper had taken quite a liking to each other during the bonfire.

Yesterday had been wonderful. Eve had been in a particularly good mood last night. She ended up going out to dinner with Jordan, and Carlos had been on duty, so Faye and Nim had an evening alone. She had searched the internet again for any sign that Jim had reported her, but found none. It was strange. She knew why he hadn't turned her in, but just the same, instead of feeling relieved about it, it was starting to give her the creeps. Like he was up to something else.

"I'm not sure what gave me more of a rush, the plane ride yesterday, or lunch afterwards. Seeing Jordan, Eve, Nim and the critters all cozy on Chanda's couch, or seeing Jordan and Eve finally kiss," she said.

"Maybe I need to remind you what the best part of yesterday was." Carlos leaned over and gave her a kiss.

"Mmm. You're right. The kiss was more of a rush than any of those other things. But you have to admit, Jordan and Eve dating is pretty sweet."

Nim smacked her sandy hand to her mouth and swung it out. Faye blew her a kiss in return, then picked up the bottle of bubbles Eve had given her and blew a cluster of them in Nim's direction.

"Maybe puppies really do attract women," Carlos said.

"Shamu is an irresistible puppy, but I think it was the note Eve had written in that card, plus setting them up with the lunch at Chanda's, that got him to open up."

"Do you know what she wrote?"

"'The smallest gesture can turn a single moment in time into forever.' Eve was convinced, back when she gave him the card, that he wouldn't even read it."

"He wouldn't tell me what it said, so I assumed that he hadn't."

"I didn't know until yesterday. She wouldn't tell me either. They certainly had us wondering."

"Don't you love a mystery." He said it flatly, like a rhetorical question.

Faye hesitated as she made circles in the sand. Was he implying something? Was he referring to her past?

The sun had passed its zenith and was hovering over the sound side of the island. The sun still set rather early in February. They weren't the only ones still on the beach, though. A few tourists had trickled into town today and were taking walks closer to the surf. More town visitors would start spending weekends on the beach, Carlos explained, in order to train for the local run in March. Running on sand was different from running on pavement or dirt. Crowds were good for business, but not for her nerves. What if one of them was someone Jim had sent to hunt her down?

"No," Faye muttered under her breath.

She was done with mysteries. She wanted to know where her sister was and she didn't want to keep living a lie. But enlisting Carlos's help would have to be an all-or-none scenario. She had run it through her head a million times. If she was going to have him help her find Clara, he'd need to know everything. And with Jim's connections in the police force, he'd quickly learn that Faye was going after him. And he'd retaliate. Take it out on Clara, no doubt.

But Carlos had told her he had connections too. Was it possible for him to help without the wrong people getting wind of it? Or was he tied to protocol? Could she risk it?

"What was that?"

"Nothing," she said. "I'm just glad Eve got through to him. In a good way. She built a bridge with words."

A bridge like the one that had carried her over rough, dark waters to reach Turtleback. A bridge to family. The kind she never thought she wanted or would be cut out for.

"I'm sure Shamu softened her heart."

"Eve's heart is soft. It's her mind that's hard," Faye said. "But you're right. Dogs are the best. Loyal, forgiving and giving."

"You need your own."

"I don't know. I can't, really. Not if I end up having to move again and again to avoid… my past." It was getting harder to lie to him. She couldn't even get the word *ex* to leave her tongue anymore. "The good-owner award is all yours. It's so wonderful that you adopt elderly dogs. You have no idea. You have a giving heart."

"You're a giver, Faye. Look at how you've dedicated yourself to your little girl. And I have no doubt—because I saw the reviews that time I checked out your website—how much your clients, both dog and owners, loved and counted on you."

She thought of the "review" Jim had left and felt sick.

"Your compliments aren't as deserved as you think."

"Have you ever given to a pet charity?"

"Well, yes, but—"

"Did you treat all your canine clients like assembly line work?"

"What? No! I knew them each by name,

sent them cards addressed to them—not their people—and talked to them as I worked. I loved every one of them. But it was my job. I got paid to work with them. It's different with you or Jordan or the others. You're not paid to have pets."

Loved. Past tense.

It hit her that she'd never be able to go back. Even if by some miracle she did, her reputation would be ruined. She'd have to sell just to cover legal expenses. And it wasn't possible to run a business like that from a jail cell. She'd probably already lost her clientele to competitors anyway.

But if by any chance she did make it back home, she'd rebuild. She had started her business from scratch before and she could do it again. Because she loved what she did. Because, she realized, she was capable. She didn't have to be afraid of failing. Her job in life wasn't to prove herself. It was to follow her passion and use it to help others.

Carlos took her hand and warmth seeped through her skin. The calloused pad of his thumb sweeping across her knuckles made her heart beat faster. She kept her eyes on the horizon. The sound of waves and bird cries a

reminder that everything could wash away…
fly away…at any time.

"I assure you, Faye. You're a giver. We all
work. We all have to earn a living. Veterinarians get paid, don't they? So do doctors. But
getting paid to do something we love and having every day come from the heart? That's a
gift. And you sacrificed it all at the drop of
a pin to do what was right for Nim. I think
that's one of the amazing things about you."

He thought she was amazing? She closed
her eyes briefly. She had given everything up
and would do so all over again, but he still
didn't know Nim wasn't hers. He still didn't
know she wasn't the innocent, abused mother
he thought she was.

"We should slow down, Carlos."

He pulled his hand back and rested his
arms on his knees.

"I'm moving too fast. I'm sorry. It's just
that, it feels like we've known each other for
longer than we have. And I want to protect
you, Faye. Help you."

"Please tell me this isn't about pity."

"Of course it isn't. You think that kiss we
shared was pity?" He took a deep breath and
stood.

—

"No. I'm sorry. I know it wasn't."

She wanted to tell him so badly. Lean on him. Let him love and protect her. Count on him.

Like you tried to count on your parents when you decided to open a business? You took a leap of faith, thinking they'd be proud and that they'd help you fund the start-up. A loan that you assured them you'd pay back, even if they could afford for you not to. And what did they do? They rejected you when you told them what the business was. They didn't approve of it...didn't think it was prestigious enough a profession... So they tried to control you by not giving you a dime. Your own parents turned their backs on you. What if Carlos does the same when he finds out the truth?

"Faye, we have something here. Maybe it started with me being concerned— No, actually. It didn't. If I'm being honest, something happened the first time I laid eyes on you. I couldn't get you out of my mind. I told myself it was out of a sense of duty, but it wasn't only that. I know it. You know it."

"Alright. I do. But I won't be here forever."

"You can be. If you'd let me help you. Tell

me all I need to know to go after him. The whole truth this time."

"I explained that I can't. I told you what I can."

"Faye. I'm not new at this. My gut tells me you're not telling me everything. The part about him being an abusive jerk, I believe. But there's something you're not saying."

She closed her eyes and tried to focus on the sound of the waves crashing ashore. Of the gulls celebrating their freedom. The beach and ocean spun like a whirlpool. Not around her, but in her head. She curled her fingers into the sand and it ran through them. The sands of time...of life. She had no hold on it. Couldn't hold on.

Her parents hadn't helped her and she still succeeded. She built a business on her own from scratch. Maybe she could take Jim down on her terms too. She could give Carlos the information he'd need to go after him and find her sister, but Faye would disappear again before he made the connection. Before he gathered enough information to realize she wasn't Nim's mother. Before he got cornered by Jim or his minions into arresting her. Maybe Eve would be willing to help her get away. But Eve used to help women and *their* children. Not women who *kidnapped* children.

She rubbed at the tension in her neck and looked around to make sure no one was within earshot. *You've got this.*

"I have a sister. A twin. Clara."

Everything, even the water and wildlife, seemed to go silent. He wiped his hand across his mouth, then crouched next to her.

"Identical or fraternal?"

He sounded like the sheriff again. Doing his job. Interrogating. Not her Carlos.

"Identical."

"What does she have to do with this?"

"He has her. Somewhere. I don't know where."

"As in he mistook her for you? So you're afraid he'll treat her the way he treated you?"

"I don't know," she said, not correcting his assumption. She got up on her knee and rubbed the sand off her palms.

"Why didn't you report him?"

"I told you, he's blackmailing me. He has power and connections. People who would believe any lies he told about me, as a mother. He refuses to accept that I have M— Nim."

That was close. And not exactly untrue. She stopped Nim from tasting a fistful of sand, then looked up. "If I don't give him his child, he'll hurt my sister. He's making me choose between my twin sister, who means the world to me, and my child, who is my life."

"I have my own connections. People I trust. Some who go much higher than the police force."

"Any move and he'll figure out where I am."

"Faye. How do you know he hasn't figured that out already? You can't live your entire life looking over your shoulder. And the longer your sister is missing, the worse her chances are."

He was referring to missing persons stats. The worse her chances of being found alive. That's what he meant.

"He left a cryptic message online. I'm sure she's alive. At least she was when he posted it."

"You're safe here. I'll start an investigation into where your sister might be. I'll need to know details. Everything about him down to his work address, property or properties, friends."

"Not friends. Don't talk to anyone. They'll only protect him."

"Let me protect you. Give me what I need to know to do this as swiftly as possible."

"But what if he gets to someone in town?"

"The residents of Turtleback are like family. We have each other's backs. No pun intended. Trust me, Faye. He can't get to them."

"He always does. I'm telling you. Whether through bribery or blackmail—all done in a subtle, slick manner—he always gets his way."

"Not this time."

"Carlos, he has my sister. He's appealing the custody ruling and is intent on winning. And who knows how he'll treat Nim after that. Even if he has enough heart to provide for her now, when she's old enough to challenge him, who's to say he won't take his temper out on her? I can't risk it."

"But you want to find your sister too, don't you?"

"Yes, of course. I'd give my life for her. I would have already done so if Nim wasn't in the picture, but she is. I've had to put her first."

"I know that. I'm not blaming you for anything. What I'm saying is that if you'll trust me and trust that the men and women I count on are on the straight and narrow, then we can beat him at his own game. You can have Clara, Nim and your life back."

Could she? Maybe this could all end. Carlos would discover the truth, and the two of them would be over, but he'd also find her sister and enough evidence—maybe—to put her brother-in-law away and toss out any charges against her on the grounds that she was protecting her niece. Either Clara would testify that she'd asked Faye to help, or, if it was too late… Maybe they could find a recording of her words. She swallowed hard against the lump in her throat. *Please be okay, Clara.* She picked up Nim and held her tight.

"His name is Jim. Jim Beauchampe."

Carlos swore under his breath.

"You're kidding me. The one I'm thinking of? *The* Jim Beauchampe? The one running for attorney general in the next election?"

"Yes. Him."

CHAPTER THIRTEEN

THE ROAD TO Eve's cottage and Carlos's had no streetlamps. Twilight cast its last ribbons of light across the road as Faye made her way back and forth to the car. It didn't take long to pack their things. There wasn't much to pack, but it took a couple of trips to get the playpen and stroller loaded. At this point, she didn't care that her registration had expired. She had set a plan in motion and there was no turning back. Carlos would be following through with the information she gave him right now. He had enough to go on to find Clara, but Faye needed to get Nim out of town. She couldn't risk her niece being taken into custody while investigations were made. She had to hide her until Clara was found and Jim was charged. And if Carlos failed and that didn't happen, well, then she'd keep moving and changing names and vehicles. She'd do whatever she had to do.

She closed the trunk on the car and the side door, then panicked. Where did she put her keys? She rummaged in her jacket pockets and found them. Thank goodness she hadn't locked them in the car. She'd have been stuck at Eve's. A sitting duck. Nim was over at Castaway Books, where Eve was hosting a bedtime-story session. It would have wasted too much time for Faye to drag the toddler all the way back to the cottage with her. She hadn't told Eve everything, but she did say there was a chance her ex knew where she was and not to let Nim out of her sight. She needed to hurry and pick up Nim. She was really regretting the whole one-road-in-and-out-of-town setup with the Outer Banks. It was like playing hide-and-seek as kids. Closets and enclosed areas felt safe, but if you were found, you were cornered.

Something stirred in the reeds off the road and she slapped her hand to her throat when a feral cat meowed and ran in front of her, disappearing into the night.

Just a cat.

Then why did she feel like she was being watched?

You're just worried because you told Carlos

more than you have before and he's acting on it. Trust him.

She jogged up the steps, looking behind her as she unlocked the door and not exhaling until she'd bolted it from the inside. Maybe it was a good thing Nim wasn't with her right now.

The duffel bag was all that was left. She started for the bedroom to grab it.

There was a scraping at the lock behind her. The sound of a key being inserted. Her pulse skyrocketed. Who had a key other than Eve? The image of the key copier at the hardware store flashed in her mind. Nim had dropped her key. Mr. Krinks had found it. Darla had mentioned that he'd been in a bad mood. She remembered her conversation with Carlos.

"The residents of Turtleback are like family. We have each other's backs. No pun intended. Trust me, Faye. He can't get to them."

"He always does. I'm telling you. Whether through bribery or blackmail—all done in a subtle, slick manner—he always gets his way."

It all happened in a flash of a second. She reached for Eve's salt lamp and prepared to throw it.

Eve walked in the door and froze.

"You're going to kill me with a salt lamp?" Faye lowered her arm.

"You scared me. You're supposed to be at the shop. Where's Nim?" Her pulse wouldn't stop racing.

"Jordan has her there. I'm going right back. We needed more diapers and wipes. Trust me. It's an emergency. It couldn't wait and it was safer not to move her. The mess would have been everywhere."

"You promised you wouldn't leave her!" Faye rushed out the door with her bag. All the diapers and wipes were in it, but she didn't care what condition Nim's diaper was in. They needed to leave town.

"Faye, I wouldn't have left her with anyone else. Jordan won't let anything happen to her. He understands," Eve yelled after her. Faye didn't respond. She got in her car, backed out and headed into town. Eve's headlights were close behind hers. Her mouth felt dry and her head buzzed. She stepped on the gas. Castaway Books wasn't far.

She just hoped Nim would still be there.

CARLOS LOWERED HIS head into his hands. The truth was right in front of him. Glaring at him from his computer. The station bustled with officers switching out their shifts. Some going and some arriving. Marg came by with a stack of mail.

"You okay, Sheriff?"

He jerked his head up.

"Just a headache."

"I keep a bottle of aspirin in my desk. I'll be right back," she said.

Aspirin wasn't going to help this one.

Had he told Faye that nothing was too complicated for him to handle? Boy was he wrong. Love was too complicated and risky. Maybe she was right. He clearly hadn't known her long enough for her to trust him with the truth.

She wasn't Nim's mother. He sat back and scrubbed his face. She'd never been married, let alone divorced. The hair color. The lies.

"Here you go." Margie handed over the bottle of pills and returned to her desk.

"Thanks," he said, belatedly.

He had told her he'd protect her no matter what. That she could trust him. Had he been lying too? Had he promised more than he could follow through with? She had him between a shark and a hurricane. Both dangerous. Now that he had this information, not taking Nim into custody would go against the law he was sworn to uphold. But he trusted her. She may have withheld the whole truth, but she must have had a reason. She wasn't a bad person. He'd have felt it. He'd have known.

He thought about her dog walking. Dogs had good instincts too. Especially that Laddie.

He needed to think. There had to be a way to protect them all...before it was too late.

FAYE PARKED HER car and hurried to the Castaway Books front door. It was locked but she could see Jordan, in jeans and a sweatshirt, sitting down with Nim in his lap, holding her under her armpits like he was afraid she'd move. She could hear Nim crying. Eve, who was only thirty seconds behind her, ran up and nudged her aside to unlock the door.

"I locked it because I was leaving. I told you I would be careful," Eve said.

"I'm sorry," Faye mumbled.

"What about diapers?" Eve asked.

"In the car. The duffel on the back seat. Don't bring it in. Just grab one from it. The wipes are there too," she said, handing her the keys. One of the suspense movies Faye had watched years ago, which had kept her awake all night, involved a killer hiding in the back seat of his victim's cars. The thought of Jim hiding in hers sent prickles down the back of her neck. "Please lock it back up," she added, as she ran inside.

Eve didn't question why she didn't get them herself. She doubled back to Faye's car as Faye ducked into the bookstore.

The place stunk to high heaven. Nim's crying got louder when she saw Faye. She stretched her little arms out for Faye to hold her.

"It wasn't me," Jordan was quick to point out.

Faye wasn't sure if he was referring to Nim's bawling or the smell. Either way, she had no sense of humor left in her. She reached out to grab Nim, who buried her tear-streaked face into the crook of Faye's neck. The poor kid wasn't feeling well.

"Maybe that tooth that's been bothering her finally erupted. One of the moms who brings her kids here mentioned that once when her baby was crying," Eve suggested, as she returned with a diaper, changing pad and a container of wipes.

"It wasn't the only thing that was erupting," Jordan quipped.

"Maybe," Faye said. "It's not her normal poop smell, though. Nim must have eaten something that upset her stomach. Sand. She may have eaten sand at the beach while she was playing. Who knows what bacteria were in it." *Please don't be sick. Let this be one bad poop.* If Nim ended up with diarrhea and needed antibiotics, that would require a doctor's visit. Of all the times for this to happen.

"Only a mother would clue into her kid's potty scents," Eve said.

"I would be careful if I were you. She's leaking," Jordan warned. Faye lifted Nim up, unfazed.

"Can I change her here?" The small bathroom in the place wasn't big enough to lay her down in. She'd learned that the last time she'd tried to change a wet diaper there and ended up having to do so with Nim standing. That wouldn't work with diarrhea.

"Yes, go ahead."

She changed Nim's diapers as smoothly as though she'd been doing it from the day she was born and put the garbage in a plastic bag that Eve handed her. She didn't want to leave the room but she had to wash her hands.

"Eve. Do you mind?" Faye asked.

"Of course not," Eve said, picking Nim up and rubbing her back soothingly.

"That smell is potent birth control," Eve said. Jordan's face fell. "I'm kidding. I mean, it is, but that doesn't mean I don't want a family. Eventually."

"Eventually," Jordan repeated, pointing a finger at her as if he was going to hold her to it.

Faye ran to the bathroom to wash up. Jordan's cell phone was buzzing when she returned. His brow furrowed. "I need to take this." He went into the back room.

He's a cop. He got a call. He looked serious. What if it was Carlos or some other officer telling him not to let you leave the place?

Her heart hadn't beat this fast since the two double shots of espresso she had the day she stole Nim.

"I'm sorry for freaking out on you, Eve. I am. And I appreciate all that you've done for us, but I need to go." She took Nim, who had calmed down slightly, from Eve. She could hear Jordan talking in a low voice on his phone, but couldn't make anything out.

"What do you mean? You're leaving? Town? Faye, it's not safe. You won't make it across the Bonner Bridge and be able to clear the Outer Banks without being stopped for your tags. Besides the fact that you're not calm and it's dark out. You said that you only suspect your ex knows where you are. You don't know for sure. I can hide you here in town. We'll watch for any newcomers asking questions. Then, tomorrow, I'll drive you out of here myself."

"No. It's too late for that." Eve didn't know that Carlos could be on the phone giving Jordan orders to arrest her. That Nim would suffer for it. She gave Eve a quick hug. "I'm sorry. Just remember that."

The door chime rattled and the air in the room went icy cold. *Jim.* She knew it was him before she even turned around. She had dreaded this moment. Dreamed about it and what she'd do. How scared she'd be. Only it wasn't fear surging through her right now. It was fury. Raw anger. She'd die before he got his hands on Nim.

"Faye."

He grimaced, likely from the air in the shop.

"Da da!" Nim's face scrunched up and she cried even louder. She twisted and flailed, throwing her weight back and nearly causing Faye to lose her hold. Faye was forced to set her down, just long enough to regain her grip, but the girl ran from her grasp and toddled straight for Jim.

"No!" She could hear his accusations now. How he found his daughter crying in an old place that smelled of sewage and how she ran to him, relieved that her daddy had rescued her.

"There you are, Mia!" He hugged her and gazed threateningly at Faye, as he kissed Mia on the forehead. "I missed you, my little number one. Daddy's never going to let you go again."

Mia, who had tried wiping her nose with her fist, patted his cheek with her hand. He shifted her to one side of his chest, lifted his shoulder and wiped his cheek dry on it.

"Nim. Come here," Faye said, stepping forward, ready to pull the kid from his arms if she had to.

"Nim, is it? Really? I don't recall seeing that name on her birth certificate," Jim said.

Jordan entered the room.

"What's going on here?" He didn't sound surprised. Faye looked between him and Eve.

"I'm here to pick up my child. From reading time, is it?" he said, glancing around the place.

He had the nerve to be snarky? Adrenaline burned through Faye's veins. She didn't care if she got hurt. She'd go after him if he tried to leave with the baby.

"Give her back to me, Jim."

"I don't think so. I'm her father. And I plan to press kidnapping charges."

"But she's her mother," Eve said. "You can't do that. Tell Jordan what he's done to you, Faye. You don't have a choice at this point. Tell Jordan how he hurt you. You should be the one pressing charges."

"I hurt you, did I?" Jim didn't take his eyes off her. "I've never laid a hand on this woman. She's been lying to you. She's not Mia's mother. She's my wife's twin. Ever read suspense thrillers about the psychotic jealous twin? Here she is in flesh and blood."

Eve flinched. She looked back at Jordan, then at Faye.

"Faye? What's going on? What does he mean you're not Nim's mother?" Eve asked.

It was happening. He was going to get away with murder. She could hear a dog barking in the distance. The bark neared, then there were more joining in. Like hounds on the hunt.

"I'm not her mother. She… Mia…is my niece. But everything else I told you is true. It just applies to my sister and how he treated her. He has her locked away somewhere. She's missing. I haven't been able to contact her. She's the one who begged me to get Mia away from him."

"You haven't had contact, yet she told you to take Mia? Sounds contradictory to me," Jim said with smug satisfaction.

Jordan stepped closer to Jim. He seemed relaxed. Like he was on Jim's side.

"Can I see your ID? Proof you're her father?"

"Don't you recognize me? The news, maybe?"

"I do. But you can't expect us to just hand her over without it," Jordan said. Eve frowned. Faye noticed that Jordan didn't mention that he was an off-duty officer. He was in street clothes. Jim wouldn't know he was a deputy.

Jim took out his wallet with one hand, pulled out his driver's license and handed it over, along with a family photo of him, Clara and Nim. All smiling. The perfect family. Faye didn't have to see it. She knew exactly which one it was.

"Look at this. Nice photo," Jordan held it up to Eve and Faye. "Looks just like you, Faye."

"But that's not her. That's what I'm saying," Jim said. "Forget this. I thought you'd have come to your senses by now and cooperate, Faye, but you had your chance. I'm calling the police."

Faye knew not to blow Jordan's cover. Jim shifted Nim to one side and reached for his pocket. He cursed under his breath when he didn't find his cell.

"My phone's in my car. You," he told Jordan, as he pushed Nim's slobbery hand off his face, "call the police."

"I don't recall 'You' being on *my* birth certificate, but sure. I'd be happy to call the police for you. If there's one thing I can't stand, it's being lied to. And here, this woman has had us thinking that she's kind, nurturing and even good with animals. Unbelievable." Jordan moved around the counter and picked up the store's landline.

"This woman is anything but. She hates her own sister so much and is so jealous of her that she stole her child and tried to pass her off as her own," Jim said.

"I love Clara and you know it," Faye shot back. "You abusive, manipulative, sick excuse for a man."

"I'm afraid it's not working. There's no signal. Eve, have you been having phone trouble?" Jordan hung up the line and came back around the counter, standing closer to Jim, as if he was siding with him.

"Yes. It hasn't been working all day, actually. I completely forgot with all this going on." Eve glanced at Faye and she knew her friends were lying.

There was a loud gurgly noise followed by a putrid smell.

"What the—" Jim held Mia away from him. His number one's number two had broken through diaper barriers and leaked all over the side of his cashmere sweater. Jordan reacted in a flash, grabbing Mia from his hands. Faye and Eve ran forward simultaneously, Faye reaching the two men first. She tried to take Mia from Jordan, but Jim, furious, grabbed Faye by the arm, digging his fingernails into her and twisting her shoulder.

"You're hurting me," Faye cried. "Let me go!"

The barking grew louder, but they couldn't see out into the darkness.

"Let her go, you son of—" Eve tried lunging again, but Jordan, holding Mia protectively, stopped her and handed her Mia—who was now crying again. He gave Eve an almost imperceptible shake of his head.

"I'll let you go." Jim sneered at Faye. "At the sheriff's department. In a holding cell. You'll never hurt my wife or daughter again." He tightened his hold on Faye.

"Let go of her right now or you'll regret it," Jordan warned.

"Shut up. You're nobody to give me orders. You," he said to Eve, "hurt Mia and I'll have you arrested too. I'm taking Faye with me to get my cell phone to call the cops and then I'm coming back in here for my child. She had better be here."

Jim twisted Faye's arm again and held her by the ear with his other hand.

"Stop it!" Faye yelled, attempting to knee Jim where it counted, but he spun her around

and tightened his grip. She stumbled and tried
to hold her ear to keep him from pulling so
hard. She could see Jordan closing the gap
between him and Jim. Jim shoved the shop
door open and pulled her outside.

He stopped in his tracks.

Faye's eyes widened, and not from the pain
he was inflicting.

The entire town stood before them. Surrounding them. Including every dog she'd
walked and a few others, with Laddie in front
of the pack and Pepper at his side. They were
snarling and barking and tugging on their
leashes. Everyone in town whom she'd ever
met, even Mr. Krinks, was there. And Carlos was standing front and center, his gun
pointed at the ground for safety, but his eyes
shooting bullets at Jim.

"Let. Her. Go."

She'd never heard Carlos's voice sound so
threatening. So welcome.

"Yeah. No one messes with our Faye," Mr.
Krinks said, folding his thick arms across
his chest.

Jim let her go and straightened his soiled
sweater.

"She's a criminal. I was about to call you.

I'm turning her in on impersonating and kid-napping charges."

Carlos signaled to another officer. The woman approached Faye and led her a safe distance away from Jim, but didn't handcuff her. Chanda, Darla and Nora all ran to her. Jim looked nervous and glanced behind him. Jordan stood blocking his way back through the store, where Eve was still harboring Mia. He gave Jim a menacing look that conveyed "don't mess with my friends" in no uncertain terms. A terse nod in Carlos's direction and Faye knew Jordan had been given a heads-up about the plan to stop Jim. The call he'd taken earlier. She could see Eve inside the shop try-ing to comfort Mia, while waiting to be told it was safe to bring her out.

A camera flashed from one of the local newspaper reporters. Carlos kept his eyes on Jim. The dogs, ordered to stay back by their owners, kept growling and snapping at him.

"Here's the thing," Carlos said, pulling out his handcuffs. "You're the one who has had charges pressed against you. Assault and bat-tery."

"Impossible."

Faye gasped and tears flooded out. Clara was okay. Alive. She'd been found.

"Why? Because you didn't think your wife could pick a lock, break out of the room in that cabin you had her in and make it down a mountain through snow on foot to get help? Let me give you a piece of advice. Never underestimate the power of a mother's love for her kid."

"You're lying," Jim said. "Faye got to you, didn't she? Have you been getting cozy with the sheriff?" He looked over at her with disgust. But his face had paled and he kept flexing his hands.

"Is Clara okay?" Faye called out. She looked past Jordan and through the shop window. She couldn't see Eve anymore, but she had a feeling that her friend had either wisely taken the child into the back so she wouldn't hear or witness anything—or to change that diaper and make sure she was alright. Faye wanted to hold Mia. Needed to hold her and comfort her. She wanted to assure her that she'd be with her mommy soon and that everything would be okay, but she didn't dare move from where the officer had her.

"She will be," Carlos said without looking

at her. He kept his eyes on Jim. "Clara, your wife and Mia's real mother, is in safe hands right now. She's in a hospital getting treated for what you did to her. Injuries so recent that they can't be blamed on Faye because she has, as you can see, an entire town of alibis. Witnesses to the fact that she's been here, taking good care of her niece. Keeping her safe. A town that was able to witness your behavior through that shop's windows. We saw how you manhandled your sister-in-law. I think we have enough cell phone videos and reporter photographs to prove it. Then there's the DNA evidence that's being collected right now at the hospital. Jim Beauchampe, your money and contacts aren't going to help you this time. I'm placing you under arrest."

The entire town cheered. Jim was hauled away after Carlos cuffed him. Eve stepped outside with Nim—Mia—when Jordan signaled to her that all was clear. The two embraced, holding Mia between them.

Faye ran over to them and took Mia in her arms, kissing her wet face repeatedly. "It's going to be okay, Mia. It's going to be okay." She didn't care about runny noses or piercing screams or sleepless nights. Lives were what mattered. Family was what mattered. Love mattered.

Carlos was at their side in seconds. Jordan and Eve stepped away to give them space.

"Are you alright? Did he hurt you? Is she okay?" He stroked Faye's hair, then her arm, then put his hand gently on Mia's back, looking over them both for any sign that they needed paramedics or first aid.

"I'm okay. We both are, thanks to you. And Eve and Jordan. And everyone here," she said, looking around the crowd, overwhelmed by all the people who had had her back. Nora, who'd been holding on to Pepper's leash, released her and the dog ran straight up, licking Mia's shoes and Faye's hands to confirm for herself that they were fine. Mia stopped crying and reached for the dog. It always amazed Faye how dogs and children could connect without words. How dogs had a way of healing a person's soul. She kneeled down and let Mia cling to Pepper. The dog, knowingly, settled down on the ground so that Mia could cuddle into her as if she were her pup. Someone came over and left a blanket for Mia. Faye wrapped it around her, adding to the warmth Pepper was enveloping her in.

"Actually, Mia might need to get checked," Faye said. "She has an upset stomach. But he didn't hurt her." Not physically, at least. Man, it felt good to be able to say that she needed a doctor without fear of discovery.

"We'll get her seen ASAP," Carlos said. "You should get checked too."

"No. I'm fine. Really. I just want to see Clara. I want assurance that Jim isn't going to get off on some technicality."

"He won't. I've already contacted everyone I know and trust. They're ready to intercept any officers or officials who have had shady dealings with him. I'm having the precinct in your hometown investigated too. I promise, it'll be safe to go back."

Her hometown.

It wasn't Turtleback Beach.

He was making that clear. Telling her she could leave now. Not even asking her to stay. Could she blame him? She knew this would happen. She had kept the truth from him. She had expected him to react even worse—as in arresting her. She should be thankful it hadn't come to that, but hearing him say those words in a to-the-point professional manner… so void of emotion or regret…*it'll be safe to go back*…felt like a different sort of jail. Like he was standing on one side of a wall of iron bars and making sure she stayed on the other. Maybe it was for the best. He was making parting that much easier for both of them. But what really hurt was that he wasn't giving her a choice. He wasn't giving her a chance. And that could mean only that he hadn't fallen in love with her the way she had with him.

CARLOS TOOK HALF a step back from Faye, needing to put distance between them but unable to pull himself any farther. He wanted to hold her and kiss her. He wanted to beg her to stay. To make Turtleback Beach her home, but he couldn't. He knew how it would turn out. He'd tried that with Natalie and she had left anyway, leaving him drained, broken and depleted. He couldn't do that again. He had protected Faye and Mia from Jim, but he had a right to protect himself too.

He was relieved that she was safe, but that only gave him the space to feel the pain. To feel the anger and frustration—not the kind an immoral man like Jim acted on but the kind that sat in his chest and tore at his heart and made him question everything. The kind that made him want to take his dog, go home and be alone. It's what he'd done years ago to quiet those emotions, only this time, he couldn't. Because something stronger and deeper had woven itself through every strand of his being. Something that was choking the anger and keeping it from letting him step any farther away from Faye or Mia. He loved her. God help him. He loved Faye. But she didn't trust him. And the fact was, she was free to go home now. Free to reunite with her sister who, he was told, was in a fragile emotional state...desperate to see her child and Faye. She was free to return to her business too. Her passion. None of that was here for her in Turtleback.

"I lied to you, Carlos. I'm so sorry. I didn't want to. I was scared."

He thought about every lie she'd given him. Every moment they'd shared. Every kiss.

"I know you were. But I told you I'd protect you no matter what. I asked you to trust me. Said that you could count on me. And that included your sister and niece."

"You did. And I should have. I wanted to. But Carlos, if you were me, what would you have done?"

"I don't know."

He wanted to say that he'd have trusted someone trying to help him, but would he have? He couldn't judge her when he hadn't gone through what she and Clara had endured. He *had* been in some pretty hair-raising ordeals during his service in the Air Force, and he'd seen his father shot and watched someone he loved slowly wither away from a ruthless disease, so on some level, he knew decisions when it came to love could be more complicated than a human mind—or heart—could handle. But he hadn't experienced exactly what Faye had gone through. So, he really didn't know what he'd have done, other than try to protect his family just as she had.

"I do trust you, Carlos. I did before this." She motioned around them, to the dissipating crowd, the spinning lights on the emergency vehicles. The sirens were silenced, and Jim was being lowered into the back seat of a police car. "I know it doesn't seem that way, but I had to be careful. I *had* to. And I didn't want to put you in a position where you would have had to make the call to break a law in order to help me. If my sister hadn't escaped, how long would it have been before you had enough evidence against Jim? Were you planning to ignore the law and the fact that I wasn't Mia's mother? Wouldn't you have had to call child protective services or hand this innocent child to her father?"

"You didn't give me a choice in the matter, did you? You made that decision for me, instead of trusting me. When I said that I'd protect you, it included anyone you care about, Faye, because that's what makes them family. That's… That's what you are to me. That's what I want you to be…for us to be for each other. Family, Faye. Because I care. Because… Because I'm so madly in love with you it hurts. The thought of you running away again and leaving Turtleback made me feel like I'd been sucked out in a riptide and pulled under. And the thought of you leaving now kills me too, but I can't make you stay. You have a life to get back to. Your sister is waiting for you. Needs you. Your job, your home, your life…your freedom… It's all waiting."

Tears pooled in her eyes and she shook her head at him.

"You're not giving me a choice in the matter either."

Her tone was harsh. Bitter. She shivered

and hugged herself, as if protecting her heart from him. Pepper whimpered and looked up at them. Mia, sitting there sucking on her thumb while holding on to Pepper's ear with her other hand, stared at them with big eyes. *Choice.* He had been upset about not being given a choice in how far he would go to stand behind Faye. He hadn't been given a choice when his father or mother were taken from this life or when Natalie had walked away. And here he was, taking that same power away from Faye.

He raked his hair back, then took off his jacket and put it around her shoulders, taking that half step closer to her. And then another. Until her breath danced in soft, frosted spirals with his. The town, the people, everything around them seemed to disappear into the night.

"What do you want, Faye?" he asked, soft enough that only she could hear.

She tugged his jacket around her and bridged the gap between them. Her arms brushed his and he placed his hands on hers, hoping she'd say that he could hold on to her forever. She looked him straight in the eyes. No more tears. No quivering. No hesitation.

"I want you. I love you, Carlos Ryker. I know I have no right to ask you to forgive me, but I love you. I choose you."

The ground seemed to wash away under his feet. The cold night air felt not so cold anymore. He brushed his thumb across her lips, then held her face in his hands.

"I want you too. I love you, Faye Donovan. I have no right to ask you to stay, but I love you. I choose you."

"We can make this work, right?"

"We'll figure it out. That's what love's all about." He wasn't sure how, but they would. If it meant quitting his job, following her and finding a new position—he'd do it. He didn't want to leave this town, but he could always come back to visit his friends here and keep his place as a summer home if that's what it took to keep Faye in his life. And Mia too, because he'd miss her. He'd be proud to be her uncle. He leaned in, wanting to kiss Faye. Unable to wait any longer.

"Does that mean you won't mind if I stay and make Turtleback my home?"

He paused.

"You want to move here? You'd move here? What about your sister? And your business?"

She looked up and down the street that ran through Turtleback. At all the dogs walking alongside their owners. She smiled.

"I think I've formed a new pack here, don't you? I could open a business here. Either close the other or hire someone to run it. And I have a feeling Clara might be willing to move here with Mia. She'd be leaving a place that holds bad memories and starting new ones here. A new life. Best of all, I'd have everyone I love here. In Turtleback. Especially you."

"Promise me one thing," he said. "That you'll give me the honor, the gift, of being able to wake up every day by your side and love you forever."

"Only if you promise me the same gift."

"Consider it done."

With that promise, he kissed her. A kiss that triggered a townful of cheers, whistles and even a happy squeal and clapping from Mia. A kiss that would lead to a million more. A lifetime of moments and memories. Life could be unpredictable, but he knew there would always be one thing that would never change. Their love. A love that would last forever.

* * * * *

#323 ENCHANTED BY THE RODEO QUEEN
The Mountain Monroes • by Melinda Curtis
When Emily Clark goes looking for true love, she expects to find a cowboy, not a Hollywood writer. But opposites attract, and city-boy Jonah Monroe might be exactly what this rodeo queen wants!

#324 A MATCH MADE PERFECT
Butterfly Harbor Stories • by Anna J. Stewart
Brooke Ardell had to walk away from her family. Now she's determined to right her wrongs with her ex, Sebastian Evans, and their daughter. Are they willing to risk their hearts by letting Brooke back in?

#325 HER SURPRISE COWBOY
Heroes of Shelter Creek • by Claire McEwen
Liam Dale never expected to see Trisha Gilbert again—and certainly not with his baby son! But he's determined to be there for his child...and for Trisha. If only she would let him in.

#326 A SOLDIER SAVED
Veterans' Road • by Cheryl Harper
Veteran Jason Ward is done with adventure, opting instead for new, quieter pursuits, but developing a crush on his writing instructor, Angela Simmons, wasn't part of the plan! Now they both need to decide which risks are worth taking.

HWCNM0320